# *REGENCY STING*

It was a perfect, and perfectly ladylike, scheme. A noble but impoverished family with a very marriageable daughter... a boorish but wealthy American relative who was conspicuously single. What could be more helpful than to bring them together and let nature run its course? Unless, of course, Anne and Jason ruined it all and, instead of marrying, fell in love...

### *Elizabeth Mansfield*

ELIZABETH MANSFIELD

# Regency Sting

A BERKLEY BOOK
published by
BERKLEY PUBLISHING CORPORATION

REGENCY STING

A Berkley Book/published by arrangement with
the author

PRINTING HISTORY
Berkley edition/January 1980

ISBN: 0-425-04497-1

A BERKLEY BOOK® TM 757,375
PRINTED IN THE UNITED STATES OF AMERICA

# Regency Sting

# *One*

THE LETTER WAS DELIVERED at eleven in the morning to the Mainwaring town house on Curzon Street and was carried by the first footman to the butler, Mr. Coyne, who was belowstairs in his shirtsleeves polishing the silver. "Why did you bring it *here*?" the butler asked in some annoyance. "Take it directly to Lady Harriet, you whopstraw!"

The footman took a step backward and shook his head nervously. "Not me!" he said stubbornly. "I've a suspicion o' what's in that letter, an' if you was to ask me, I'd say that it should be *you* what takes that kind o' news to her."

The butler frowned at his subordinate and took the letter from him. One look at the sender's name—Lucious R. Brindle, Solicitor—was enough to inform Coyne of the letter's contents: Lady Harriet's brother, the Viscount Mainwaring, had passed on. "I don't see why you're in a quake over this," the butler said, unmoved. "Lord Mainwaring's demise should come as no surprise to her ladyship." It should come as a surprise to *nobody* in London, the butler thought, for William Osborn Hughes, Viscount Mainwaring, was known to have suffered several severe attacks of apoplexy during the past few months. It was generally believed that the Viscount would not outlast the summer of 1810, but here it was almost November, well past the expected time.

"You mean her ladyship's *expectin'* this news?" the footman asked.

"So I would imagine," the butler said shortly. "Therefore, if you please, put the letter on the salver and take it to her."

"But...she's still sitting wi' Lady Mathilda Claybridge."

"I know that, you nodcock. But they've been closeted for more than an hour. Lady Mathilda was wearing a sour face when she came in, and I've no doubt the visit is no joy for her ladyship. Lady Harriet will be glad of an interruption."

"But what if Lady Harriet don't take the news in good part? What if she turns on the waterworks or somethin'?"

"Waterworks? Lady Harriet? You *are* noddy. Lady Harriet ain't the sort who excites herself or has the vapors—you know that. The way you carry on, one would think Lady Harriet was *fond* of that stiff-rumped old—" Coyne caught himself up and fixed his eye on the footman severely. "Just do as I say. Bring her the letter, and don't make such a pother."

The footman, with obvious reluctance, put the letter on a newly polished silver tray and started from the room. At the doorway he turned and looked back at the butler with a pleading, frightened-puppy look. "I ain't never had to break such news before. Please, Mr. Coyne, won't you—?"

Coyne exploded. "Look here, you blockhead, do you see what I'm wearing? An *apron*. I'm in my *shirtsleeves*. This teapot has not yet been finished, and I've *all* the Storr plate yet to do."

"But Mr. Coyne...*please*..."

In utter digust, Coyne snatched the tray with the letter from the hand of the craven footman. "Oh, give it over. I'll do it myself. Here, help me off with this apron and get my coat. And while I'm gone, you can finish the teapot. But if I find so much as a smudge on it when I return, you'll be out on the street before the day is out!"

In the drawing room above, Lady Harriet Hartley was clenching her fingers in her lap and telling herself over and over to remember to remain calm. She had long ago trained herself to keep her emotions in control. Her father had frequently indulged in choleric fits of anger and had died in his thirties of a heart seizure. Her elder brother was also abnormally short-tempered and as a result suffered from severe bouts of apoplexy. Harriet therefore had realized early that if she were to avoid a similar fate, she must not permit herself to indulge in tantrums, tears or tempers. And when she found herself, as at this moment, in situations which promised to irritate her nerves, she pressed her hands together in her lap, pressed her feet flat on the floor, attempted to regulate her breathing and talked to herself soothingly.

Lady Mathilda Claybridge was just the type of woman to irritate Harriet's nerves. She was small, thin and given to jerky little movements of her hands when she spoke. Her voice was high and her speech quick, and one half-hour in her presence made Harriet yearn for the company of a plump, even-tempered, placid matron like herself.

It had taken Mathilda more than half-an-hour to get to the point of her visit. After much roundaboutation, she had confessed that she was unhappy about her son Arthur's interest in Lady Harriet's stepdaughter, Anne. It had taken a great deal of patient questioning on Harriet's part to discover the reason. Mathilda Claybridge, recently widowed, had learned that her husband had gambled away a great deal of his fortune and had left the estate hopelessly encumbered. "So you see, Harriet," she had admitted at last, "it is absolutely fatal for Arthur to ally himself to a penniless girl like Anne. You know, my dear, that I'm very fond of Anne. Truly I am. There is no young lady in London I admire more. Why, how often have I said to you that I wish my Marianne had some of Anne's style and elegance?"

"Very often, Mathilda, my dear, very often," Harriet murmured politely.

"Of course. And I am most sincere when I say there is no one I'd rather have as a daughter-in-law—"

"Daughter-in-law?" Harriet sat upright in surprise. "I had no idea that matters between Anne and Arthur had progressed so far! Has Arthur made her an offer?"

"No, I don't think it has yet come to _that_, but it's plain as pikestaff that it's May Moon with them both. That's why I've come today. We must do _something_ before things go too far. That is...unless..." Lady Mathilda paused and reddened in embarrassment.

"Unless...?" Harriet urged.

"This is very difficult for me to say, Harriet, but I believe we must be aboveboard in this matter, don't you?"

"Yes, let us be aboveboard, by all means."

"Good. Then I shall ask you frankly—does your brother intend to deal with Anne...er...shall we say 'handsomely'?"

It was at this point that Lady Harriet began to clench her fingers, check her breathing and warn herself to keep calm. "If by that you mean to ask if he will leave her a legacy, I can only tell you that I have no idea _what_ my brother's intentions are," she said flatly.

"I see. I suppose there is no hope that Anne's father, your late husband, left any—"

Harriet shook her head. "No, Mathilda. I think you know quite well that the Hartleys never had a feather to fly with."

"Well, then, you must see—"

"I'm afraid I _don't_ see. What is it you want of _me_, Mathilda?"

"I want you to help me keep them apart."

Harriet sighed. "But how?"

"We must forbid them to see each other."

"Nonsense. That's just the sort of thing that drives lovers into each other's arms."

"Not if we are firm. Believe me, Harriet dear, I've given this matter a great deal of thought. I can think of no other way. I'm convinced that, if I have your support, and if we both remain firm, we shall brush through."

Harriet was dubious. "I would like nothing better than to encourage Anne to turn her thoughts elsewhere, but I cannot like—"

It was at that moment that Coyne scratched at the door. Lady Harriet called an eager "Come in," and he entered with his silver tray. His step was measured, his face composed, his manner unconcerned. He had been the Hartleys' butler ever since Lady Harriet was first married, almost twenty years ago. He knew that she was not given to emotional outbursts. He was convinced that she would read the letter and take the news of her brother's demise with her customary complacency.

As he expected, Lady Harriet smiled at him with unmistakable gratitude in her eyes. Plainly she was not enjoying Lady Claybridge's visit. He offered her the letter with his leisurely bow, and she opened it in her usual, unhurried, placid manner. As she glanced over the contents, she blinked, paled, and made a choking sound. She read the words a second time. "I must remain calm." she muttered under her breath, the letter beginning to tremble in her hand. "I must remain *ca-a-a-a-lm*!" The last word was more like a shuddering sigh, and the placid, complacent Lady Harriet toppled to the floor in a swoon.

Lady Mathilda uttered a little, shocked cry, and the butler stared at her ladyship's prostrate form goggle-eyed. He could not believe what he saw. In all these years, he had rarely seen his mistress in a taking. She had hardly ever raised her voice. She had never hurried, nor shed tears, nor given way to the vapors. And she had certainly never *swooned*.

As soon as he could recover from the shock, he knelt beside her and began awkwardly to chafe her hands. His movements nudged Lady Claybridge to her senses. Mathilda Claybridge had frequently indulged in fainting spells, and she tremblingly reached into her reticule for the hartshorn she always carried. A great deal of chafing and sniffing of hartshorn was necessary before Lady Harriet could be brought round, but at last she opened her eyes and permitted herself to be helped to the sofa. She fell back against the cushions, pressing her hand against her heaving chest. "Oh, my *heart*," she murmured. "I must remain *calm*."

"May I get you a glass of brandy, your ladyship?" Coyne asked, bending over her in concern. "A sip of brandy is most efficacious in these circumstances."

"No, thank you, Coyne," she said weakly.

"Yes, Coyne, it's the very thing," Lady Claybridge said. Coyne ran out of the room and down the hall to the dining room where a decanter of brandy was kept on the sideboard. As he passed the library, the sound of his footsteps was heard by Lady Harriet's seventeen-year-old son, Peter, who had been sitting there reading his Cicero. Disturbed, he placed a finger in his book to mark his place and wandered down the hall. As he passed the drawing-room doorway, he caught a glimpse of his mother stretched out on the sofa, with Lady Claybridge standing over her in an attitude of tender solicitude. Never having seen his mother indisposed, he adjusted his spectacles to make sure his eyes were not deceiving him. "Good heavens, Mama, what's amiss?" he asked, half in alarm and half in annoyance at having been distracted from his studies.

"Oh, Peter," she said tearfully, attempting to sit up, "please come in. There's something I..." Then, with a glance at Lady Claybridge, she bit her lip and relapsed into silence.

Lady Claybridge smiled reassuringly at Peter. "Your mother has merely had a little fainting spell—"

"Fainting spell? *Mama*?" Peter asked incredulously.

"It was nothing," Harriet said quickly. "Mathilda,

you've been very kind, but I...I'm quite myself now. There's no reason for me to detain you..."

Lady Claybridge looked quickly from mother to son. "Yes, of course," she said, rising. "You needn't look so dumbfounded, Peter dear. After all, a little fainting spell can scarcely be considered at all serious. Ah, here's Coyne. He can see me out."

"Of course, my lady," Coyne said, coming into the room with the brandy, "as soon as Lady Harriet has had her restorative."

"No, thank you, Coyne, I won't need that dreadful stuff. Do take it away and show Lady Claybridge to her carriage."

Lady Claybridge went to the door. There she hesitated. "You won't forget what we talked about, will you, Harriet? I am counting on your support in the matter."

"No, no, I won't forget," Harriet said abstractedly.

As soon as they were alone, Peter sat down beside his mother and studied her curiously. "I've never known you to do such a thing. What's wrong, Mama?"

Harriet looked at him tearfully. "Oh, my dear," she said in a quavering voice, "what a *catastrophic* blow we've had!"

She handed him the missive which she'd been clutching even during her period of unconsciousness. Peter adjusted his spectacles and read it quickly. Then, completely unmoved, he looked up at his mother. "I don't see why you're in such a taking," he remarked. "Everyone *expected* Uncle Osborn to stick his spoon into the wall at any time during this past year."

"*I* didn't expect it," his mother said weakly. "He wasn't much past sixty, he was the strongest and hardiest man in the family despite his apoplexy, and although he was the eldest, he was always used to say that he would outlive us all. Besides, it is not at all kind in you to use so dreadful an expression. Stick his spoon into the wall, indeed! Have you no respect for the dead?"

"Dash it, Mama," Peter said defensively, "you surely

don't expect *me* to carry on over this, do you? Because I
see no cause to put on a long face over the demise of a man
I hardly knew. I admit that he was generous with money,
if one cares for such things, but I *detest* the sort of sham
which prompts one to praise—after he dies—a man one
despised while he was alive."

Lady Harriet shook her head and sighed hopelessly. I
must remain calm, she told herself. Peter was not being
rude. Although little more than a boy, her son was an
independent-minded, scholarly youth who had adopted
strong latitudinarian principles. He cared for little but his
books and his imminent entrance into Oxford. She was
utterly devoted to him and very proud of his scholarly
abilities, but she had to admit that she did not always
understand him. She knew that his slender physique and
his lack of sporting prowess were a disappointment to
him. It was too bad that his father had died when he was
so young, and that her now-deceased brother had never
taken an interest in the boy. He needed the influence of a
strong man. But her brother had always been selfish and
reclusive, and it was too late now to change things. "I
suppose I should not have expected you to grieve for your
Uncle Osborn," she said regretfully, "but you may find
that you have other reasons to mourn. You should grieve,
if not for your uncle, then for Anne—and for yourself."

"Why? What do you mean?"

"Did you not read the letter through?" she asked,
trying with a perceptible effort to regain her composure,
but not quite succeeding. "Osborn left *everything*
to . . . to . . ." Here, her self-control broke down again.
". . . to that *rebel!*"

"Rebel?" Peter asked, perplexed. "What rebel? Do you
mean your brother Henry's son?"

"Of course I mean Henry's son!"

"Well, really, Mama, you can scarcely call *him* a rebel.
He can't be more than twenty-five or six. The American
uprising was over before he was *born*!"

"What has *that* to say to anything?" his mother

demanded with unaccustomed irritability, unable to recapture her normal complacency. "His father—my rackety second brother, Henry—was a rebel, wasn't he?"

"Not at all," Peter explained, shifting the book he carried to his other hand and seating himself beside his mother. "As I understand it, my Uncle Henry was a perfectly respectable British officer of the line who discharged his duties quite honorably. Just because he chose not to return to England with his regiment after the war does not make him a rebel."

"Any man who would choose to remain abroad and give up his homeland is a rebel in my view. Besides, he *married* a rebel, did he not? You'll have to admit that, even if *Henry* couldn't be called a rebel in the strictest sense, his *son* is a rebel—on his mother's side, at least."

Peter shrugged. "A tendency to rebellion," he said, repressing a smile, "is not inherited. Anyway, I don't see why you're upsetting yourself over all this *now*, Mama. It isn't at all like you."

"It's because I cannot understand why Osborn left everything to an *American*, while *my* son is given nothing at all," she answered, pulling a handkerchief from the bosom of her dress and sniffing into it piteously.

"But you *must* have understood all these years that the inheritance had to pass on down the *male* line—"

"I suppose I *should* have understood," his mother admitted miserably, "but I kept hoping... all sorts of foolish hopes that Anne would marry well... that Osborn would live for years and years... or that he would make proper provision..." Her voice quivered pathetically. "Oh, dear, I *must* be calm," she warned herself.

Peter put his book aside and patted her hand comfortingly. "Never mind, Mama. We shall manage. Father did not leave you destitute, after all, and Anne will soon be married to that Claybridge fellow..."

Harriet felt a wave of irritation and frowned at her son in uncharacteristic impatience. "For a brilliant young scholar, as you are reputed to be, you certainly entertain some idiotic notions. Your father left us with barely enough to enable us to live in genteel poverty. This very *house* is Mainwaring property. It was only because your Uncle Osborn detested London and preferred to stay buried away in Derbyshire that we were able to remain here all these years. And now, that American savage is very likely to order our removal as soon as he sets foot in London. We shall have to take rooms in Hans Town or some other such dowdy neighborhood. We shan't be able to afford more than a cook, a butler and one maid for our household staff! And how will you like doing without stables and carriages or even one single horse?"

"Oh? Will things be as bad as that?" Peter asked, startled.

"Worse! And as for Anne, she will *not* marry Lord Claybridge. It is out of the question, especially now."

"Why?" Peter asked curiously. "You've *always* been against the match. I don't say I especially care for the fellow, myself. Seems a rather dull sort to me. But if Anne is so taken with him, I don't see why you oppose their marriage." Peter habitually took Anne's part. Although she was five years his senior, and only a half-sister to him, the affection between them was very strong. Anne's mother had died when she was three years old, and her father, Sir Archer Hartley, had married Harriet Mainwaring shortly thereafter. Peter was born two years later. Hartley himself had died the following year, and Peter, as soon as he was old enough to realize that his mother (although lovingly devoted to both her stepdaughter and her son) was not always capable of understanding him, turned to Anne. The two had developed a closeness which had lasted through the years.

"Of course you don't see," Harriet answered irritably. "You don't see *anything* beyond your Latin epistles and your Greek philosophies. Don't you understand why Mathilda Claybridge was here this morning? Arthur Claybridge has not a feather to fly with! Mathilda told me herself—"

"Told you what?" came an irate voice from across the room. They looked up to find Anne herself poised in the doorway. Above average height to begin with, she had drawn herself up even higher in her anger and was glaring at them from beneath a high-crowned bonnet on which even the ostrich plumes seemed to be waving in irritation. "Well, Mama," she demanded coldly, "what was Lady Claybridge saying about me?"

# Two

"I MUST REMAIN CALM," Lady Harriet muttered warningly to herself, and she let her eyes dwell for a moment on the enchanting picture her daughter made as she stood framed in the doorway. An artist would have found the girl striking at any time, but now, with her eyes sparkling with anger, her shiny brown curls peeping out from beneath a completely fetching bonnet, and her cheeks pink from either the November wind or her reaction to the bit of overheard conversation, an artist would be bound to find her almost breathtaking. Harriet had heard more than one smitten gentleman describe Anne's eyes as "speaking" and her nose as "perfection itself." (Of course, Lady Dabney had once remarked that Anne's mouth was rather too full in the underlip, but Lady Dabney's daughter was as plain as a sparrow and broke out in spots at the slightest provocation, so what could one expect from the envious old cat?) As far as Lady Harriet was concerned, Anne's mouth was as enticing as her other features.

The underlip in question was, at this moment, rather too much in evidence. Peter, not blinded by motherly affection, recognized the expression instantly. "Why are you standing there *pouting*?" he asked, peering at her through his spectacles in brotherly disapproval.

Anne surveyed him coldly. "I do *not* pout," she said imperiously.

"Then what *is* it you're doing that makes your underlip stand out like that?" he asked, undaunted.

"I am merely waiting for an answer to my question. Why, Mama, were you discussing my affairs with Lady Claybridge behind my back?"

"Anne, dear, do come in and sit down. I cannot be easy while you stand there glowering at me. And never mind the Claybridge matter now. I have some other news that I'm afraid may be even more upsetting to you. Here. Read *this*! But first, be sure to tell yourself to remain calm." And she handed the letter to her stepdaughter.

Anne pulled off her gloves, tossed them on a chair and scanned the letter. "I don't see anything in this to upset me," she said, looking up at her stepmother candidly. "There's nothing terribly shocking in the fact that an old man who was subject to apoplectic attacks has died. I'm sorry, Mama, if *you're* grieved, but Uncle Osborn never did anything to earn *my* affection."

"What ungrateful children I have reared, to be sure," Lady Harriet said with mild disgust. "Who do you think provided you with the niceties of life—even the very elegant bonnet you wear at this moment?"

"Oh, *that*!" Anne dismissed a lifetime of largesse with a scornful wave of her hand. "Who cares for such things? You would not want me to sell my affection for a...a mess of potage? I didn't like him, and I will not wear the willow for him."

"Hear, hear," Peter said supportively, grinning at his sister in approval. "I must admit, Anne, that you've quite a bit of pluck, for—"

"—for a girl!" she finished for him, responding to his grin with a quick, affectionate smile.

"You *both* are impossible," Harriet declared disapprovingly. "Your attitudes are not only improper—they are positively shameful. I'll admit your uncle was something of a curmudgeon—"

"*Something* of a curmudgeon? Really, Mama, even *you* must admit that Uncle Osborn was a brittle-tempered, puffed-up blackguard!" Anne declared.

"At his *best*!" Peter added teasingly.

"And positively apoplectic at his worst," Anne went on.

"Under the circumstances, that is a dreadful thing to say!" poor Harriet remonstrated.

"But true," Anne insisted. "At least, that's how he was whenever *we* saw him—"

"Which was not more often than once in two years," Peter said.

"And, Mama, I once heard him say that you set up his bristles. *You*, who never said an unkind thing to him!"

"And he never bothered to invite us to dine with him—not *once* in the last decade!"

"And when we *did* see him, he'd kick up a dust if we so much as giggled in his presence—"

"And remember, Mama, how he fell into a pucker when you invited him to dine with us and then had no Madeira for him to drink?"

"And he never condescended to dine with us again—"

"Stop!" Lady Harriet threw up her hands. "Very well, I shall admit he was a curmudgeon. But all this has nothing to say to the nub of the matter, which is that we are left without a groat."

"Without a groat?" Anne asked in surprise.

"Not one," her stepmother answered, the tears filling her eyes again.

"Oh, dear. That *is* a problem," Anne murmured, chastened.

Lady Harriet sniffled into her handkerchief. "*Now* do you understand why I'm so distraught?"

"I daresay I had *better* understand," Anne admitted, putting her arm comfortingly around her mother's shoulders. "I think I may even shed a tear or two *myself*."

Peter looked from one to the other in disgust. "Confound it, Mama, and you, too, Anne . . . it's not as if we were *destitute*."

"We are *almost* destitute," his mother said lugubriously. "I don't even know if we'll have the means to send you to Oxford next year."

Now it was Peter's turn to be taken aback. Entering Oxford had been his dream for years. Most young gentlemen attended the university because society expected it or parents demanded it, but some few, like Peter, actually welcomed the scholarly life. Peter had no talent for sporting pursuits, and no taste for the gambling, the drinking and the carousing that most young men of his age and station seemed to enjoy. He had never even *considered* an alternative to life at Oxford. There was no other world he wanted. As he met Anne's eyes, he lowered his own so that she would not read the sudden fear that he knew was reflected there. "No . . . money for Oxford?" He could barely say the words.

"Nonsense, Mama," Anne said with what she hoped would be reassuring firmness. "I'm certain that something can be contrived . . ."

"Can it? I really can't see what—" Harriet began doubtfully.

"We can use the small legacy from my mother!" Anne said in sudden inspiration.

Peter adjusted his spectacles manfully, picked up his book and rose in offended dignity. "You surely don't imagine," he declared, "that I would take your money!"

"Of course you will," she insisted warmly, looking up at him with earnest affection. "I shall have no need of it, especially after Arthur Claybridge and I are married."

Lady Harriet caught her breath and took a quick look at her stepdaughter's face. "Anne, you must be practical. You and Lord Claybridge . . ." She hesitated, wondering how to soften this additional blow to her beloved girl's prospects.

"What about Lord Claybridge, Mama?" Anne asked, arrested.

Lady Harriet pressed her feet flat on the floor and twisted her hands in her lap. With her breathing in strict control, she said firmly, "You and Lord Claybridge will never marry. I'm sorry, dearest, but it is out of the question."

Anne jumped to her feet. "But, Mama, *why*?"

"Oh, my poor dear, don't you *know*? The Claybridges are almost as deep in the suds as *we* are! Mathilda Claybridge confided to me today that her husband's gambling debts have left their estate much encumbered. They are relying on Arthur to make an advantageous match. That tiny legacy from your mother scarcely qualifies *you*. So you see, my dear, a marriage between you and Lord Claybridge can never be."

Anne stared at her stepmother in disbelief. "This can't be true! Arthur has told me *nothing* of this!"

"You see, dearest, until today, there was the *hope* (even if only a faint one) that Osborn would deal generously with you—with us all! But now . . . I hate to say this, Anne dear, but now our only hope is for you, too, to make a good match."

Anne sank into the nearest chair. "I cannot believe that our circumstances can have altered so drastically overnight."

"But they have," Harriet said hollowly. "The fortune that has been keeping us secure and comfortable all these years is now in the hands of my American nephew."

Anne and Peter exchanged troubled glances. "Yes," Anne said thoughtfully, "I can see now that we have much to think about."

There was a long moment of brooding silence. At last Peter's voice broke through the gloom. "We needn't fall into the dismals yet awhile," he suggested bravely. "After all, the heir is not even here in England. At least, not yet."

"Yes, that's right," Anne agreed, brightening.

"Why, with the tensions between our government and

America so great at this time, the fellow may not be able to come to England *at all*!" Peter pointed out hopefully.

"What tensions?" his mother asked.

"Don't you pay any attention to politics, Mama? The Americans have been hinting that they may throw their support to the French. Napoleon, you know, has been trying to entice them to cut off intercourse with us again, and it looks as if he may be succeeding. I understand he sent the American President a letter last summer—it's known as the Cadore letter, I believe—in which he promised the Americans all sorts of shipping concessions. Of course, if they take Napoleon's word for anything, they're nothing but fools. But Mr. Madison is a great lover of the French, I hear—"

"Who's Mr. Madison?" Harriet asked.

Peter threw his mother a pitying glance. "The American President, of course. As I was saying, Mr. Madison is said to favor the French, so the tensions between us and the Americans are quite strained at the moment."

"Are you saying, Peter," his sister asked interestedly, "that there may be another *war* with America?"

"No, I very much doubt that things will go *that* far, but there very likely will be a declaration of non-intercourse from the Americans (as there was once before) which will very severely limit American shipping to England."

Lady Harriet's worried look lightened perceptibly as the import of Peter's words sank in. "Do you really think it is possible, then, that the new heir may not come?"

Peter shrugged, but Anne nodded eagerly. "Of course it's possible!" she exclaimed enthusiastically.

"Let's not fly into alt, my dear," Peter cautioned sensibly. "I only suggested a possibility. A possibility is not a *probability*, you know."

"I know, I know," Anne assured him cavalierly, "but so long as the new heir doesn't show himself, we need not feel depressed. I see no reason to fall into the vapors because of something that may not even come to pass. Until the new Viscount manages to find his way across the ocean—if he ever does—we may go on as we always have."

"I don't know," Lady Harriet said dubiously. "I shall have to speak to Mr. Brindle about the details of our present financial situation. But I must remind you, Anne dear, that *you* cannot go on as you always have, no matter *what* Mr. Brindle tells me."

"What do you mean, Mama?"

"I mean that you are no longer to be permitted to enjoy the company of Lord Claybridge. I'm sorry, love, but Mathilda was quite firm on that point."

"Oh, pooh," Anne said with an insouciant wave of her hand which seemed to dismiss Lady Claybridge's strictures from the very air. "Who cares *what* she says. Arthur is of age and in full possession of his titles. He has no need to jump at his mother's commands." Somehow the optimism engendered by Peter's political analysis would not be dampened, and Anne went on with her cheerful hopes for their futures. "Life is full of surprises, is it not?" she pointed out airily. "Why, *anything* may happen! The new Lord Mainwaring may not come, and we may be given the entire Mainwaring fortune! Then Peter could go to Oxford without a care, you, Mama, would be secure for life, and I should be able to marry Arthur with even his *mother's* blessing."

"On the other hand," Peter interjected, wishing to keep his sister from putting too many hopeful eggs into a very fragile basket, "the new Viscount may very well manage to find his way to England and make his claim to the inheritance."

"Yes, he may. We must not blind ourselves to the possibilities," Lady Harriet cautioned. "A fortune like the Mainwarings' is not likely to go a-begging."

"But you know, Peter, that American ships have difficulty reaching here in these times," Anne insisted, "even when the political climate has been *less* strained. Certainly, now, it will be close to impossible."

"Yes, that's true."

"There! Then there is good reason for optimism."

"I suppose so," Peter agreed, wishing to do his part to dispel the gloom which had enveloped them. "It is even possible that the news from Mr. Brindle about Uncle Osborn's death may never even reach the American shores."

Anne clapped her hands in pleasure. "That's *true*! There will be the same difficulty for a British ship to reach an *American* port. See, Mama? There are *many* reasons for hope. As I've said, anything may happen! The news may never reach him . . . or he may not be able to book passage across the ocean . . . or, even if he does, why . . ." She smiled widely as a new possibility came into her mind. ". . . why, if we have any luck at all, the fellow may *drown at sea*!"

And on that happy thought, they went upstairs to dress for dinner.

# Three

ANNE'S OPTIMISM in the drawing room did not outlast the short climb up to her bedroom door. Since she was neither devoid of sense nor given to self-delusion, she soon realized that it was extremely unlikely that the inheritance would not be claimed. A man would be insane to forego the titles and fortune of the size and importance of the Mainwarings'. She must face the facts and try to find a way out of the dilemma the heir's arrival would cause.

In the meantime, she decided to put a brave face on it. As she went about her usual daily routine, her expression and demeanor were the same as always. Even the sharpest-eyed of the London gossips could not discern a sign of anxiety in the self-assured, stylish Miss Hartley.

But it was abundantly plain to Anne's bosom-bow, Charity Laverstoke, that something was amiss. Charity, called Cherry by her intimates, was nothing if not sympathetic. Offering sympathy was what she did best in the world. To anyone who related troubles into her ear she would devote her most complete attention, her most melting gaze and her most tender feelings. She was so soft-hearted that the afflictions of passing *strangers* could bring tears to her eyes. Cherry had large, wide eyes, a heart-shaped, full-cheeked face and thick, silky-brown hair which she wore in unstylish braids wound round her head. Even the lines on her body, while not exactly plump, were comfortingly soft.

Knowing that her beloved friend was troubled, Cherry looked for an opportunity to see Anne alone. When Anne arrived one afternoon to take Cherry up for their weekly ride in Hyde Park, Cherry insisted that Anne come up to her bedroom while she finished dressing. There she urged Anne to perch on her four-poster bed with its feminine pink-and-gold draperies, and, jumping up alongside her, encouraged her friend to reveal what was on her mind.

Anne, hoping that her inner tensions would be relieved by speaking of her problems to her best friend, unhesitatingly explained the financial difficulties which had suddenly beset both her family and that of the Claybridges. It was her new awareness of Arthur's home situation which troubled her most deeply. "It may be," she concluded despondently, "that we will *never* find a way to marry!"

"Oh, Anne, my dear!" Cherry cried, her chin quivering in heartfelt concern. "How utterly, completely *dreadful*!"

"Yes, I know," Anne agreed brusquely, "but don't start to cry, Cherry, for tears never solved anything. They'll only redden your eyes, and we'll have to spend half-an-hour applying cold cloths and face powder to make you look presentable."

"I d-don't intend to cry," Cherry said bravely. "Besides, things may look dark now, but at least we can console ourselves with the knowledge that Arthur will never look at another female but you. You *do* know that, don't you?"

"I believe he loves me, but—"

"Of *course* he loves you! Anyone with half an eye can see that!"

"But he's never formally declared himself, you know, and ... now it's been almost a *week* that I've not seen him . . . !" Anne admitted with a slight quiver in her *own* voice.

Cherry put an arm around her consolingly. "Don't be gooseish. You *know* he loves you. He's keeping away because he doesn't want to upset his mother, that's all. Before long, he won't be able to stay away—you'll see."

"Perhaps. But even if he *does* love me, it's a fact that love does not always lead to marriage, Cherry. Especially when the family exerts pressure on one to make an advantageous match."

"Advantageous matches!" Cherry snorted scornfully. "How I hate them!"

"Yes, but they are so often necessary," Anne sighed. Finding that there was not much relief in going over these depressing circumstances, Anne squared her shoulders and lifted her head. "Never mind, Cherry. Let's not talk any more. My tiger cannot keep the horses standing in this weather. Do put on your bonnet and come along."

Cherry obediently took her bonnet from a tall, pink-painted wardrobe and sat down at her dressing table to tie it on. "Has Arthur's family asked him to make such a match?" she asked, looking at her friend's reflection in her dressing-table mirror.

"Since he's forbidden to see me, I cannot be sure, but according to Mama's conversation with Lady Claybridge—"

"Arthur is too honorable to agree to make such a match!" Cherry said loyally, placing the chip-straw bonnet on her head and tying it on with a knitted scarf.

"You are *not* going to wear that ugly scarf with that light bonnet, are you?" Anne demanded with a wince.

"Don't you like it?" Cherry asked, turning her attention to the mirror. "It's the finest swansdown I could find. I paid more than—"

"I don't care *what* it cost. It's too heavy to tie properly." She rummaged around in Cherry's drawer and pulled out a wide ribbon of green grogram. "Here, use this, and tie it in a bow under your ear."

Cherry did as she was bid. "There, is that better?"

"Yes, it looks lovely. Or it would, if you didn't insist on those insipid braids. I do wish you would let me cut and dress your hair one day. You could look so charming—"

"Not as charming as you," Cherry remarked admiringly. "I have no sense of style. If I didn't have you to advise me, I should look a hopeless dowd."

Anne was stabbed with sudden guilt. How could she speak so patronizingly to her dearest friend? "Don't be so silly!" she said, giving Cherry a quick hug. "One would think you had to consult me every time you dressed! You must know that you're quite capable of turning yourself out to perfect advantage without my advice. You've done it any number of times." Then she added bluntly, "I don't know why you always belittle yourself, Cherry."

Cherry lowered her eyes in shamefaced agreement. "I don't know why, either. I never have had the least self-confidence."

"But why?" Anne asked earnestly. "You are as sweet and as good and as pretty as a girl can be. And your hair is lovely. I'm an odious toad for suggesting that it needs styling."

Cherry blushed with pleasure but shook her head. "You needn't offer me Spanish coin, you know. I know that braids are for governesses and abigails. I've just become so accustomed....But why are we discussing this? Who cares about my hair? Perhaps if I could find a man to look at me as Arthur looks at you—!"

"You will, love," Anne assured her with another hug. "And soon, too!"

Cherry looked at herself in the mirror in critical appraisal. "Do you really think I should cut my hair? No, don't answer. I don't want to discuss *me*. It's *your* problem we should be discussing. What will you do if Arthur cannot make you an offer?"

Anne sighed. "I don't know. Oh, Cherry, I can't bear to think of it! Let's not dwell on *this* subject either—it will only bring us *both* to tears. Come, the horses are waiting."

It was indeed unthinkable to Anne that her dreams of marriage to Lord Arthur Claybridge might not come true. She had never loved a man before, and she was convinced that she could never love another man. The tender feelings he aroused in her, she knew, would never fade. There had been many young men who had attempted to win her affections in the two years since her come-out, but her heart had been stirred by none of them. Only Arthur had been able to move her in that special way that the poets and the writers of romance describe so lyrically.

She had met Arthur in a truly romantic way. He had been thrown by his horse and was lying unconscious alongside the bridle path that threaded its way through Hyde Park. Anne and Cherry, accompanied by two gentlemen whose names Anne no longer remembered, had been strolling nearby and had heard his moan. They'd hurried to his assistance. Anne had knelt down beside him and loosened his cravat. Her escort had run for some water. By the time Lord Claybridge had come round, Anne had placed his head in her lap and was staring down at what she judged to be the most beautiful face of any man she'd ever seen. When his eyes had fluttered open, and he'd fixed his melting blue gaze on her face, even the onlookers could tell that love had instantly struck.

Lord Arthur Claybridge possessed the kind of good looks that even in a man are called beautiful. His features were perfectly proportioned, like the head on a Greek coin. His dark-gold hair had a natural curl, and a lock of it persisted in falling over his forehead and tempting every female to smooth it into place. Although not above average height, his body, too, was perfectly proportioned, and he moved with unaffected grace. Anyone having seen him once would be willing to swear that there was not a handsomer creature in all of London.

In the year since their first meeting, neither Anne nor Arthur had eyes for another. As often as possible they were in each other's company. Arthur's nature was as flawless as his face; he was always thoughtful, earnest and sincere. He made no attempt to hide his feelings—the sincerity of his declarations of undying affection was unquestionable. If sometimes Anne (who could not claim to equal her beloved in perfection of character) became impatient with his consummate earnestness, if sometimes she became bored with his unfailing reliability, if sometimes she chafed at his lack of humor, she had only to look into those beautiful blue eyes, and her resistance would melt.

Into this romantic atmosphere, the intrusion of financial and familial woes was bound to come as a rude shock. The questions of encumbered estates, disinheritances, marriage settlements and fortuitous financial alliances had never been discussed in their ardent meetings. Even now, when each of them had been made aware of the seemingly insurmountable problems a marriage between them would create, Anne realized that Arthur was reluctant to spoil the purity of their relationship with discussions of sordid business matters.

As Anne confided to Cherry, her greatest concern was that he would give her up without discussing the matter with her at all. She believed that his affections were as intense as ever, but the nobility of his nature might dictate that he sacrifice himself to an advantageous marriage rather than force poverty upon his family and hers. As the two friends climbed into the carriage and rode off to the park, they could not tear their minds from that dreadful prospect. "Do you *really* think Arthur will break it off?" Cherry almost whispered in her consternation.

Anne shook her head and forced herself to smile. "No, of course not. I admit that prospects for our marriage look bleak at the moment, but I am not without hope. As I said to Mama and Peter, one can never say what the future may bring. Why, *anything* may happen!" And on that faint note of optimism, the girls tried to put aside their depression and face the November wind with what courage they could muster.

\* \* \*

Lady Harriet, too, tried to keep a spirit of optimism alive, but in the days that followed her practical mind warned her that optimism was in vain. The new heir was bound to come, soon or late. The titles and wealth were too sizeable a prize to be ignored. The fellow would appear, and she made up her mind to prepare for the event. Her best course lay first in remaining calm, and second in encouraging Anne to find an eligible suitor. But how this was to be accomplished when Anne had set her heart on the impecunious Lord Claybridge, she did not know.

Besides, a proper marriage for Anne needed a great deal of time and arranging, and it would take place—*if* it would take place—too far in the future to be of immediate comfort. Therefore, Lady Harriet decided to consult with the late Lord Mainwaring's man of business before determining what other courses of action would be necessary. To that end, she took herself in hand, one cold November day, and dressed herself as cheerfully as her state of mourning permitted. She brightened her black gown with a shawl of lilac mohair, tied on a flowered bonnet with a black veil and told her coachman to take her to the city.

As they rode through the gloomy streets, Harriet wondered if the flowered hat was too gay for her state of mourning. Would Mr. Brindle look on her with disapproval? But she needn't have worried, for Mr. Brindle proved to be a cheerful, rotund, rosy-cheeked gentleman whose optimistic nature was quite at variance with his profession.

He ushered her into his private office, apologizing profusely for its disarray and urging her into a seat with great ceremony. As soon as he had taken his place behind his desk, she put back her veil and, after calming herself with a few deep breaths, faced him bravely. "Without roundaboutation, Mr. Brindle, I want you to tell me just what is my financial situation," she said bluntly.

"Just as before, dear lady, just as before," he said with

an upraised eyebrow. "Didn't my letter make that clear?"

"No, it did not. As I understood what you'd written of the terms of the will, I am left with *nothing*."

"In a manner of speaking, that is true," Mr. Brindle explained, "but in actuality it is not quite the case. You *are* to have an income, but the exact amount of it is left to the discretion of the new heir."

"But that is as bad as being left with nothing, is it not?"

"Only if the new heir were an unfeeling monster," Mr. Brindle explained with a kindly smile. "In my experience, Lady Hartley, most heirs take on the responsibilities borne by their forebears as a matter of honor. You may have every expectation that the new heir will be as generous to you and yours as your brother was."

"Do you think so?" asked Lady Harriet, much relieved. "But perhaps Americans are not motivated by honor in the same way that the English are."

Mr. Brindle suppressed a smile and appeared to consider the matter seriously. "Perhaps so," he said thoughtfully, "but in this case, I have every reason to be optimistic. You see, although we have not yet located Mr. Jason Hughes, the heir, we have managed to learn a bit about him. He was born and is thought to reside in the state of Virginia, although there is some information that he may be traveling on their western frontier—Kentucky, I believe—where he has recently acquired a sizeable tract of land. He is well thought of by his business associates and friends. They describe him as honest, kind and generous. It is, therefore, quite unlikely that the fellow would cut you off without a penny."

"How delightful!" Harriet gave a heartfelt sigh. "This is the best news I've had since Osborn passed on. But tell me, Mr. Brindle, what am I to do until the heir is found and informs us of his intentions toward the family?"

"I see no reason why your income should not continue in the manner instituted by the late Viscount. I've already made those arrangements, since I am the executor of the will until such time as the heir is located."

Lady Harriet smiled at the lawyer warmly. "I don't know how to thank you, Mr. Brindle. You have dispelled a worrisome cloud from my mind. There is only one more matter which troubles me. Do you think we may remain in the Curzon Street house?"

"Since the Mainwaring townhouse is the only family residence in London, I have no idea what Mr. Hughes' wishes will be in that regard. But you may certainly remain there until Mr. Hughes arrives and makes his intentions known."

Lady Harriet nodded and rose to leave. The news she had learned was much more promising than she'd expected, and she left feeling years younger than when she arrived. Without bothering to replace the veil in front of her face, she permitted Mr. Brindle to escort her to her carriage. Before driving off, she asked him curiously if he had learned anything else about the new Viscount.

"Not much, I'm afraid," he told her. "Only that he is thought to be under thirty years of age and unmarried."

Unmarried! Lady Harriet sat back against the coach seat and savored the news. *Unmarried!* If only he would take a fancy to Anne! All their problems would be solved in such a case. Her sensible mind cautioned restraint, but throughout the entire trip home, she found herself daydreaming about it. She realized that every unmarried female in London would set her cap for the American, even if he proved to be as boorish and uncouth as most Americans were reputed to be. The fortune and the Mainwaring titles would be enough to minimize, in the eyes of every matchmaking Mama, any drawbacks of appearance or manner which the American might possess. The new Lord Mainwaring would have his choice of young ladies. But Anne might very well win him, if she chose to do so; she would have the advantage of being the first female with whom he would become acquainted. If only the girl could be persuaded to forget her attachment to Lord Claybridge.

But Lady Harriet was not so foolish as to embark on a

program of persuasion. She knew that her urgings would have little effect on her stepdaughter. In matters of the heart, most young ladies were wont to be obstinate, and the more one tried to separate them from the young men for whom they developed a *tendre*, the more likely they were to hang on. So Harriet wisely refrained from confiding to Anne her hopes for a match that would keep the Mainwaring fortune in the family. And she tried to remain calm.

November and December passed much as they always had. As the weeks went by, another hope began to grow in Lady Harriet's breast: perhaps the American was not coming after all! She developed a new interest in the *Morning Post* and would peruse its pages eagerly as soon as it arrived. (It was indeed wonderful how one's interest in politics increased as one's own fortunes became affected by the affairs of state.) The dispatches from America were infrequent and lacking in detail, but Harriet was able to learn that the Americans had curtailed their shipping to England because of their dislike of an English edict known as the Orders of Council. She had no clear idea what it all meant (and when she'd asked Peter to explain it to her, the explanation was so complicated that it quite made her head swim), but she understood enough to realize that travel to England from America was now almost impossible. By the time the new year had come and gone, and the unknown heir had not made an appearance, Lady Harriet became convinced that he would never come at all.

But one day in late January, a note arrived from Mr. Brindle informing her that Mr. Jason Hughes had been located by a British agent in America and was on his way to London. Lady Harriet's hope was crushed beyond repair. He was coming! Terrible things might happen. He might cut them off without a cent. He might turn them out of the house. The fearful worries that had assailed her at the time of her brother's demise returned in full force.

Now her only hope was to push the new heir into the arms of her stepdaughter. If only he were a pleasant, presentable gentleman, it would not be too cruel a thing to do to Anne. Lady Harriet knew only too well the benefits of an advantageous match. If only *her* mother had encouraged her to make one, she would not now be in this position. With this salve to her conscience, she began immediately to draw up a workable scheme. If she proceeded cleverly, all might not be lost.

Harriet decided that it would be wise to keep from the rest of the family the news of Jason Hughes' imminent arrival. Thus Anne was completely ignorant of her stepmother's hopes for her. Once she'd been informed that the family income was likely to continue indefinitely, she assumed that the dire predictions which her stepmother had made at the time of Lord Mainwaring's death would not come to pass. Besides, the situation with Arthur drove from her mind any concern she might otherwise have felt for the future of her family or the possible arrival of the gentleman from Virginia.

In the months since Lord Mainwaring's death, she had seen Arthur so infrequently that she could number the occasions on the fingers of one hand. And on those few occasions, his tongue had been guarded, and she'd learned nothing of his plans. It was only his gloomy aspect and the urgent appeal in his eyes that told her how much he'd suffered at her absence. There was a desperation in his tone the last time he'd seen her that told her he was at his wit's end. He'd even made a suggestion, quite veiled and vague, of a runaway match.

Anne's nature rebelled at the suggestion of a Gretna Green marriage. Such runaway affairs only caused pain and disappointment to the families and gave to the marriage an air of disreputable squalor. She would have liked a proper, formal, stylish wedding, during which all of London society could wish them joy, not a surreptitious, sordid affair which she and Arthur would always remember with shame. Yet, if there were no other way . . .

On a cold February afternoon, with the sleet making icy traces on the windowpane, Coyne delivered into Anne's hands a letter which had been brought to their door by a street urchin who had made it clear to the butler that the missive was for Miss Hartley's eyes and hers alone. One look at the designation told her it was from Arthur. She dismissed the butler, telling him that she did not want to be disturbed, and ran upstairs to the small sitting room at the head of the stairs in order to read the letter in strictest privacy. The note begged her to arrange a clandestine meeting so that he could discuss with her "Certain Matters" which were causing him "great Mental distress."

The note touched her deeply, but she had no love for meetings of this kind. In addition, she could not help but feel that Arthur should have the courage to demand to see her openly and honestly, no matter what his mother should say. All afternoon she paced the room, trying to decide what course to take. Unable to make up her mind, she returned to the window and, in the gray afternoon light, she read the letter for the third time.

A step on the stairs made her start guiltily. She folded the note in awkward haste and thrust it into the bosom of her dress. Snatching a book from the mantelpiece, she ran quickly to the sofa, sat down and assumed an expression of deep concentration on the book.

To her surprise, the door did not open unceremoniously upon her half-brother or her stepmother, as she'd expected. Instead, someone knocked firmly. "Is that you, Coyne?" she asked in annoyance.

"No, ma'am," came an unfamiliar voice.

With a puzzled frown, she put aside the book and went to open the door. She found herself facing a complete stranger who stood smiling down at her from a height of more than six feet. She gaped. The man seemed enormous in his odd clothing. His sunstreaked hair was wet with rain and much too long to be fashionable. His skin was darkly tanned and made his gray eyes seem shockingly light. His loosely fitting coat, buckskin breeches and blunt-toed boots were the garments of a man of the outdoors and seemed woefully out-of-place in a London sitting-room doorway.

She was suddenly aware that her heart had begun to hammer in fright and her knees to shake, but whether these symptoms of shock were caused by the unexpectedness of his appearance, the compelling gleam of his electrifying gray eyes or something else, she couldn't determine. "Wh-who *are* you—?" she stammered.

The gleaming smile widened, and the man made a brief bow. "Jason Hughes, ma'am. If you're Miss Anne Hartley, I'm your cousin-by-marriage from America."

"I . . . I am . . . Miss Hartley," Anne managed to acknowledge, staring at him in astonishment.

"Well, then, I'm mighty pleased to meet you, ma'am," the giant said cheerfully, proffering a large hand. Speechless, Anne automatically extended her hand to be kissed, but instead the man grasped it and shook it vigorously.

"How . . . do you do?" Anne said breathlessly, unable to keep from staring at him. "Are *you* the new Viscount Mainwaring?"

"I reckon so. The lady downstairs—your mama, I take it?—"

"My stepmother, Lady Harriet."

"Yup, she's the one . . . she said I was to tell you that, since I'm to be the new Viscount, you'll have to do somethin' with me."

"*Do* something?" Anne asked in complete confusion. "I don't understand . . ."

"I reckon she wants you to turn me into an English gentleman," he explained with a broad smile.

Anne, trying to digest his words, merely continued to gape at him. The young giant in the doorway, responding to her expression of dismay, grinned widely and nodded down at her in sympathetic amusement. "Yes, ma'am," he said with a wry twist of his lips, his voice choked with suppressed laughter, "I can't say I blame you for lookin' so staggered. Judgin' from the look of me, you've got yourself a job and a half!"

# Four

"MAY I COME IN, or is it the custom for English ladies to keep their gentlemen callers coolin' their heels in the corridors?" the American asked after a long moment, during which Anne found herself being surveyed with an appraising stare as direct, curious and rude as hers had been.

"Of course you may come in," she said coloring, and stepped aside to let him pass. "Please sit down." As he looked around the room and lowered his long frame into a chair, she added tartly, "What a strange expression. And not very apt. You can scarcely consider yourself a 'gentleman caller.' One can't be a caller at one's own home. This *is* your own house, you know."

"*Is* it?" Mr. Hughes asked innocently. "I didn't know that. The letter said only that I was to report here on my arrival."

"Nevertheless, it is yours. Are you going to put us out into the storm?"

Mr. Hughes tilted his head up to flick a cool glance at her as she stood over him. "You don't mean to call that little drizzle out there a storm, do you? If I'm to take some

real enjoyment from puttin' you out, I'd best wait for a
gale, or a nice, freezin' snowstorm."

Realizing she'd been bested, Anne merely tossed her
head and took a seat opposite him. "Have you just arrived
from America?" she asked loftily.

"Yes'm. Landed at Southhampton two days ago and
made straight for London. I intended to stay at
Fenton's—a fellow on board ship told me it's a right
proper hotel—but your stepmother insists I'm to stay
here. I hope you don't mind."

"I have no right to mind. As I told you, this is *your*
house."

Mr. Hughes frowned at her. "I know I *look* like a giant,
ma'am, but I'm no monster who tromped down a
beanstalk. I don't drive widows from their homes nor eat
little children for breakfast. I can quite easily take
residence at the hotel if my presence here causes you the
slightest discomfort."

"I . . . I'm sorry," Anne said contritely. "I've been quite
rude. You see, I . . . I had no warn—I mean, I had not been
informed that you were coming. If Mama has invited you
to stay here, of course you are welcome to do so."

"Thank you," the American said briefly. "*But*—?"

"But?"

"I thought I heard a 'but' at the end of that very polite
declaration," Mr. Hughes said, a mischievous twinkle
gleaming in his surprisingly light eyes.

Anne shrugged. Americans were obviously quite frank
and direct in their conversations. She decided to answer
him in the same spirit. "I was only going to say that I shall
certainly do my part to make you feel welcome among us,
but—"

"Aha! But . . . ?"

"But I hope you don't take Mama seriously when she
says I'm to . . . er . . . take you in hand."

"Take me in hand? Do you mean 'make a gentleman of
me'?" Mr. Hughes laughed loudly. "No, ma'am, I know
better. That's no job for a slip of a girl like you."

Anne, considerably taller than the average young lady, had never heard herself described as a 'slip of a girl' and relented enough to smile back at him. "Then we understand each other," she said.

"Better than you think," Mr. Hughes said, rising. "If you please, ma'am, will you call the butler to show me to my room? I can see that I'm keepin' you from some important readin'."

Anne was nonplussed. "Important reading?" she echoed.

"A letter. I must have interrupted you."

"B-But ... *how did you know* ... ?"

"Well, you see, ma'am, it's stickin' out of your dress a mite. If you'll excuse me, I'll get out of your way and leave you to it."

The color in Anne's cheeks took several minutes to recede after Mr. Hughes had followed Coyne out of the room. The fellow was the rudest creature she'd ever met! How *dared* he refer to a letter that was obviously not meant for him to notice? What right had he to look at her bosom, anyway? The more she thought about it, the more furious she became. Her stepmother had no right to send him to her without warning! She would tell Lady Harriet what she thought of such behavior—and *right now*!

In the meantime, Lady Harriet, absently working on her embroidery in the drawing room below, had every expectation of a confrontation with her stepdaughter. She had adjusted her embroidery frame so that she could face the door as she worked. In a very few minutes, she knew, Anne would burst indignantly into the room. She realized full well that Anne was bound to react strongly to her sudden confrontation with the new Viscount. But Harriet was unperturbed. She smiled placidly as her plump fingers worked with unhurried precision, adding tiny silk stitches to the intricate floral pattern stretched on the frame before her. She was quite calm. The arrival of the Viscount had not upset her at all. In fact, she'd found the young man delightful. She'd needed only ten minutes in his company to realize that he was the perfect man to fulfill her plans.

Mr. Jason Hughes of America was not exactly handsome, but there was something magnetic about his face. Harriet realized instantly that he was exciting enough to attract the most exacting of females. But she also recognized that his blunt manners, his drawling, informal speech and his years-out-of-fashion mode of dress all cried out for remedial attention. The American was in need of a good coat of town-bronze. And who was more capable of supplying the needed polish than Anne herself?

In addition, the situation gave Lady Harriet a perfectly acceptable excuse for keeping the American hidden away from society for a time. He had to be made presentable. The task would take some weeks, she surmised, during which it would be necessary to keep him in seclusion. And since Anne was to be the principle instructor in his transformation, she would, of necessity, be much in his company. How perfectly natural, therefore, for Anne to win a secure place in Jason Hughes' affection! By the time the young man was ready to meet all the eager young females who would be vying for his attentions, Anne would have already been established in first place.

Harriet smiled in satisfaction. Her plans seemed to be most fortuitously taking shape. Her nephew was a very likeable fellow. Her first brief meeting with him had been fascinating. Lady Harriet had kept him sitting beside her in the drawing room, plying him with questions. In response to her accusations that his father had callously forgotten his sister and brother in England, he'd assured her that his father had spoken of them often. He'd explained that Henry Hughes had married the daughter of a Virginia planter at the end of the war and had removed his bride to the city of Norfolk, where he'd made a mark in the shipping trade and where Jason had been born. About eight years ago, Jason's father had succumbed to a liver ailment and died. Two years later,

Jason's mother had remarried, and Jason, having attained his majority, had struck out on his own.

Although Lady Harriet was most curious about the details of Jason's life, she'd noticed that he was somewhat reticent about revealing anything but the most basic facts of his background. Unwilling to pry, and eager to arrange a meeting between the young man and her stepdaughter, she'd refrained from questioning him further. She'd sent him upstairs with instructions to introduce himself to Anne. And now she waited, keeping an interested eye on the door, for Anne to come in and reveal her reaction.

Lady Harriet had not long to wait. Jason had not been gone above a quarter of an hour when the drawing room door was flung open and Anne strode in. Her high color indicated that the girl was furious and bemused, but she faced her stepmother with her temper in check and eyebrows raised in challenging hauteur. "Just what are you up to, Mama?" she demanded unceremoniously.

"Up to? Whatever do you mean?" Lady Harriet countered calmly, fixing her eyes on her needlework.

"You sent that man up to me without a *word* of warning! How *could* you, Mama? I almost jumped out of my skin when I found him standing in the doorway—the fellow's a veritable *giant*!"

"I'm sure you can't blame me for *that*," Harriet pointed out reasonably.

"You know I don't mean that," Anne said impatiently. "I don't see why you sent him up at all. Why didn't you tell Coyne to warn me that he'd arrived? And what do you mean by telling him that you expect me to make a gentleman of him? How could anyone make a gentleman of that insufferable creature? What are you about, Mama? Have you some scheme up your sleeve?"

Harriet looked up innocently. "I have no idea why you should think me scheming merely because I would like my nephew—who has just arrived from a colonial backwater where he has obviously experienced nothing of civilized life—to learn to measure up to the demands of his titles.

You must have noticed, dearest, that his clothes and manner of speech are not quite what one would expect from an English peer."

"Of course I've noticed. I couldn't *help* noticing. But why should you *care*? A few months ago, you would have been happy to learn that he'd disappeared from the face of the earth!"

"I've changed my mind," Harriet declared calmly. "Now that I've seen him, I find I'm quite attached to him."

"*Attached* to him? Are you serious? You've barely met him!"

"Nevertheless, I *have* met him and find him charming—in a rough, untutored way. I've discovered that I have strong maternal feelings for the lad and would like nothing better than to have him become part of our family."

Anne stiffened and looked at her stepmother furiously. "Part of the *family*? And how do you plan to accomplish that, pray? And what has it to do with me?"

"It has only *this* to do with you—that I wish you to offer Mr. Hughes a bit of advice and assistance on matters of clothing and social activities and so on. After all, the young man has never set foot in London. He's never had any dealings with proper society. I merely wish you to teach him how to get on."

"And why have *I* been given the honor of instructing him?" Anne asked icily.

"My dear, you have always been admired for your sense of style. Everyone always says that Anne Hartley is bang up to the mark. Who else in the family is more qualified?"

The suspicious glare did not leave Anne's eyes as she dropped into the nearest armchair. "Mama, I have no desire to involve myself in this. It is no matter to me *how* the fellow gets on in society! And I don't see why it should matter to you."

"But it *does* matter to me," Harriet declared, keeping her voice placid. "He's my own brother's son, after all. My own blood, you know. And he's come across the ocean to take his place as head of this family—"

"Yes, but you've been praying that he would *remain* on the other side of the ocean—"

"Never mind. Now that he's here, I find that I like him very well. I'm glad he's come to head the family—it's a position that *I* don't feel at all qualified to hold. He seems a generous and capable man—just what this family needs."

"Ha!" snorted Anne bitterly, "you've much to learn about his character. But if you think he's so perfect, why do you want to change him?"

"I don't want to change him—only to give him some town-bronze. You can't wish for the head of our family to make a poor impression on the *ton* of London."

"I don't care *what* sort of impression he makes!"

Lady Harriet frowned. Then, carefully inserting her needle into the fabric for safekeeping and taking a deep, calming breath, she rose with as much dignity as her plump figure permitted and confronted her stepdaughter purposefully. "You *must* care, my dear, for all our futures depend on Mr. Hughes. We must, therefore, assist him in every way possible to adapt to his new station in life. He must be made content and comfortable in his new surroundings, but this will not come to pass unless he is accepted without restrictions by all of London society."

"But I don't see why *I* need be involved in—"

"You must be involved because there is no one else so well-qualified to instruct him."

"Nonsense! *You*, my dear Mama, are every bit as qualified as I!"

Harriet was momentarily at a loss. "Perhaps I am," she admitted reluctantly, "but it is better for him to be instructed by...er...someone closer to his own age."

"Then what about Peter?" Anne persisted. "At least Peter is a *male*—"

"Peter!" exclaimed Harriet with a snort. "What a notion! I suppose he can help, of course, but you know very well that the boy is completely at a loss when it comes to matters of style and social intercourse. For a boy who is universally considered to be brilliant, he has many areas of complete ignorance."

While his mother was ruthlessly maligning him behind his back, Peter, in the upstairs hallway, was making himself known to the new head of the family. The American was following the butler down the hall when Peter stepped out of his study for a brief respite from his books. He took one look at the enormous stranger, blinked behind his spectacles and gaped at the man open-mouthed.

The butler took the opportunity to introduce them. "May I present Master Peter Hartley, your lordship?" he asked with appropriate formality. Then, his formal duty done, he dropped his usual imperturbability to murmur into Peter's ear, "It's the new Viscount, Master Peter. Can you credit it? He's just arrived from *America*!"

Peter, embarrassingly aware the new Lord Mainwaring could scarcely have missed noticing Coyne's solecism, glanced quickly at the Viscount's face to catch his response to the butler's lapse. Coyne had known Peter from birth and stood on comfortably intimate terms with the boy. Although Peter was aware that the butler should have kept a closer guard on his tongue in front of the new head of the household, he hoped that the American would understand Coyne's justifiable excitement.

But there was no sign on the American's face that he'd taken any notice of Coyne's dereliction of duty. He merely put out his hand. "You're Lady Harriet's son, aren't you? I'm Jason Hughes."

Peter found his hand being shaken with enthusiasm. He peered up through his spectacles at the tanned face of his American cousin with undisguised curiosity. "This is an unexpected surprise, my lord," he ventured. "I had supposed that passage from America would be impossible to obtain in these times."

"Difficult, but not impossible, as you can see," the

American answered in his pleasant, drawling colonial accent. "And please, don't call me 'my lord.' We don't cotton to titles in the States."

Peter couldn't help smiling at the unfamiliar usages; "*cotton to*" and "*the States*" had such an American sound. "Then what *am* I to call you?" he asked shyly.

"Won't just plain 'Jason' do?"

Peter considered. "It seems an unwarranted liberty to use your given name on such short acquaintance—"

"But we Americans enjoy taking liberties, you know," Jason assured him with a warm smile.

"So I've heard," Peter smiled back, "but you're not in America now, you know. I don't think Mama would approve of my calling you Jason so brazenly."

"Well, let's not stand about in the hall debatin' the point," Jason suggested. "Why don't you keep me company while I unpack my gear, and we'll discuss the matter?"

"Unpack your *gear*?" Peter asked in surprise, eagerly falling into step alongside his enormous cousin. "Why don't you let Coyne—?"

The butler, leading the way to the large bedroom in the northwest corner of the house (the room which Lady Harriet had hastily chosen as the most appropriate one available on such short notice, despite its drafty windows and smoky fireplace), looked back over his shoulder with a grimace of disapproval. "His lordship insists on doing his own unpacking," he said, with an ill-concealed air of offense.

"No need to get miffed," Jason said placatingly. "There ain't much to unpack, you see."

The butler didn't answer, having arrived at his destination. He opened the bedroom door cautiously and looked inside. Relieved to discover that the maid (whom he'd hastily dispatched to remove the dust covers and tidy up the room) had accomplished her task, he stepped aside and permitted his lordship to enter. Jason looked around with interest at the square, moderately sized but ornately

paneled room. His shabby portmanteau had already been
placed on the upholstered bench which stood at the foot
of a large, canopied bed. A fire had been started in the
grate, the furniture had been dusted, and the curtains had
been drawn back to permit the gray afternoon light to
filter in.

The butler, well aware that the bed hangings were
threadbare, the chair upholstery shabby and the room
enveloped in gloom and chill, nevertheless hoped that the
new Viscount would not be overly disturbed by these
defects. He need not have worried. The Viscount surveyed
his new quarters with an approving smile. "Now, ain't this
*grand!*" he exclaimed, impressed.

Peter, whose bedroom was larger, warmer and more
comfortably furnished than this one, glanced quickly at
Jason's face, but there was not a sign of insincerity written
upon it. Mr. Jason Hughes of Virginia must have had a
humble background, Peter surmised, if he found *this*
room grand.

When Coyne had bowed himself out, Peter perched on
the bed and watched in fascination while his cousin
unpacked his meager belongings. Three or four changes
of linen, a riding coat, a few outmoded day and evening
coats and three pairs of breeches were all that Jason had
brought, except for a strange-looking furry garment
which Peter took to be a greatcoat. Peter wondered what
sort of life his cousin had led in America. From all
appearances, it was not the comfortable, elegant, easy life
which he would have led if he'd been brought up in
England.

Jason, meanwhile, looked about him for a place to
store his things. The only piece of furniture which seemed
suitable was an odd-looking chest with more than a dozen
small drawers in it. "What *is* this thing?" he asked Peter.
"May I put my things in it?"

"It's a gentleman's dressing table," Peter explained,
getting up from the bed to demonstrate the chest's many
intricacies. "You see, although it appears to be merely a
chest of seventeen drawers—"

"Seventeen? Amazing!" Jason marveled.

"Not all of these are drawers, however. This is really a mirror which pops up when you open it. This one here unfolds and becomes a writing desk, see? And this one, on the left, is compartmented to hold your cuff links, watch fobs, and such trinkets. And *this* one—"

"Stop, or I shall be hopelessly confused!" Jason laughed. "It's truly a wonder, but are any of those just plain *drawers*?"

"Of course. All the lower ones. And you needn't worry about becoming confused. Your valet is the only one who has to bother with it."

"But you see, I have no valet," Jason explained with a shrug.

Peter resumed his perch on the bed and adjusted his spectacles thoughtfully. "Don't they have valets in America? Or were you too poor to have one?" he asked with frank interest.

"Money was never a worry to me," Jason answered with equal directness. "Don't know if there are any valets in America or not—no one I ever knew had one. Can't you English fellows dress yourselves?"

Peter laughed. "Not the dandies. Why, some of them take three hours to tie their neckcloths!"

"You don't mean it!" Jason said, looking up from his portmanteau in disbelief.

"It's true," Peter assured him. "I've heard that some of them spend half the day dressing for dinner."

Jason merely shook his head and stooped over to store his shirts in one of the lower drawers. Peter noticed the grace and agility of his movements as he bent down. "You must be well over six feet tall!" he exclaimed admiringly. "Do all American men grow so tall?"

Jason straightened up. "I'm six feet three or so," he grinned, "and as big a gawk back home as I'll no doubt be here."

"And weigh fourteen stone, I'd wager," Peter estimated, looking over his cousin speculatively. "What a fighter you'd make in the ring!"

"I don't get much chance to box—a man my size has trouble findin' a challenger," Jason grinned. Then, looking at his bespectacled cousin in surprise, he added, "Don't tell me that you've a liking for boxing! Your mother gave me to understand that you're the scholarly sort."

"That's about all I'm good for," Peter admitted with a sigh. "I ride a bit, of course, but I'm not fit for much else. Certainly not boxing."

"Size doesn't have much to do with prowess in the ring, you know," Jason said, feeling a flicker of sympathy for his slim young cousin. "So long as you're matched with an opponent of equal weight, it's speed and footwork that make the difference."

"I've always thought so," Peter said, brightening, "but there's never been anyone around who could show me how—"

Jason understood immediately what Peter could not quite explain. The young, bookish son in a household of women—it was not the atmosphere in which a boy would learn to develop the manly arts. "I'll be glad to teach you a few of the skills and tricks of boxing—not that I'm a great expert, mind."

"Would you *really* be willing to teach me?" Peter asked with a shy eagerness.

"I wouldn't have offered if I didn't mean it," Jason said bluntly.

Peter's face colored with pleasure. "I never thought I'd be saying this, Cousin Jason," the boy said with obvious sincerity, "but I'm very glad you've come."

Downstairs, Lady Harriet was finding it beyond her capabilities to convince her obstinate stepdaughter to undertake the education of the American. The girl's resistance was unshakable. "I tell you, Mama," she insisted, "it would be a waste of time! The fellow is ill-mannered and rude, and he subjected me to vulgar scrutiny and near-insults. Don't look at me so! I'm not being obstinate, I assure you. I am merely trying to explain to you that I cannot accept what I am certain is a hopeless task. I haven't the time nor the ability to undertake the excessive effort which would be required to make a respectable peer of him. Even Mr. Hughes admitted to me—How did he put it? Oh, yes!—that it would be *a job and a half*!"

"Nonsense," Lady Harriet murmured placidly, resuming her seat at the embroidery frame and picking up her needle, "the fellow cannot be so bad—"

"Not so *bad*? Why, he's positively *primitive*! He can't even speak proper English!" Anne rose from her chair and walked purposefully to the door. But before she stalked from the room, she turned to her stepmother and added dramatically, "Turning that man into a Pink-of-the-Ton would be like turning a *frog* into a *prince*! And for *that* trick, Mama dear, you'd need more than a daughter with a sense of style. You'd need a fairy godmother with a *magic wand*!"

# Five

ANNE RETURNED to the upstairs sitting room and, finding it deserted, entered, closed the door carefully and returned to the window to read her letter once more. Although the light by this time had all but disappeared, she knew the wording almost by heart. But repeated readings did not lessen her feeling of distaste. Why did Arthur feel so strongly the need for secrecy? Why couldn't he call at her home, as he was used to do?

The letter gave some explicit suggestions for a meeting between them. He'd requested that she arrange for a meeting at Cherry's home in Half-Moon Street. He would send for her answer that evening. With a shrug, she lit a candle, brought it to the writing table and penned two quick notes—one to Arthur and one to Cherry. She would accede to his wishes this once, but she determined to make it clear to him that she would brook no furtive meetings. It was a mode of behavior for which she had no taste.

The meeting took place the following morning. Anne arrived at the house on Half-Moon Street early, so that she would have a moment to confer with Cherry about strategies. Cherry greeted her at the door in pleased excitement. She was overjoyed to be party to such romantic doings. "Come in," she chirped eagerly, dismissing the butler with a wave of her hand. "Oh, how lovely you look today. That blue pelisse is positively—"

"Never mind the pelisse, Cherry, please. Has your mother gone to her card game, as usual?"

"Yes, but you needn't have worried about her. She would not think it strange that Arthur Claybridge chances to drop by when you are with me. After all, you are here so often, and Arthur is such a very good friend—"

"I know. You're quite right. I'm behaving like a confirmed ninny-hammer." The two girls walked down the hall to the Laverstoke drawing room. "It's only that I cannot like meeting Arthur in this surreptitious way."

"I find it *very* romantical," Cherry sighed enviously.

"Oh, Cherry, you are such a goose! I very much fear that the only reason for this 'romantical' meeting is . . . well, I hate to say it, but it's the only thing I can think of . . . Arthur's *cowardice*!"

"Cowardice! Anne, how *can* you think such a thing!"

"What else am I to think? Why must he suddenly find it necessary to meet me *here*? Why can't he stand up to his mother and see me openly?"

Cherry drew off Anne's pelisse, picked up her gloves and bonnet and threw them all on a chair. Then, seating herself next to Anne on the sofa, she looked earnestly at her friend, her wide eyes clouded with sympathetic concern. "Don't think ill of poor Arthur, dearest. I'm sure he'll explain it all when he comes. You mustn't jump to conclusions—you're undoubtedly misjudging him shamefully. Just give him this chance to explain."

"But that's why I'm here, is it not?"

Cherry patted her hand. "Good. Everything will be fine, you'll see. In the meantime, I'll go to see about a tea tray. How long shall I leave you with him? Do you think half-an-hour—?"

"No, Cherry, you're not to go at all. You're the best

friend I have in the world—as Arthur knows perfectly
well—and there's nothing he can say to me that can't be
said in your presence."

"No!" Cherry said with surprising firmness. "I *can't*
stay here! Arthur won't be able to speak freely . . . and I'd
find the circumstances most uncomfortable. It's really out
of the question to expect me to remain . . ."

"Honestly, Cherry, you vex me. If the situation were
reversed, and it was *you* who were meeting a man
clandestinely in *my* drawing room—"

Cherry smiled, her wide eyes suddenly glowing in
pleasure at the imaginary scene that Anne's words had
conjured up before her. Clasping her hands together at
her breast, like an actress at Drury Lane, she breathed,
"Oh, Anne, if *only* it would happen! What an absolutely
*thrilling* conjecture!" Then, putting aside the vision
firmly, she said, "If it *were* to happen, I should certainly
expect you to leave me and my . . . er . . . *gallant* to
ourselves. And for as long as possible!"

Anne couldn't help giggling. "Cherry, what a *goosecap*
you are! Sometimes I think your brain has been addled by
too much reading of romantic novels. It's Fanny
Burney—she's bad for you. I'm convinced of it."

"Just because I've read her *Evalina* two or three times?"

"Two or three times? What a bouncer! You practically
know it by heart!"

The question of Cherry's presence or absence during
the forthcoming meeting was forgotten in the badinage
over Miss Burney's novel, and Arthur arrived before the
issue was settled. Arthur's appearance on his entrance
into the drawing room was every bit as romantic as
Cherry had anticipated. His hair was windblown, his eyes
troubled, his manner agitated and his voice breathless.
"I've kept you waiting, haven't I?" he asked in a tone of
severe self-censure. "I'm most terribly sorry. I could not
leave the house as early as I had planned."

Although the apology had been addressed to Anne,
Cherry could not help replying. "But you are not late at

all," she assured him gently as she took his hat, picked up Anne's outer garments from the chair and started out of the room.

"Cherry, you needn't bother to remove our things," Anne said with a meaningful glare. "Call for the butler."

Cherry met the glare with a mischievous smile. "I'll only be a moment," she murmured and slipped from the room.

The lovers were alone. Arthur seized his opportunity and crossed promptly to Anne's side, sitting down beside her on the sofa and grasping both her hands. "Anne, my dearest girl, I am in the greatest despair! I don't know what to do!"

Anne looked down at his lowered head, his tousled curls and his posture of dejection and was conscious of a feeling of impatience. She had not the capacity for sympathy that Cherry had, she suddenly realized. Cherry would have murmured something endearing and stroked his hair. But Anne was so strongly overwhelmed with curiosity about the *reasons* for his unhappiness that she was unwilling to spend any time or effort to soothe his pain. "What is this all about, Arthur?" she asked abruptly.

Arthur looked up at her. "I've had a terrible row with my mother. I haven't wanted to trouble you with this before, but I've known for some time that the family's finances are hopelessly tangled. I've been doing what I can to straighten matters out, but I'm not greatly talented in matters of business management. And now Mama feels that it is my place to ... to ..." He could not go on but lowered his head again.

"To make an advantageous match," Anne finished for him drily.

He looked up in surprise. "Yes, that's *it*. How did you guess—?"

"I've been hearing the same thing ever since Lord Mainwaring died and Mama realized that Peter would not be the heir."

Arthur was horrified. "Do you mean that Lady Harriet

wants *you* to . . . to marry for convenience? My God! Why haven't you *told* me?"

"I don't know. I hoped something might happen..."

Arthur jumped up and began to pace about the room. "This is worse than I thought! Good God, to think of . . . of your being pushed into wedlock with . . . with who knows what sort of creature! And merely for his wealth! It makes me *ill*! This is insupportable! I cannot—will not—give you up!"

"Give me up?" Anne stiffened. "Is *that* what you have come to tell me? That you've decided to give me up?"

"No, no! How can you ask such a thing? I admit that my mother desires me to do so, but I am not a helpless child, but a grown man . . . the head of my family . . ."

"Exactly. The head of your family. Your mother has not the authority to make such demands of you."

He turned away, sagging in despair. "But Anne, I can no longer bear the life I lead at home . . . the endless quarreling and nagging to which I'm subjected. I must do *something* . . ."

She met his eyes and, as always, the intensity of his gaze, the twitch of the muscle in his cheek, the lock of hair that fell so appealingly over his forehead caused her heart to contract. She beckoned him to sit down beside her and, surrendering to an impulse, she brushed back the unruly lock from his forehead and let her hand rest for a moment on his cheek. With a groan, he took the hand and pressed it to his lips. "What are we to do?" he asked miserably.

"I don't know," she whispered in equal unhappiness. "Have you thought of anything . . . anything at all?"

"Yes, I have," he answered suddenly, sitting up with a purposeful set of his shoulders, as if he were making up his mind to something. "Gretna."

"*Gretna*? A runaway marriage?" This time it was Anne's turn to rise and pace the room. "I haven't wanted . . . I've never liked it. All that dissembling and dishonesty. The secrecy, the furtiveness . . . as if we'd done something of which we were ashamed."

"I know. I've thought of that, too. But I see no other way—"

"But Arthur, it would solve nothing! Where would we go afterwards? Where would we live? And *how*?"

"I *have* thought of that, my dear. I am not completely impractical. There is a living about to become available at a vicarage in Shropshire. I have a family connection there. The income is not great, but there is a house. And if I sell the family estate in Devonshire, which my business agent has been suggesting, my mother and sister might contrive tolerably well in their life here in London without my support."

Anne stopped in her tracks and stared at Arthur as if she'd never seen him before. "Do you mean . . . are you saying that you would take *holy orders*?"

He smiled at her air of stupefaction. "Yes, of course. I would *have* to, wouldn't I? Don't look so dismayed. I am qualified. I've often thought that, if circumstances had been different . . . if my family were not so well placed in society, or if I were not the only son . . . that I might have been quite content to take that path."

Anne could not help staring at him. No gentleman of her acquaintance had ever shown the slightest interest in entering the clergy. Members of the *ton* were usually either uninterested in religious matters or, at best, casual in their observances. That anyone in her circle would consider taking holy orders was almost unthinkable. "But should you *enjoy* such a life?" she asked, aghast.

"Yes, I think I would," he answered. "But *my* enjoyment is not the point. It is *you* I am thinking of. I would enjoy *any* life that made it possible for you to be my wife."

Anne, whose mind had been dwelling on the picture of herself in a little cottage in Shropshire, the wife of a country vicar, did not realize, for a moment, what she'd just heard. "What did you say?" she asked, a smile dawning at the corners of her mouth.

"I said I would enjoy any life that made it possible for you to be my wife."

"Oh, dear," she said, a mock expression of dismay on her face, "I've missed it. What a disappointment!"

"Disappointment?" Arthur asked, blinking in confusion.

"Yes. I think that I've had a *proposal of marriage*, and it was made in so casual a fashion that I almost failed to notice it."

Arthur's puzzled look remained frozen on his face for a moment and then changed to discomfiture. "Of course!" he muttered. "I should have done it properly. I've botched it, haven't I?"

"Don't be silly, Arthur," she responded, sitting down beside him again. "I was only joking."

"But you are quite right," he insisted. "Is it too late for me to get down on my knees and make a formal proposal?"

Anne laughed. "Sometimes I think you're as gooseish as Cherry. I would only giggle if you went down on your knees."

"But I haven't yet told you that you are the most beautiful, wonderful, delightful girl I've ever known, that I love you most devotedly, and all the other things a man should say when he asks a woman to be his wife."

"Well, you've told them to me now. And very nicely, too."

Arthur smiled at her in some relief. "Have I? Very well, then, I suppose we may dispense with the kneeling." There was a pause while he watched her expectantly. But Anne, a smile still lingering on her lips, was looking down abstractedly at her hands folded in her lap. "Haven't you anything to say to *me*?" Arthur prodded. "It's *your* turn now."

"My turn?" She blinked and forced herself to attention. "What do you mean?"

"I've asked you to marry me, my dear. You're supposed to give me some response, you know."

Anne's smile faded. "You know I love you, Arthur. With all my heart. But a Gretna marriage . . . a vicarage in Shropshire . . . it's all a bit . . ."

"Sudden?" Arthur supplied.

"Yes, sudden." All at once, she shook her head, stared at him a moment, and then a peal of laughter escaped her.

Arthur stared. "What is it? What has amused you so?"

Anne was laughing too hard to manage an answer. At that moment, there was a discreet knock at the door, and Cherry entered, followed by the butler with a tea tray.

Cherry had envisioned a number of tableaus which she might have discovered on her entrance into the drawing room: Anne and Arthur at opposite ends of the room, staring at each other in white-lipped anger; Anne and Arthur locked in a passionate embrace; Anne seated on the sofa, hands folded, and Arthur kneeling beside her; Anne sobbing miserably in Arthur's arms. What she *never* imagined was that Anne would be laughing uncontrollably, and Arthur would be gaping at her in bewilderment. "What on earth is making her so merry?" Cherry asked Arthur curiously.

Arthur shrugged. "I wish I knew," he muttered.

After the butler had left, Anne caught her breath with an effort and endeavored to explain. "Forgive me, but it's so *funny*! I had determined, years ago, that when a gentleman made me an offer, the one thing I would *never* say was 'Oh, sir, this is so sudden!' And just now, quite without realizing it, *I said those very words*!"

Cherry giggled briefly, but then her mouth dropped open. "But... but that means...!" She looked from one to the other with shining eyes. "Arthur! You've *offered* for her!"

Arthur nodded, smiling at Cherry's delight. "Yes, but I've not yet had an answer, beyond 'this is so sudden,' of course."

"Oh, dear," Cherry said in chagrin, "I came in too soon! I'll go out again and give you more time—"

"No, Cherry, it's not necessary," Anne cut in. "Please stay and serve Arthur some tea."

"But... Anne, are you not going to give him an answer?" Cherry asked, perplexed.

"No. I must go home and think. Arthur knows how much I wish to marry him, don't you Arthur? But your plan is so unexpected that it leaves me quite astounded. I must have time to consider it calmly..."

"What plan?" Cherry asked, curiosity taking precedence over good manners.

"Arthur will tell you about it over tea. I must go. Don't disturb yourself, Cherry. The butler will get my things." And giving Arthur's hand an affectionate squeeze, she went to the door. "Tell me, Arthur," she inquired, pausing in the doorway and turning to him, "would you not prefer to be married and return here in London if it could be arranged, rather than go off to Shropshire?"

"I...suppose so," he replied hesitantly, "if it is what you would wish. But I don't see how such a plan can be contrived..."

"Neither do I. That's what I want to think about," Anne said. With a wave of her hand to Cherry, who stood gaping after her, Anne took her leave.

"Shropshire? What is she talking about?" Cherry asked, as she took a seat at the tea tray and began to pour.

Arthur, bemused and discontent with the outcome of his tête-à-tête, felt the need to unburden his heart to an understanding friend, but his masculine reticence made him hesitate. However, when two comforting cups of tea had been drunk, and when Cherry had taken a place beside him on the sofa and fixed her wide eyes on him with their expression of compassionate concern, he found himself confiding the whole of his conversation with his beloved into her eager ear. She nodded and smiled encouragingly every time he sighed; she was most heartening when she heard his plans and most flatteringly impressed by his hitherto-unexpressed ambitions to enter the clergy. When he at last took his leave, his step was jaunty and his head high. It had been, he decided, a most satisfactory morning.

## *Six*

THE SHORT WALK BACK HOME did not give Anne much time to think, but it was long enough for her to realize that she was completely unsuited to be a vicar's wife and to live in dowdy obscurity in a cottage in Shropshire. Her reaction, she knew, was ignoble and mean-spirited. Cherry would be appalled. Her friend would no doubt have glowed with joy at the prospect of love in a cottage. Anne could almost hear her: "Just think, dearest, how *lovely* it would be! You could plant roses round the door, and bake your own bread! Just imagine it—when Arthur came in after making his rounds of the parishioners who were ill, he'd find you in the kitchen up to your beautiful elbows in fragrant dough . . . and he'd try to embrace you, and you'd spill flour on his shoulder and across his cheek . . . and you'd both laugh . . ."

Ugh! The entire picture made Anne shudder. How could she bear it in Shropshire, so far from the balls, the opera, the shops, the libraries, the gossip, the excitement, the gaiety of London? How could she exist in a place where she would be forced to wear last year's gowns, chat with the farmers' wives and find herself patronized by the local gentry? The prospect was utterly repellent.

On the other hand, could she bear to *refuse* Arthur? To live without him—perhaps to see him wed to another? *That* was the dreadful alternative.

She arrived home before she could even begin to find a solution to the problem. She came in quietly, hoping to make her way to her room unnoticed, to give herself an opportunity to think without being disturbed. But in the foyer, she came upon a scene which drove everything else from her mind.

Coyne and Lady Harriet were confronting a creature Anne took at first to be an enormous gypsy. But of course, she immediately recognized her strange American cousin-by-marriage. He was dressed in the most peculiar coat she'd ever seen. It was made of an unrecognizable animal skin and sewn with the fur on the inside. It had no collar or lapels, but it was edged all around—even on the bottom—with the fur. In his hand, the American carried a round-brimmed, round-crowned black hat. He looked very much like a backwoods trapper she'd once seen in a sketch in a book of American explorations. "Good God!" she exclaimed. "You're not going *out* in that coat, are you?"

Lady Harriet turned to her with an expression of intense relief in her eyes. "I'm so glad you've returned, love," she said with less than her usual placidity. "We've been trying to make Jason understand that he should not step out into the world just yet."

Anne giggled. "Yes, I can quite see why."

Jason frowned at her in mock reproof. "I'm happy to be able to provide you with a fittin' subject for ridicule, ma'am. But I wish you'd stop your laughin' long enough to help me convince your mama that no harm will come if I take a bit of a stroll. I've set my heart on purchasin' a suit of armor, and I'd like to look at the shops—"

"No harm?" Anne cut in bluntly. "You'll have the whole of London laughing by nightfall if even *one* person sees you in that rig."

"Let 'em. Ain't no skin off *my* nose."

Anne, trying to make sense of his unfamiliar aphorism, blinked up at him, only to become aware of a glint of amusement in his eyes. "Are you laughing at *me*, sir?" she demanded, putting her chin up haughtily. "If I've been slow in responding to your witticism, it is only because your American language is so barbaric."

"Nonsense, girl," he came back, grinning. "There wasn't a word in that sentence you don't know."

Challenged, Anne went over the sentence again. "'Ain't no skin off my nose.' Oh, I see! It's similar to 'Sticks and stone may break my bones, but words—'"

"Exactly," he said approvingly, "but shorter and more to the point."

Anne smiled back. "I admit it's a colorful expression."

"That may be," Lady Harriet said, "but it's not very much help in the matter we're discussing. It may be no skin from *your* nose if you become the laughingstock of London, but it shall certainly bruise *mine*. I won't have the Mainwaring name made ridiculous."

Jason turned back to her and said politely, "I know how you feel, Lady Harriet, but no one knows me here. No passerby will be able to make the connection between this peculiar foreigner and the Mainwarings."

"They'll make the connection later, however, when you've been introduced to society. Such a sight as you make now will not easily be forgotten."

"Do I look as bad as that?" Jason asked ruefully.

Lady Harriet softened immediately. "Oh, dear. I didn't mean to offend . . . that is, of course *you* don't look bad. I find you quite handsome, truly I do. It's only that *coat*—"

Anne nodded in agreement, circling Jason and studying his appearance with amused, half-admiring revulsion. "I've never *seen* such a dreadful garment. Why on earth do you want to wear it?"

"Because it's warm!" he declared impatiently. "I own nothing else that is suitable for this obnoxious climate. This Virginia boy is accustomed to much milder weather."

"But I'm sorry to have to tell you, 'Virginia boy,' that nothing like it has ever been seen on the streets of London. If you don't want to make a cake of yourself, you'll remain indoors until a greatcoat can be made for you."

"But that may take *days*!"

"Weeks, more likely."

*"Weeks?"* He looked at Anne in dismay. "You can't ask me to remain cooped up in the house for weeks!"

"It *does* seem a bit cruel," Lady Harriet admitted.

"Of course, he may go outdoors on milder days," Anne suggested, "if he wears one of his less exceptional coats. And he may take some hope in the realization that the time necessary for making his greatcoat can be considerably shortened if he speaks to the tailors in the proper way."

Lady Harriet looked at Anne hopefully. "Oh, Anne, dearest, would you help him to do that?"

Anne caught herself up short. "Now, Mama, I *told* you I wanted nothing to do with—"

"Anne!" her stepmother cut her off in embarrassment. "You needn't be so tactless, with Jason standing right here."

"Oh, that's all right, ma'am," Jason assured her. "Your daughter has already informed me to my face that makin' me over into a proper gentleman is too hopeless a task for her to undertake."

"Never mind, dear boy," Lady Harriet said soothingly, "we shall manage very well without Anne's help. As far as *I* can see, you are quite a proper gentleman already and only want the proper clothing."

Anne merely snorted in a scornful—and very unladylike—manner.

Jason, ignoring her, grinned at his aunt. "Thank you, ma'am, for those comfortin' words. If I had to rely on the good opinion of your daughter, my self-esteem would suffer a real beatin'."

"What gammon!" sneered Anne. "I'm beginning to suspect that your self-esteem is as oversized as *you* are, and I'm convinced it can stand up quite well under any blows from *me*."

"Anne, stop this at once! You are upsetting me, and you know my heart won't stand it. If you won't help him, you can at least leave the boy in peace," Harriet ordered. "Come, Jason, give that coat to the butler and let's confer in the library about ways and means to set you up properly in your new role."

Jason, with a sigh, surrendered to female pressure. He took off the offending garment and handed it to Coyne. The butler made sure also to remove the ugly, round hat from Jason's hand, after which he quickly made a retreat down the hallway, determined to hide the clothes forever from the light of day.

Lady Harriet, meanwhile, with an encouraging smile, started up the stairs, with Jason meekly following. With his foot on the bottom step, he remembered that he had not taken his leave of Anne. He turned around and found her staring at him with a look of earnest speculation. "Is something the matter?" he inquired.

"I was only thinking..." she said slowly, "that perhaps I *might* take it upon myself to instruct you—"

Lady Harriet, halfway up the stairs, swung around eagerly. "What? Oh, Anne dear, would you *really*?"

"Under certain circumstances," Anne said cautiously.

Jason looked from one lady to the other, his eyes glinting with rueful amusement. "I don't want you ladies to fight over me, now," he muttered drily.

Harriet either missed or ignored his sally. "What circumstances?" she demanded of her daughter.

"That is to be a matter between his lordship and me, Mama, if you don't mind."

Lady Harriet gave Anne a piercing glance. "No, I don't mind at all," she said.

"Does anyone care if *I* mind?" his lordship asked no one in particular.

"No," said Anne shortly. "And since Mama has given her permission, I'd like you to come with me to the morning room where we can discuss the matter."

Jason looked up at Lady Harriet. "Do you wish me to go with her, ma'am?"

"Yes, I *do*, Jason. She can be of enormous help to you," Harriet urged.

Jason nodded and obediently turned back to follow Anne into the morning room. "All right, girl, what's this all about?" he asked as soon as they were alone.

Anne closed the door carefully. "Won't you sit down, my lord?" She motioned to the round table set before the bow window.

"No, I don't think I will. Here I am in my shirtsleeves, and there you are all rigged out in that blue coverin' and that bedazzlin' bonnet—why, ma'am, it makes you much too intimidatin'. Maybe I'd better stand."

Anne met his bantering look with a suspicious one of her own. "I'm quite sure, sir, that it would take more than a mere bonnet to intimidate you. Nevertheless, I shall remove it, and my pelisse as well, and then we may *both* be comfortable."

"Stripped to our shirtsleeves, like a couple of boxers, eh?" grinned the Viscount.

"Please, my lord, let us be serious," Anne requested, seating herself at the table and gesturing to the chair opposite. "I have a proposal to make to you."

Jason seated himself. "Well, go ahead, girl. Shoot!"

"First, my lord, may I ask you a few questions which are rather...er...personal?"

"Sure. Fire away."

Anne smiled and shook her head. "What a wild country you come from, Mr. Hughes. All this 'shooting' and 'firing away' convinces me that Americans are more apt to converse with guns than with words."

"Not at all, ma'am," Jason answered promptly. "The expressions are merely metaphorical, I assure you. Please proceed with your questions. You've aroused my curiosity."

"Very well, then. First, I'd like to know if it is *you* who wants to make a mark in London society, or it is *Mama* who is urging you to do so."

"Oh, it's me, I assure you. Lady Harriet is very willing to assist me, but I would like nothing better, I promise you, than to be turned into one of those—what is it Peter calls them?—out-and-outers."

Anne looked at him suspiciously. "Then why do I feel that you're mocking me? That you really have no desire *at all* to make yourself over?"

"Is that a question you wish me to answer, or is it merely rhetorical? Because I can't possibly answer it, you know. How can *I* explain why *you* don't trust my word?"

"Then you *truly* want my instruction in how to get on in London?"

"Yes, truly."

"Do you mind telling me *why*? You don't seem the sort of man who would enjoy dressing to the nines, paying morning calls on insipid girls, riding decorously through the park at five in the afternoon, dancing at Almack's, doing the pretty for the dowagers, gambling at White's—"

"Good Lord, girl, if it's your object to talk me out of it, you're on the verge of succeedin.' Is *that* the life of a London gentleman?"

"It is, more or less, an accurate summary, I think. Why do you want to do it?"

"Are you askin' my *motive*, ma'am? What makes you think I have one?"

"I don't believe you're the sort of man who would do things without a reason."

He regarded her askance. "Do you want the truth?"

"Yes, I do. And nothing but . . ."

"Well, then, the truth of the matter is that I wish to find myself a wife."

"A *wife*?" she asked, startled.

"Yes. Why do you find that so surprisin'?"

"I . . . I don't know. I didn't think . . . Are you *bamming* me, my lord?"

"If that's your English way of askin' if I'm pullin' your

leg, I tell you bluntly, girl, that we'll get nowhere in this conversation if you insist on disbelievin' me."

"But... couldn't you have found a wife in America?" Anne asked.

"I didn't *want* a wife when I was in America," he answered promptly, smiling at her with that teasing glint back in his eyes.

For no reason that she could determine, Anne felt a flush creep up into her cheeks. "Then why *now*?" she nevertheless persisted in asking.

"Let's just say that if I'm to be a proper lord, I ought to have a proper lady."

"I see. And *that's* why you feel the need for... er... town-bronze?"

"A bit of polish? Of course. Would a lady—like you, for example—take any notice of me the way I am?"

"Oh, she'd *notice* you, certainly," Anne responded with a teasing smile, "but I agree that she might not wish to *wed* you—at least not as you looked in that dreadful coat you were going to wear today."

"Exactly. That's why I need some polishin'."

"Very well. That's just what I wanted to determine. Now, if I were to give you that polish... and even help you to win a suitable young lady... would you be willing to make a... a kind of... exchange?"

He gave her a level look. "In America we call it horse-tradin'."

"Yes, that's it exactly! Horse-trading. Are you willing?"

"Depends on what it is you want from *me*, doesn't it? What's *my* part of this arrangement to be?"

"Well, it's a little... difficult... to explain..."

"Is it? Don't tell me that I'm intimidatin' *you*, now. You've nothin' to fear from me, girl. Out with it."

"Very well. You see, there's a certain young man—"

"I thought there might be," he muttered drily.

She cast a quick glance at his face, lowered her eyes and

went on. "—and we wish to marry. But our families oppose the match—"

"Lady Harriet doesn't like him?"

"Let us say she thinks we wouldn't suit."

"I see. The fellow's a bounder, is that it?"

"Not at all! The gentleman in question is honorable and respectable. His lineage is impeccable and his character is... well, practically *flawless*."

"Flawless, eh? Is *that* why you don't suit?" Jason quipped irrepressibly.

She merely glared at him. "I don't think we need go into further detail. I merely wish to have your support in pushing through my marriage plans."

"*My* support? What sort of support can *I* give?"

"Well, sir, you *are* the head of the family. Your approval would certainly weigh with Mama. And as for Arthur's family—"

"Arthur, eh? Does *his* family object to the nuptials as well?"

"Yes, I'm afraid so. You see—"

"They don't find your character flawless enough for their son?" he quipped roguishly.

She put up her chin proudly. "That's not it at all. It's simply that Lady Claybridge wishes him to make a more advantageous match."

"Ah!" Jason said, his eyes watching her speculatively. "And how could *my* support be of influence on—what was the name?"

"Lady Claybridge. Well, you see, if she thought that you, the great Lord Mainwaring, favored the match, she might believe that I had expectations of a settlement..."

Jason looked at her shrewdly. "Then my support is not merely to be verbal, but *financial*, is that it?"

Anne had the grace to blush. With a lowered head, she said in some embarrassment, "As head of the family, you know, it is quite in order for you to make a settlement on an unmarried female in your care."

"Do you mean to say," Jason demanded, "that such things are often done? That Englishmen need to be *bribed* into marriage?"

"*Bribed*?" Anne's head came up abruptly. "How *dare* you, sir! It is not *at all* a question of bribes. It is merely our custom. Do you mean to imply that American girls go into marriage without bringing a penny with them?"

"I don't believe dowries are *customary* in America, but I guess that the practice exists—"

"You 'suppose' the practice exists," she corrected.

"What?" Jason asked, not following the sudden irrelevancy.

"In England, we say 'suppose,' not 'guess'."

"You needn't start instructin' me just yet, ma'am. I haven't yet agreed to make the trade."

"Oh," murmured Anne, chastened.

"I was known as a pretty good horse-trader, back home. I've got to figure out if I'm gettin' the worst of this bargain. How much is your 'settlement' likely to cost me?"

Anne felt her cheeks begin to burn. "I . . . couldn't say. That would be up to you to decide."

"Hmmm. One couldn't be tight-fisted in such matters, could one? The groom might have debts to settle, a family to be made secure . . . things like that. What would you say would be proper in this case?"

Only a boor, Anne decided, would have subjected her to this vulgar questioning. "I don't know," she answered coldly, the color in her cheeks high. "A young lady is not usually privy to the sordid details of the arrangements."

He looked at her mockingly. "Bein' sordid, am I, ma'am? Offendin' your ladylike sensibilities?"

She raised her chin and met his eye for a moment, but then her eyes wavered and fell. He was right to mock her. It was *she* who had been vulgar, trying to extort money from a veritable stranger! "I wish you would stop calling me 'ma'am' in that irritating way," she muttered irrelevantly. Then she looked up and faced him. "I didn't mean to imply that you are being sordid, sir. I am sorry."

But Jason did not let the digression distract him. "Horse-tradin' ain't a ladylike business, Miss Hartley. You're askin' me to fork over what will undoubtedly be a large sum of money in return for a few English lessons and meetin's with my tailors. Do you think I'd be makin' much of a bargain?"

Humiliated, Anne looked down at her hands folded in her lap. "No, I suppose not. I should never have made such a suggestion. It was quite vulgar of me." She rose to leave. "I ask your forgiveness, and I will be quite happy to assist you in any way I can—"

"Shucks, girl, no need to surrender. I've decided to *agree* to the trade. I'd be makin' a fine bargain. For my agreement to supply you with a marriage settlement (which will cause me no difficulty, for they tell me that my fortune is impressively large), you agree to turn me into a fine gentleman (which you tell me is a near-impossible job—)"

"I begin to think," Anne said wondering, "that I exaggerated."

Ignoring the interruption, Jason went on. "—and that you'll find a suitable girl for me to marry. I think we have a bargain, ma'am."

"Do you really mean it, Mr. Hughes?"

"Here's my hand on it." He held it out to her with a smile. "But the girl you find for me must be suitable, mind."

"Of course," Anne assured him, putting her hand in his. "What sort of girl did you have in mind?"

Instead of shaking her hand, Jason held it for a moment. "Someone like you, I think," he said, looking into her eyes with his light-eyed, level stare.

She felt suddenly breathless. "L-Like *me*?"

The mischievous glint reappeared. "Except not as short-tempered—"

Anne's eyebrows shot up. "Short-tempered? I?" And she pulled her hand from his.

"And a little less stubborn—"

"Less stubborn," she said in cold agreement, getting to her feet and glaring down at him.

"And a bit sweeter-natured—"

"Go on."

"Taller, of course—"

"Of course."

"And..." Jason let his eyes roam over the girl who stood before him glowering. "...a bit fuller in the chest, I think," he concluded outrageously.

"Very well, Mr. Hughes," she said in her most businesslike tone, "I'll do my best to find someone such as you describe. There must be a girl *somewhere* who fits your description, who is also foolish enough to agree to accept whatever I can make of you." She put out her hand again. "Done?"

He shook it warmly. "Done!" he smiled.

She turned and went to the door. But before she could leave, his voice stopped her. "Oh, Miss Hartley, wait. There's one thing more," he said casually.

She turned back. "Yes, sir?"

"Since we are to be associated in this...enterprise, I hope you will discontinue the habit you seem to have acquired of calling me 'sir' or 'Mr. Hughes'."

She smiled at him maliciously. "I'm afraid, sir, that I cannot oblige. I do not call people by their Christian names unless they are bound to me in an intimate, affectionate relationship," she responded with pompous affectation.

"Oh, I don't want you to call me *Jason*," he told her, rising and crossing to the door.

"Then, what—?" she asked, caught by surprise.

"Call me 'my lord.'" he answered grandly. "I find your way of saying it very much to my liking." And, grinning wickedly at her open-mouthed astonishment, he strolled out of the room.

# *Seven*

THE FIRST STEP in the transformation of the American 'primitive' into an English peer-of-the-realm was to be, Anne decided, a haircut. This decision was unanimously applauded by everyone consulted—Lady Harriet, Peter, Coyne and even the second footman (who was known to have ambitions to enter the barbering trade and was thus asked by the butler for his opinion). Coyne was directed to send for the most talented *coiffeur* in London, and thus it was that, on the following morning, a Mr. Tobias Fenderwinzel, followed by his assistant laden down with equipment, presented himself at the door of the house on Curzon Street.

Mr. Fenderwinzel could not be called a barber. His skill with the scissors was beyond mere barbering. He was the most sought-after *coiffeur* in London, and he priced his services accordingly. Although he stood only five feet tall and was very slight of build, he carried himself pridefully and clothed himself with marked though modest elegance. He entered with all the dignity of a surgeon (perhaps never having admitted to himself that barbers had been prohibited by law some years before from practicing surgery). He handed his high-crowned beaver to the butler with the insouciance of a visiting earl. But when Coyne tried to reach for the black bag the barber carried (a bag exactly like the kind which surgeons use to carry their instruments), Mr. Fenderwinzel wouldn't let it out of his hands.

The barber was shown into the morning room where he removed his coat, donned an enormous, gleaming-white apron and, with the help of his assistant, proceeded to rearrange the furniture. They cleared the center of the room, placed a cloth on the floor to protect the carpet, and then set a chair upon it. The assistant unpacked a worktable, which he placed to the left of, and a little behind, his 'barber chair.' Then the assistant spread a damask cloth on the table. Mr. Fenderwinzel, waving his assistant aside, opened his instrument bag and removed an amazing number of combs, scissors, clippers, brushes, mirrors and powders. All these he laid out neatly on the table in a carefully prearranged and precise order.

When all was in readiness, Mr. Fenderwinzel nodded to Coyne, who had been waiting in the doorway. The butler took himself to the drawing room where the entire family had gathered to discuss the stylish direction which the barbering operation should take. Lady Harriet suggested a cut in which the back would be tapered, the sides straight and the front locks brushed forward, *à la Brute*. Peter, who had earlier muttered that he didn't see what all the fuss was about, nevertheless made an appearance to suggest that a very short, brushed-back mode, *à la militaire*, was the most appropriate style for a man of Jason's size and character. Anne insisted that the only suitable cut was the medium-length, curled-all-over-the-head style, *à la Grecque*. Jason took no part in the discussion but merely sat quietly, and uncomplainingly permitted them to stare at him, circle around him and discuss him to their hearts' content. If any of the family took notice of the scarcely restrained look of amusement in his eyes, they made no comment on it.

When Coyne announced that the barber was ready, they all rose and followed the butler to the morning room. The butler, noting with surprise that the entire group showed an inclination to remain and watch the proceedings, hurriedly placed chairs for them in a semicircle facing the 'barber chair.' As soon as they had been seated, he ceremoniously led Jason to the chair of honor.

Mr. Fenderwinzel had been standing at the window, his back to the company, flexing his fingers in preparation for the operation to come. The assistant eyed the family with obvious dismay, coughing worriedly in an attempt to attract his employer's attention, but the barber would not be disturbed. When his fingers were adequately exercised, Mr. Fenderwinzel raised his hands like an orchestral conductor about to begin the concert and turned from the window. His mouth dropped open at the sight of the family sitting in rapt attention before him, with Coyne standing behind them, and the second footman surreptitiously peeping in at the doorway. Mr. Fenderwinzel paled. "Wh-What is 'appening 'ere?" he demanded of the butler furiously. "Did you sell *tickets*?"

"Mind your tongue, Tobias," Coyne hissed. "This is the *family*."

"I don't care if it was the Prince 'isself, sittin' there!" the barber cried. Trembling with agitation, he bowed to Lady Harriet and the others nervously. "I am honored at your interest, ladies and gentlemen, I assure you, but this 'ere ain't no *theater*. I do *not* work before an *audience*!"

"I *beg* your pardon," Anne said angrily, jumping to her feet and trying with difficulty to ignore the choking sounds of laughter issuing from Jason and Peter, "but I've never heard such an arrogant, insolent—"

"Hush, dear," Lady Harriet said mildly, "there's no need to take a pet. If the man is indeed the artist that Coyne thinks he is, he is quite right to demand peace while he works. If we make the fellow nervous, he will not do his work well. Jason will not benefit if we insist on remaining. Let's go and leave the barber to his work."

"Exac'ly so, my lady," the barber said, giving her a deep, appreciative bow.

"But, Mama—" Anne objected.

"Take a damper, my dear," Peter cut in. "Let's do as Mama says."

"Very well," Anne agreed reluctantly, "but make sure you cut it *à la Grecque*," she admonished the triumphant little *coiffeur*.

Harriet turned at the doorway. "No, no. The *Brutus*, I think, don't you, Mr . . . er . . . ?"

"Fenderwinzel. Tobias Fenderwinzel, my lady," the barber said politely, and, with another bow, he crossed the room, ushered them into the hallway and locked the door behind them.

It was two hours before Jason was seen again. By that time, Anne had become so impatient she was pacing the room like a caged lioness. Peter had long since retired to his study. Lady Harriet had drawn her embroidery frame from the corner and was placidly stitching away at it when Coyne knocked at the door. "Mr. Fenderwinzel," he announced.

The little *coiffeur* had removed his apron, donned his coat and packed his bag. His mouth was twisted into a slight but decidedly self-satisfied smile. He made a low, formal obeisance and announced importantly, "Lady Hartley, Miss Hartley, I present for your approval, his lordship, the Viscount Mainwaring!"

Every eye turned to the door, but no one was there. The barber clucked, shook his head, muttered a curse under his breath and ran out into the hallway. In a moment he returned, his face red with chagrin. "'E was to follow right be'ind me," he explained in agitation. "Where 'as 'e gone?"

Harriet blinked. "I'm sure I haven't the slightest idea—"

"Dash it," Anne muttered, "he doesn't want us to see him! The coward must have run *out*!"

"*Has* he gone out, Coyne?" Harriet inquired.

"I couldn't say, my lady," Coyne said with a shrug. "I

assumed he had followed Mr. Fenderwinzel. I never thought to look."

"'E didn't go out, Mr. Coyne," said the second footman, popping in from the hallway where he'd been lurking. "I seen 'im walkin' down the 'all."

"Did you indeed?" said the butler coldly. "And what are you doing hanging about out there in the hallway, pray?"

The footman colored. "Well, I . . . I was just wantin' to take a peek at 'is noddle."

"Well, you can take yourself downstairs, *right quick*! I'll have a word with you later," Coyne muttered sternly.

Anne expelled a breath in disgust. "In the meantime, may I trouble you *all* to go and *look* for him?"

"Look for whom?" inquired Jason from the doorway. His voice was provokingly innocent, and so was his expression as he lounged against the door-jamb polishing a large apple on his shirtsleeve. Anne was about to deliver the sharp set-down which had leaped to her tongue at the sound of his voice, when her eyes took note of his appearance. She gasped in pleasure. The gasp was echoed by everyone else in the room but the barber. For Jason had truly been transformed.

Even in his ramshackle American clothing, Jason had taken on the look of a veritable Corinthian. Mr. Fenderwinzel had cut his hair short at the sides and curled it very slightly toward the face. The top was cut somewhat longer, and the barber had brushed it into an attractively careless disarray. The effect was both elegant and casual. "Oh, Mr. Fenderwinzel," Anne sighed in awe, "you really *are* an artist!"

"Jason," Harriet declared beaming, "you're *beautiful*!"

"Beautiful, eh?" Jason shook his head in amazement, took a bite of his apple and chewed reflectively. "And to think that only this mornin' I was a homely gawk," he marveled. "Ain't it wonderful what a bit of a haircut can do?"

"A *bit* of a 'aircut?" came an agonized cry from the barber. "A *bit* of a 'aircut?" With agitated little steps, he crossed the room to confront the Viscount. "A Fenderwinzel *coiffure* can never be called a bit of a 'aircut," he declared pugnaciously, "as you'll learn when I send my bill!"

The sight was ludicrous—the little barber's proudly elevated nose barely reached the level of the top button of Jason's waistcoat. Anne choked with suppressed laughter, and even Lady Harriet was forced to smile. Jason, however, looked sincerely apologetic. "I beg your pardon, Mr. Fenderwinzel. I sure didn't mean to disparage your work. Any man who can make a lady call me 'beautiful' is more than an artist—he is a *magician*. I'll be glad to pay whatever you think is right."

"Thank you, my lord," the little barber said, mollified. "It was an honor to be of service." With a bow to the Viscount and another to the ladies, he went to the door. "Whenever you 'ave need of my services again, my lord, I 'ope you'll not 'esitate to call on me."

Fortunately, Coyne closed the heavy doors behind him so quickly that, when Jason and the ladies gave way to their laughter, Mr. Fenderwinzel didn't hear it.

The haircut now successfully completed, Anne turned her attention to the problem of the Viscount's clothing. After much thought, she decided to send Jason to Nugee, instructing his lordship to put himself completely into the tailor's hands. He was to order a complete array of morning and evening coats, breeches, trousers, waistcoats, shirts, neckcloths and other linen—everything. He was further enjoined to speak to no one but the tailors, and the coachman was ordered to return his lordship to Curzon Street directly at the conclusion of the business with the tailors.

An hour later, the coach returned, but Jason did not emerge. The puzzled coachman reported to Coyne, who reported to Miss Hartley, that his lordship had quietly left Nugee's establishment when no one was looking and had not been seen since. After waiting through four interminable hours for Jason to make an appearance, Anne heard a knock at the door. Believing that Jason had at last arrived, she followed Coyne to the door, ready to pounce on the fellow in fury. But standing in the doorway was Lord Claybridge.

"*Arthur*," Anne cried, "what are you—?" Then, with a glance at the butler, she said in a much more restrained tone, "Do come in," and she dismissed Coyne with a wave of her hand.

"I can only stay a moment," Arthur whispered hurriedly. "I don't want Lady Harriet to know I'm here. I merely stopped by to find out how you've been keeping. I haven't had a glimpse of you since that morning at the Laverstokes'."

"I know. I'm most dreadfully sorry, but I've not had a moment's peace since Lord Mainwaring arrived. The fellow is a dreadful here-and-thereian. Why, at this very *moment*—"

"Do you mind if we don't waste time speaking of him? I've been on tenterhooks since last I saw you. Anne, my dear, have you come to a decision about . . . about what I asked you?"

"What you asked—? Oh, that. Yes, I think I have news that will please you, Arthur, but I haven't time to tell you about it now. Standing here whispering in the hall is not the way to discuss matters as important as this. Meet me at Cherry's house next Saturday morning, and I'll tell you the whole."

"Next Saturday? Must we wait so *long*?" Arthur asked, dismayed.

Hearing a step in the upstairs hall, Anne urged him to the door. "It's the soonest I can arrange. Please go now, Arthur. And don't worry. Everything will be fine, I promise you."

She pushed him out the door and closed it after him in the nick of time, for Lady Harriet appeared at the top of the stairs. "Has someone called?" she asked.

"No one of importance," Anne answered evasively. "I was hoping it was your nephew. He's not yet returned. What *are* we to do?"

"Do?" Lady Harriet murmured in an untroubled way. "I don't see that there *is* anything we can do."

"Mama, you cannot have *heard* me. Mr. Hughes has *disappeared*! He has not been seen since ten this morning. Aren't you at all *concerned*?"

"If my nephew was able to make his way across the Atlantic Ocean and to find his way here without any help from you or me, I'm convinced that he cannot need it now. Jason is a very resourceful young man. I'm not in the least concerned about him."

"He may be resourceful, but he's the most irritating and unreliable make-bait it has ever been my misfortune to encounter! Where can he have gone? I told him quite clearly to stop at Nugee's and nowhere else! What can he be doing for so many hours? He knows no one in London, he has neither horse nor carriage, and there's not a shilling in his pockets, so far as I know. In these circumstances, I cannot *imagine* what he can be doing, unless he's been set upon by thieves or cutthroats, in which case, if anyone were to ask me *my* opinion, he has met a fate he very richly deserves."

"Thieves and cutthroats?" Lady Harriet repeated with a slight quaver. "Oh, dear, you are making me nervous, and you *know* how damaging that can be to one's heart. I must remain calm." She took three deep, soothing breaths. "Anne, my love, you must learn not to indulge in fits of temper or ill-humors. I know you're angry with Jason only because you've worked yourself up this way. But you needn't be alarmed. Jason can take care of himself. When he returns, he will no doubt have a perfectly rational explanation for his absence."

With that small comfort, Anne had to be content. After another hour, unable to delay dinner any longer without causing untoward disturbance in the kitchen, the ladies went upstairs to dress for dinner. Jason returned home not five minutes after the ladies had closed their doors behind them. He came into the house and greeted Coyne as if he had not a care in the world, calmly sauntered up to his room and began to change for dinner. Coyne, however, knew how disturbed Miss Anne had been over his disappearance, so he tapped at her door and whispered to her that his lordship had returned.

"Oh, he has, has he?" she declared with a militant sparkle in her eye. "Thank you, Coyne, for informing me." And she brushed by him and marched down the hall in the direction of his lordship's bedroom. The angry swing of her stride told Coyne better than words that the forthcoming confrontation boded no good for the unfortunate Viscount.

Jason, in his shirtsleeves, opened the door in answer to Anne's knock. He had already removed his neckcloth and had almost completely unbuttoned his shirt. But he showed no embarrassment at his state of undress. He merely smiled at her and stepped aside for her to enter. Too angry to take notice of the inappropriateness of his appearance, she glared at him and stalked past him into the room. As soon as he had closed the door, she rounded on him. "What do you *mean* by disappearing all afternoon without a word? Don't you remember my instructions? I told you to return immediately from Nugee's!"

"Did you now?" he asked innocently. "Fancy my forgettin'!"

"Is that all you have to say? Where have you been?"

"Orderin' my clothes, like you asked."

'Don't think you can flummery me, my lord! The coachman told me you slipped out of Nugee's before you'd ordered anything."

"That's true, but I ordered the things elsewhere," he explained.

"*Elsewhere*?" She glared at him with renewed fury. "What is the point of my trying to advise you, if you will not *listen* to me? Nugee's coats are the very height of fashion."

"Maybe, but they wouldn't have suited me."

"Oh, wouldn't they?" she asked acidly. "I thought *I* was to be the judge of that."

"Even *you* wouldn't have approved of what they were plannin' for me. A mornin' coat with shoulders padded up to here—as if a great oaf like me needs padded shoulders!—and wide lapels made of *velvet*—"

"Velvet lapels are very much the thing," she informed him, "although I'll admit that I would not have approved the padded shoulders either."

"Especially in—what did he say the color would be?—oh, yes, robin's-egg blue."

The image that flashed into her mind of Jason in a robin's-egg-blue coat was indeed ludicrous. "I see. Well, what did you do about it?"

"I just walked out. Found a tailor not far away and ordered everything, just as you instructed."

She put her hand to her forehead in a gesture of hopelessness. "Oh, that's just *fine*! We shall be presented with armloads of apparel that will be good for nothing but depositing in the poor-box. One cannot go to just *any* tailor, you know. There are fewer than half-a-dozen in all of London who can be relied upon to suit a gentleman."

"Oh?" Jason murmured meekly. "Do you really think the clothes will not be satisfactory? Mr. Weston assured me—"

"Weston? You went to *Weston's*?" she asked in disbelief.

"Yes, ma'am," he said with a look of worried innocence.

"Are you trying to make me believe that you found your way to Weston's purely by *accident*?"

"Why? Have you heard of him?"

She stared at him suspiciously. "Yes, I've heard of him. Many men consider him the best in London."

"Indeed? Then why didn't you send me *there*?"

"Well, some say he's somewhat conservative. I thought Nugee might design clothes for you that were more dashing."

"Yes, a robin's-egg-blue coat with wide lapels sounds *very* dashing," he agreed.

"But not quite right for a man your size," she admitted reluctantly. "I suppose you're right. Weston is an excellent choice for you. I just can't believe that you could have stumbled upon him by accident like that!"

"Well, Peter *did* happen to mention—"

She would have liked to hit him. "You *humbug*! You knew *all the time*—!"

Jason merely grinned.

"Not only going ahead and doing exactly as you please, but staying away all day ... going to who knows what sort of disreputable places and doing all sorts of disreputable things—with never a moment's concern for what *we* would think when the coach came home without you! Are you so thoughtless or so addle-pated that you didn't realize we would all be at sixes and sevens, wondering what had become of you? Do you have *no* sense of responsibi—?" She was prepared to go on at much greater length, but she heard a laugh escape him and it infuriated her. "What do you find so amusing, you ... you *clod-crusher*!"

"It's *you*, girl. I'm laughin' with admiration, you might say. Pure admiration. You sure know how to phrase a scold! Why, I haven't heard such a good jawin' since I was five years old and jumped with my muddy shoes all over my mama's satin bedspread. I had no idea, ma'am, that you held such motherly feelin's for me."

"*Motherly* feelings!" she retorted scornfully. "*Murderly* would be more apt." But her voice lacked conviction. He had made her conscious of treating him like a child, and somewhere deep inside her she felt very foolish.

"They had *better* be motherly feelin's, ma'am," he said with his mischievous twinkle, "for otherwise how would you explain your presence in my bedroom, with me standin' here half dressed—?"

"Half—?" She blinked in sudden awareness of his bared chest, suntanned and hairy, showing itself in a brazen V from his opened collar to the waist of his breeches, and she blushed to the roots of her hair.

"No need to color up, my dear," he said, grinning wickedly. "I knew that, feelin' so motherly as you do, you would take no lascivious notice."

"*Lascivious*—!" she sputtered, backing to the door awkwardly. "You *might* have buttoned up, you know. Well, you'd better hurry and dress, or dinner will be late," she added lamely and made a hasty retreat. But even as she pulled the door closed behind her with a resounding slam, she heard his obnoxious guffaw.

# *Eight*

IN HER EMBARRASSED HASTE to remove herself from Jason's room, Anne forgot to ask her rebellious charge how he'd spent the hours of the afternoon *after* he'd ordered his clothes from Weston's. She'd realized fleetingly that he could not and would not have spent an entire day choosing coats and waistcoats. But his teasingly barbarous behavior in his bedroom had driven all other matters from her mind, and she didn't think of it again until she'd gone to bed that night. She surmised that he'd gone searching for the suit of armor he always spoke about and gave the matter no more thought.

By the next morning, however, there was no longer a need to question him about his mysterious afternoon; the whole of London was talking about it. No fewer than four of Lady Harriet's friends called to inform her of the story that was circulating with alarming rapidity through the salons of London. The new Viscount Mainwaring, they said, had been seen racing a horse through the park against the notorious rakehell, Miles Minton. At first, Lady Harriet vehemently denied that the story could be true. In the first place, she said, her Jason didn't know Sir

Miles. In the second place, there were no horses in their stables suitable for racing. But when the ladies all insisted that Sir Miles' opponent had been an American of noteworthy size, her confidence was shaken. And when Peter came running in to ask where they had acquired the absolutely splendid stallion he's just seen in their stables, she realized the story must be true.

It was from Peter, however, that Anne learned the details. Peter had run to ask Jason about the horse and had heard the entire tale from the best source—Jason himself. The Viscount told Peter that, after he'd finished at Weston's, he'd walked over to Tattersall's stables. Tattersall was a dealer in horseflesh whose reputation extended even to America, and Jason, who was interested in acquiring a horse capable of bearing a rider of his weight, was eager to look at his stock. He'd taken one look at the stallion and had purchased it on the spot.

Just as the transaction had been completed, Sir Miles Minton had appeared on the scene. Sir Miles was a gentleman of shady reputation who could always be counted on to be involved in any disreputable sporting event or to be a participant in the most dubious of wagers. He had had an eye on the stallion for himself but, always in debt, had not had the necessary blunt. Looking the American over and taken in by his easy smile, his drawling speech and naive manner, Sir Miles had decided the Viscount was a flat. He persuaded Jason to wager, on the outcome of a one-and-a-half-mile race through the park, his new horse against Sir Miles' magnificent saddle.

Jason had admitted to Peter that he'd been foolhardy, but the horse looked prime, and he, having been cooped up for so long, was ripe for a lark. He'd accepted the wager in the full realization that he had not the measure of either his opponent's skill as a rider or the strength of either one of the animals to be run in the contest. But, he'd told Peter with a shrug, Sir Miles had more flash than bottom, and Jason had won easily.

Peter's account was relayed by Anne to Lady Harriet,

who had at last to admit to herself that the gossip she'd been hearing all morning was—in every one of its particulars—quite true. Jason had made a mull of things—his presence in London was no longer secret, and his recklessly rash encounter with the notorious Sir Miles was an *on-dit* in every London drawing room. After her usual self-warning to remain calm and five minutes of breathing exercises to regulate her pulse, she sat down to think of ways to determine how to salvage the situation.

Lady Harriet did not think of herself as a particularly clever woman (her inability to understand her brilliant son had taught her that), but she knew that she was endowed with a sufficient supply of common sense. Her common sense had taught her that one can find answers if one asks the right questions. In the case of Jason's escapade, two problems were immediately apparent. The first was that Jason's period of leisurely seclusion was quite at an end; the door knocker was bound to be kept busy by the curious, eager to get a glimpse of the new Lord Mainwaring, and the invitations would come flooding in. Thus, the first question Lady Harriet had to answer was how to prevent Jason from having to face the *ton* too soon—before he'd been properly trained. The second problem was that Jason's reputation had been sullied by his thoughtless association with a loose fish like Sir Miles. The question here was how the ill-effects of this encounter were to be minimized.

Lady Harriet could not, even after lengthy cogitation, find satisfactory answers to either of her questions, but she answered them as best she could. She had intended to keep Jason at home for at least a month; now that would be impossible. But two weeks she must have. She looked through her social calendar in order to select the most appropriate fête for Jason's debut. Her choice was a large, formal ball being given by Lady Dabney in two weeks' time. She and Anne would ready him for that occasion. In the meantime, Coyne would be instructed to tell every caller for the next two weeks that they were not at home.

As for Jason's injured reputation, Lady Harriet could only hope that his additional two weeks of seclusion would be time enough for the gossip to die down. For the time being, the family must give all their time and attention to preparing Jason for his debut.

His clothing was the most urgent need. Jason's trip to Weston's had been only the beginning. An amazing number of shopping expeditions were necessary to outfit him properly. A visit to Schweitzer and Davidson's for riding clothes and sporting togs was undertaken. Then an entire day was spent at various shops on St. James Street: at number six, there was Lock's, where, under Anne's direct supervision, Jason was urged to order a shocking number of high-crowned beaver hats with curly brims in various shades of gray, brown and black, glossy black top hats, and a chapeau-bras (which Anne told him was merely to be carried under his arm when in evening dress); then, down the street, at the corner of Picadilly, there was Hoby's, where Jason was fitted for long boots, Hessians, Hussar boots, top boots, Wellingtons and highlows (which, Anne explained, were absolutely necessary to wear with trousers); and finally the glover's, where his hands were much admired for their great size and were measured for more than a dozen pairs of gloves in brown, white, blue, fawn and York tan.

At the end of an exhausting week, Jason firmly declared that he would not step foot in another store; nor would he submit to being fitted, taped, ruled, weighed, measured, turned round, surveyed, inspected, studied, scrutinized or otherwise examined. He would visit no other store. He would even give up the hunt for the suit of armor, which was the one and only item he'd wanted to purchase for himself. He completely abandoned his intention to search the stores for it. He was through with shopping forever!

Shortly thereafter, the deliveries began. Packages, bandboxes, cases and cartons were delivered in a steady stream. The poor Viscount began to complain to his instructress that there would soon be no space in his bedroom for *him*.

"What we must do, my lord," she responded, "is to move you to a bedroom with a dressing room. And we must find you a proper valet to take care of your things."

"Valet? Never!" Jason declared. "I'm quite capable of dressing myself."

"Don't be obstinate," Anne said superciliously. "You must have someone to pull off your boots, for one thing—"

"I've always managed to pull them off before—"

"What? Those outsized monstrocities you've been wearing? *Anyone* might be able to manage those. But wait until you try to remove the ones Hoby is making for you. They'll fit like a second skin, you know."

"Nevertheless, I'm certain I can manage. Shucks, ma'am, does becoming a lord make a man suddenly incompetent?"

Anne did not bother to respond. However, she told Coyne privately to place an advertisement for an experienced gentleman's gentleman in the *Morning Post*.

While the various tailers, bootmakers, hatters and glovers diligently labored to provide the Viscount Mainwaring with the necessary apparel, Anne worked on the man himself. For at least two hours a day, Anne instructed him in speech ("One doesn't say 'shucks,' my lord. One says 'Hang it,' or 'I daresay.'"), in deportment ("One does not drink coffee at tea time, my lord—not ever! And the tea is taken, not with 'crackers' but with 'biscuits,' if you please."), and in dancing ("Right foot forward, toe extended, tap, back; left foot forward, toe extended, tap, back—no, *no*! Count the beat! Take me around the waist and turn me—but can you manage to do it with a little less energy, my lord? This way you are likely to fling me across the room!").

Anne found the hours spent with her pupil to be very engrossing, although she was often irritated by Lord Mainwaring's cavalier attitude toward the subject matter.

He listened to everything she said with great attention, but she was always aware of a disconcerting lack of seriousness in his manner. The gleam of amusement was always present in his eyes, and his demeanor suggested that the whole matter was nothing but a game to him. But since he never disputed what she told him, never absented himself from a lesson nor failed (at least in the attempt) to follow her instructions to the letter, she could not find a reason to scold or to complain that he lacked the appropriate gravity or the proper regard for the importance of what they were doing.

The dancing lessons were the most difficult for Anne to handle. Lord Mainwaring would attempt to dance to the music that Lady Harriet patiently provided at the pianoforte, but he could not seem to move his feet in time to the rhythm. He counted out the beat valiantly in time to the music, but even though he kept count with his voice, his feet followed a beat of their own. Lady Harriet, watching from her place at the keyboard, would often break into giggles at his clumsy, galloping steps, which would cause the Viscount to laugh, and then he would lose count altogether. Anne would sometimes find herself joining in the laughter, but more often she would frown impatiently. Since Lady Harriet had decided that Lord Mainwaring would make his first appearance in society at the large ball to be given by Lady Dabney, now only one week hence, and since Anne was convinced that Jason could never master the art of dancing in so short a time, she saw nothing amusing in his awkwardness on the dance floor.

She increased the number of hours of dancing lessons, hoping that, by frequent repetition of the simpler country-dance figures, he might manage to get through a couple of dances at the ball. They were thus engaged on Saturday afternoon when Coyne interrupted to whisper to Anne that her friend, Miss Laverstoke, had called and was waiting in the sitting room. Instructing Lady Harriet to continue her playing, and insisting that his lordship continue to practice, she ran across the hallway to see Cherry.

Her friend was seated on the sofa, twisting her hands worriedly in her lap. "Is there anything amiss, Anne dear?" she asked as soon as Anne had entered and closed the door.

"Amiss? Of course not. Why do you ask?" Anne queried cheerfully, taking a chair opposite Cherry and looking at her with eyebrows raised.

"Then why didn't you come to Half-Moon Street this morning?" Cherry asked in perplexity.

"This morning? Why should I have come this morning? I thought we had arranged to drive out tomorrow afternoon."

"Yes, we had. But did you not tell Lord Claybridge to meet you this morn—?"

"Good God! *Arthur!*" Anne pressed her hands to her mouth in dismay. "I forgot all about him!"

Cherry gasped. "Oh, Anne, you *couldn't* have! I assured him repeatedly that some urgent matter must have prevented you—"

Anne jumped from her chair and paced the room in distress. "How could I have *forgotten*? It slipped my mind completely! Oh, Cherry, was he very angry with me?"

"He was quite upset, but only because he was sure that something dreadful had happened to keep you. Or that you had decided not to marry him and were too tenderhearted to face him with the truth."

"But that's ridiculous. I told him the other day that I had *good* news for him."

Cherry stared at her friend as disapprovingly as her sympathetic eyes permitted. "I don't understand you, Anne. How could you do something so unkind? He had been *counting the days!*"

Anne was conscience-stricken. "I don't know how I could have done such a thing. It's only that my responsibilities to Lord Mainwaring have occupied so much of my mind and my time—"

As if on cue, there was a knock at the door and Lord Mainwaring looked in. "Excuse me, ma'am," he said to Anne apologetically, "but Aunt Harriet wants to know how long you intend to keep me hoppin' about?"

"You see?" Anne muttered to Cherry in an undervoice. "I can't leave him for a minute. Come in, my lord. I'd like you to meet my friend, Miss Charity Laverstoke. Cherry, this is Jason Hughes, the new Lord Mainwaring."

Cherry was awed. Staring, she shyly extended her hand. "H-how do you d-do, my lord?" she murmured breathlessly.

Jason advanced and took her hand. Just as he was about to shake it, Anne shook her head vigorously at him and cleared her throat. With a quick glance at his mentor's forbidding frown, he grinned and lifted Cherry's hand to his lips. "Charmed," he said politely, as he released it.

Anne nodded at him approvingly and returned to her chair. "Do sit down, Lord Mainwaring, and join us. Perhaps you can tell Miss Laverstoke something about America. Wouldn't you love to hear about life in the wilderness, Cherry?"

"Oh, yes!" Cherry said with shy eagerness.

"As much as I'd enjoy regalin' you with wilderness tales, Miss Laverstoke, I'm afraid I must decline. I've been instructed to practice my dancin', you see. I need all the practice I can get, for, naturally, a man who's spent all his life in the wilderness could not have grown adept at such a *civilized* activity. With your permission, ma'am, I shall leave you to your conversation." With a wicked glint, he nodded to Anne, bowed to Cherry and left the room.

Cherry blinked at the door, speechless.

Anne laughed. "Don't sit there open-mouthed, Cherry. Say something."

"Oh, *my*!" Cherry breathed at last.

"I know what you mean," Anne nodded. "Overpowering, isn't he?"

"Yes, he is. I must admit, Anne, that the Viscount is certainly...er..." Cherry searched for a word. "...an original, isn't he?"

"That is *just* what he is," Anne agreed.

"Are you truly giving him instruction in dancing?" Cherry asked, wide-eyed. "I would be terrified to—"

"Nonsense. What is there to be terrified of?"

"I don't know, exactly. He's so...*large*! And so...self-assured. And those eyes of his—they seem to penetrate right through one."

"Yes, they do, don't they?" Anne's smile faded into a thoughtful frown. "I always feel as if he is reading my thoughts and laughing at them."

"Yet he doesn't frighten you?" Cherry asked admiringly.

"No, of course not. He's really rather agreeable, you know. In fact, Cherry, I've been thinking...he'll be making his bow in society in a very short time, and he's bound to make a mark, even if he doesn't master all the proper social graces. He'll be considered an enormously splendid match for some girl. Why shouldn't it be *you*?"

"*Me*? You must be joking!"

"Of course I'm not joking. Why *shouldn't* it be you?"

"Why, I'd be terror-stricken just to be asked to *stand up* with him at Almack's!" Cherry declared.

Anne frowned at her. "Really, Cherry, you can be such a wet-goose! Just because Jason is somewhat *tall* is no reason to be afraid of him. He is truly an easygoing, amicable sort. Peter thinks the world of him."

Cherry wavered. "But even if I could find the courage to...to...Anyway, he didn't seem to take particular notice of me a moment ago," she pointed out frankly.

"Never mind that. He's given me the task of finding a wife for him, and *you*, Cherry, are my first choice. And the sooner I arrange to bring the two of you together, the better."

Cherry stared at her friend in fascinated horror. "But,

Anne, I . . . I wouldn't know what to *say* to such a man! And I'm not the sort who could attract . . . I'm sure we wouldn't suit."

But Anne would not be deterred. "Leave it all to me, Cherry. Tomorrow, we shall all go driving in the park together. Will you ask Arthur to come along with us? It will be the perfect opportunity for me to apologize to him, and for you and Lord Mainwaring to become acquainted."

Cherry found a number of objections to the plan. What if Arthur did not like being part of a foursome? What if Lord Mainwaring should object? What if he should become bored? Cherry had nothing suitable to wear. What if her mother should ask questions? What would people say if they were observed?

To all these points, Anne made scornful replies. Her mind was made up. With a long list of instructions for her friend on the arrangements with Arthur, on the time of day which would most suit the situation, and on the outfit Cherry was to wear, Anne walked with her friend to the door. "Oh, Anne," Cherry said with a fearful sigh, "I hope you know what you're doing."

"Leave everything to me, dearest, and don't fret. Lord Mainwaring will be charmed, I promise. And if he is not, then . . . well, perhaps then you'll let me cut your braids. If all else fails, that may be the very thing to do the trick."

Cherry's hand flew to her hair. "Only if all else fails," she pleaded. Then, before Anne could think of anything else to cause her to quail, she hastily took her leave.

# *Nine*

THE MANY ELEMENTS which were needed to insure a successful outing seemed to fall into place for Anne. First, Lord Mainwaring good-humoredly accepted Anne's sudden invitation to ride in the park without questioning her motives. Then Cherry sent word that 1) her mother had given permission for her to go, and 2) Arthur had agreed to join them. Lastly, the weather seemed to bestow its blessing upon the excursion; the sun was surprisingly warm and the wind obligingly mild for a day in March.

At the appointed hour, Anne came down the stairway to find Lord Mainwaring already in the foyer awaiting her arrival. She observed with pleased surprise his very creditable appearance. He was wearing the new coat which Weston had delivered the day before. It was of dark green superfine, superbly cut to fit smoothly over his broad shoulders and to emphasize his narrow waist. His buckled, Manchester-brown breeches clung without a wrinkle to legs which she hadn't realized were so shapely, and his new topboots gleamed. "Why, Lord Mainwaring," she exclaimed approvingly, "you look positively British!"

"I reckon you mean that as a compliment, ma'am," he said sardonically, "so I thank you."

"You *suppose* I meant it as a compliment, my lord," she said in her most obnoxiously schoolteacherish tone. "*Suppose*, not *reckon*." And she swept past him and out the door.

Together they went to the waiting phaeton. Jason, glancing at the well-sprung phaeton and the lively grays, requested permission to take the reins. "Of course, my lord," Anne told him. "After all, the horses and carriage are yours." Nevertheless, she felt a twinge of misgiving as Jason climbed up beside the coachman, for the grays that had been harnessed to the carriage were an exceptionally high-spirited pair. She sat back in her seat nervously as they started out, but it took only a few minutes during the short ride to Half-Moon Street through the heavily trafficked streets for her to realize, with relief, that Jason showed remarkable skill with the ribbons.

When they arrived at Half-Moon Street, and Cherry and Arthur came out to meet them, Anne did not have to hint to Jason that his company would be desired inside the phaeton. With surprising graciousness, he surrendered the reins to the coachman and joined the group.

The introductions were made, and Anne signaled Jason to help Cherry into the front seat. While he was complying with this unspoken request, Anne beckoned Arthur to climb up beside her. Jason, therefore, had no choice but to sit next to Cherry. Since both seats of the phaeton faced forward, Jason found himself faced with the problem of making conversation with a tongue-tied, blushing girl who had not enough courage to turn her eyes to him. After a few attempts to draw her out on such subjects as the weather, the number of carriages clogging the streets, and her very fetching bonnet, he gave up and relapsed into silence.

On the seat behind, Anne tried to whisper apologies to Arthur for having forgotten to meet him the day before. He responded politely, but he was obviously very offended, and his manner was stiff and cool. The possibility that their conversation might be overheard by the occupants of the seat in front of them hampered further discussion, and their ride to the park was passed in a silence as awkward as the one being endured by Cherry and Jason.

Fortunately, the ride was not long. When they arrived, Anne suggested that they walk through the park to exercise their legs, a suggestion that was approved eagerly by the others. They climbed down, and the coachman turned the carriage out of the road to a place where he could wait for them to return. For a moment, they stood looking about, unable to decide which of the many charming walking paths they should take. It was at that moment that a high-pitched laugh echoed from the lane to their right. Instinctively, all their heads turned. There, too far away to greet but close enough to be seen clearly, stood a gentleman in the uniform of a cavalry officer, helping a ravishing young lady to dismount from a horse. The lady was wearing a close-fitting riding costume in dark red and a very dashing riding hat which was cocked to one side of her head and sported a captivating white plume. "Now *that* is someone I'd like to meet," Jason muttered to Anne without taking his admiring eyes from the lady in question.

Anne, quite aware of the identity of the horsewoman, glared at Jason in irritation. Why did that odious Lexie de Guis choose this particular time to make an appearance? Alexandra de Guis, daughter of a French emigré and an English lady, was the one girl in all of London whom Anne wanted to keep from Jason. Lexie, the reigning beauty of the season, and of several seasons past, and called "La Belle" by all the bucks of the *ton*, could capture a man's heart by the mere flick of an eyelid. Not only beautiful, she was clever, poised, stylishly elegant and tantalizingly unreadable. Men adored her and women detested her.

Anne was determined to keep Lexie from making

Jason another victim of her long list of conquests. She therefore promptly took Jason's arm and turned him into the lane to their left. "*This* way looks more inviting, does it not, Cherry?" she said gaily, and hurried them away from a possible encounter with the riders. If she was aware of the raised eyebrows and amused expression on Jason's face, she took no notice of them.

As the strollers walked deeper into the park, the lane narrowed, leaving room only for two abreast. Anne linked her arm in Cherry's, and the two ladies preceded the gentlemen down the path. "You look just as you ought," Anne whispered to Cherry with approval. "I *told* you that the feathered bonnet would be charming with your spencer."

Cherry, still feeling shy and uncomfortable, nodded without conviction. "Yes, Lord Mainwaring was kind enough to comment on it."

"Did he?" Anne asked gleefully. "I *knew* he'd take notice of you!"

Cherry looked at her friend lugubriously. "He was only being polite. After all, he had to say *something*, especially since I couldn't think of a thing to say to him."

Anne cast a quick look over her shoulder. Arthur and Jason seemed to be conversing comfortably enough. "Cherry, I don't know why you must behave in this missish way. There are *dozens* of things you and Lord Mainwaring could say to each other."

"What things?"

"Oh, for goodness sake, Cherry, look about you! Everything you *see* can be commented upon. Isn't the prospect of the park itself, with its tiny buds of green about to burst into life, worth remarking upon? How about the trees? You could ask if they are like the trees in America. Asking about America could very well supply conversational material for *weeks*! And then, you could ask him how he does with his dancing—after all, he *did* tell you about it yesterday. And there's his new coat. Weston delivered it yesterday. Doesn't he look complete to a shade? I never quite believed that clothes could effect such a change in a man, but there he is, quite up to snuff."

"Really, Anne," Cherry said with a touch of reproval in her voice, "you cannot expect me to compliment him on his *coat*!"

They came to a fork in the path, one branch leading upward to a grassy knoll where there was a bench with a fine view of the prospect below, and the other downward to a lake where a number of swans floated in graceful arrogance. "We must make a decision," Anne said, turning to face the gentlemen who had caught up with them. "Since you are the newcomer in the park, Lord Mainwaring, you may choose our direction. Shall it be the lake with the swans or the knoll with the bench?"

"Oh, let's see the swans, by all means," he answered decisively.

They turned into the downward lane. As they did so, Anne took Arthur's arm, forcing Lord Mainwaring to drop back and fall into step beside Cherry. After a moment, however, Anne stopped. "Oh, dear, there's something in my slipper," she murmured, limping. "Please take me up to the bench, Arthur. I'm afraid there's a pebble lodged in my shoe. Cherry, dear, go along with Lord Mainwaring. We'll catch up in a moment."

The imploring look cast at her by Cherry and the mocking gleam she saw in Jason's eyes told her that her ruse had not fooled them, but since no objection to her suggestion was voiced aloud, she had her way. In another few moments, she was seated on the bench, with Arthur kneeling before her in an attempt to remove her shoe. "Never mind that, Arthur," she said impatiently. "Just sit down beside me. I want to apologize to you."

She launched into a penitent, heartfelt explanation of her thoughtlessness the day before, and Arthur, melting at the sincerely contrite expression in her eyes, forgave her. She then told him eagerly about the arrangement she had made with Lord Mainwaring concerning her marriage settlement. If she had expected Arthur to be overjoyed by her news, she was doomed to disappointment. "But I never asked ... that is, I have no wish for a settlement or anything else from Lord Mainwaring," Arthur said with obvious disapproval.

"But, Arthur, I don't understand!" Anne was completely taken aback. "Isn't that the very thing your mother wants for you?"

Arthur shook his head impatiently. "I'm not interested in what Mama wants. What *I* want is to marry the woman I love without assistance from a man who is a stranger to us both."

"He's not a stranger to *me*. He is, in a way, responsible for me. Have you taken him in dislike, Arthur?"

"No, not at all. He seems a very decent sort. That, however, does not mean that I can endure living on his charity."

"You are being much too *nice* in your attitude, my dear. Besides, we *cannot* marry without Lord Mainwaring's financial assistance."

"Yes, we can, as I explained to you before. I've thought it all out. If I take the living in Shropshire (and, by the way, I've already taken steps to sell the country estate which will support my mother and sister), we can manage very well without his lordship's generosity."

"Do you mean the vicarage? Surely, Arthur, you were not serious about that! It was a suggestion made only out of desperation, was it not? Now that I've found a more acceptable solution—"

"It is not a more acceptable solution to me. I was *quite* serious about the Shropshire plan, and the only flaw *I* see in it is the necessity to make a Gretna marriage."

Anne stared at Arthur as if she'd never seen him. Could he really *want* the life of a country vicar? Or was the thought of the need for assistance from a stranger so repugnant to him that anything, even a Shropshire vicarage, would be preferable? "Oh, dear, I see we've come to an impasse," she said slowly, "but we cannot solve the problem now—not with Cherry and Lord

Mainwaring waiting for us. We'll have to continue this another time." With a troubled frown, she rose from the bench.

"But you haven't let me remove the pebble from your shoe," Arthur pointed out.

She glanced up at him with a mixture of impatience and guilt. He was always so disconcertingly *honest*! "Really, Arthur, you are sometimes incredibly naive. There *was* no pebble." And to avoid his reproachful stare, she hurried down the path.

When she and Arthur finally caught up with their friends, Anne found to her chagrin that Cherry and Jason had been joined by another couple—none other than Lexie de Guis and her companion. Their horses had been tied to a nearby tree, and from the flirtatious smile on Lexie's face, the interested gleam in Jason's eye and the bored expressions on the faces of Cherry and the cavalry officer, Anne deduced that the meeting had occurred quite soon after she and Arthur had left. As they approached, they heard Jason remark to the lady, "Shucks, ma'am, most of the men in America are much taller than I. Why, back home, they find me positively puny."

Alexandra de Guis threw back her head with a peal of hearty laughter. It was some moments before Anne managed to divert her attention. "Good day, Miss de Guis," she said loudly.

Lexie turned to her at last and flashed a brilliant (and, to Anne, triumphant) smile. "Ah, there you are at last, Miss Hartley. We've been passing the time waiting to say good day to you. May I present Captain Edward Wray? Edward, I don't believe you've met Miss Hartley or her escort, Lord Claybridge."

While the men shook hands, Lexie tapped Anne's arm with her riding crop. "You are a naughty puss, Miss Hartley, for keeping this charming cousin of yours hidden away. Not that I blame you," she added with a sidelong glance at Lord Mainwaring, "for if I were in your place, I might have done the same. But you must not be permitted to do so any longer." With that, she again turned to Jason, smiling up at him enticingly. "Did you hear that, my lord? Take warning. Now that I've discovered you, your period of seclusion is over." Then she took her escort's arm. "But come, Edward. We must go. The horses should not be kept standing any longer."

She strolled off on Captain Wray's arm without a backward glance, but every eye followed the pair until they had mounted and ridden off into the trees. As the four strollers turned and climbed the path back to the carriage, Anne had all she could do to hide from the others her intense vexation. The afternoon had been a failure for three of the four of them, but the fact that the fourth had so obviously managed to enjoy himself immensely somehow made her feel that the day had been worse than a failure—it had been a positive disaster.

# Ten

THE SUN HAD SET and the afternoon had grown quite
cold by the time Cherry and Arthur had been deposited
on Cherry's doorstep in Half-Moon Street. Arthur had
glumly watched the coach disappear down the street and
had sighed, tipped his hat to Cherry and started toward
his own equipage when she stopped him. "Would you like
to come in for a cup of tea before you start for home?" she
asked.

Willing to postpone the depression which he knew
would settle on him once he was left alone to review his
unsatisfactory conversation with his beloved, Arthur
acquiesced. As Cherry led him into the house, took his hat
and ordered the tea things, she was aware of a perceptible
lightening of her spirits. For the first time that day, she
was conscious of a feeling of contentment. She settled
herself behind the teapot and permitted herself to wonder
why she had been so ill-at-ease all afternoon. Certainly
Lord Mainwaring had done or said nothing to discompose her. Yet she had not felt at all happy in his company.
On the other hand, here with Arthur, even though he was
bound to spend the entire time confiding to her his

troubles with Anne, she was almost blissfully content. It was a most curious reaction, one which she would explore at length as soon as she had the opportunity to think. In the meantime, she turned her attention to her unhappy guest, listened to his woes with her wide eyes brimming with commiseration and offered him comforting murmurs of hope whenever he paused for breath.

In the coach, meanwhile, filled with utter disgust, Anne glanced surreptitiously at her companion. Jason was leaning back contentedly against the squabs, his hands behind his head and his legs stretched out comfortably before him. His lips were turned up in a small, reflective smile and his eyes were lit with an abstracted glow, as if he were reliving a fond memory. Anne ground her teeth in irritation. Had that detestable Lexie caught him *already*?

But she would not surrender without a struggle. "Cherry is quite a lovely girl, is she not?" she asked suddenly, with a falsely cheerful lilt in her voice.

"Mmm," Jason murmured absently.

"You must certainly agree that she is pleasant and even-tempered."

"Mmm," Jason nodded.

"Not a bit stubborn either, is she?"

"Not at all, as far as I could see," he agreed.

"Sweet-natured, too. As sweet-natured as one could wish."

"Oh, yes, very sweet-natured."

"And adequately tall, I would say, wouldn't you?"

"I suppose so," he assented uninterestedly.

"And...er...quite full in the chest, too, don't you think?"

Jason shifted around, took his hands from his head and sat up at attention. "*What* was that you said?" he asked, his eyes taking on their mocking gleam.

"I was talking about Cherry's...er...form. It seems perfectly to suit your...specifications," Anne suggested boldly.

"My specifications? Are you suggestin' that you find

Miss Laverstoke a likely candidate to be my *wife*?"

"But of course! I think she'd make a perfect—"

"You're way off course, girl. I'm not the man for your friend Cherry. She's a lovely young woman, I'll admit, but she's the sort who'd like to mother a man. I'm not lookin' for a mother."

"Of all the *unkind*—! Really, Jason—"

"My lord," he corrected promptly.

"Very well, *my lord*. I just wish to point out, *my lord*, that motherly women make the very *best* wives, even, *my lord*, to such obnoxious husbands as you, *my lord*, are likely to be."

"That may be, but I have quite another sort of wife in mind."

"You don't say. And what sort is that?"

"The sort like that Miss de Guis. Now, *there's* a female worth considerin'!"

Anne fumed. "I don't see that Miss Alexandra de Guis fits your specifications *at all*!" she snapped.

"Don't you? Come now, girl, be honest. She's very pleasant, taller even than *you*, you know, and her form is . . . well, it's nothin' short of spectacular."

"Men!" Anne sneered. "You are all fools! But if you can sit there and say that Lexie is sweet-natured and even-tempered, you're a greater dunderhead than even *I* took you for!"

Jason grinned down into her indignant, flashing eyes. "As long as the girl is as sweet-natured and even-tempered as *you* are, my dear, she will be good enough for me. And now, may I suggest that we get out of the carriage? We came to a stop several minutes ago, and the coachman is starin' at us through the window as if we're a couple of loonies."

There was nothing Anne could do but gnash her teeth and follow his suggestion.

Despite her exasperation with him, Anne continued to prepare Jason for the forthcoming ball. The dancing was

still a failure—it seemed to Anne that the fellow was
growing more clumsy with practice—but his speech was
steadily improving. Although an occasional "shucks" still
passed his lips, he had learned to substitute "perhaps" for
the dreadful "maybe" that Americans used, and he had
given up saying "I guess" or "I reckon" every time he
expressed an opinion. In particular, however, Anne
instructed him in the proper demeanor before royalty, for
it was rumored that the Prince might put in an appearance
at the festivities. It was less than two months since
"Prinny" had been made Regent, and his presence at a
ball would be accompanied by a great deal of pomp and
ceremony. It was vital that Jason not bring unfavorable
notice upon himself by committing a social gaffe before
the Regent.

Jason, however, demanded that he be excused from his
lessons for at least a couple of hours in the afternoons.
These he usually spent in Peter's company. The two
would closet themselves in the library to play chess,
discuss Peter's studies or (if they were sure that the ladies
were out of earshot) drill Peter in various boxing
exercises. Peter thrived under Jason's attention. His
appetite improved, his moods became more cheerful, his
pallor lessened and his confidence increased. Jason
rapidly filled the void that the absence of a father or
brother had created.

One afternoon, their chess game was interrupted by a
disturbance in the corridor outside their door. Peter
opened the door to find Coyne engaged in verbal dispute
with a lanky, gaunt-cheeked personage whose black,
long-tailed coat had seen better days, whose gray-
streaked mustaches drooped forlornly at the corners and
who carried a much-handled newspaper in his hand. "Is
there some difficulty, Coyne?" Peter inquired.

"No, Master Peter, it's nothing at all," Coyne said in
contradiction of the quite obvious tension in the hallway.
"I'm sorry you were disturbed. I shall see this person to
the door immediately."

"Oh, y'will, will yer?" the 'person' sneered. "I can tell yer y' *won't*—not till I've 'ad some satisfaction."

Coyne clenched his fists. "That's enough now, my man. You are *not* qualified for the position, and that's *that*. So let's get along," he said, and tried to move the fellow on down the hall by grasping the lapel of his coat and pushing him backward.

The man resisted stubbornly. "Le' *go*!" he shouted. "I demand to see 'is lordship."

"You will *not* see his lordship," Coyne said between clenched teeth, "so you may just as well take yourself off."

"Le' *go* o' me! Why did y' put the advertisemint in the paper, if y'r not wantin' to 'ire no one?"

Jason, listening to the commotion from his seat at the chessboard, found his interest caught. "Don't make a ruckus out there in the hallway, Coyne," he called out. "Bring the fellow in here and close the door."

Without releasing his grip on the man's lapel, the butler pulled the man into the library. Peter followed, shut the door and leaned against it in order to observe in unobtrusive comfort the unfolding of what promised to be an amusing scene. The intruder, before even glancing round the room, thrust Coyne's hand from his coat, smoothed the injured lapel carefully, favored Jason with a measuring stare and bowed deeply. "Are *you* 'is lordship?" he asked.

"I am. The question is, who are *you*, and what do you want with me?"

"Me name's Orkle, me lord. Benjamin Orkle. An' I'd be 'appy to acquaint yer lordship wi' all the fac's, if y' gi' me a chance to tell yer..."

"I'm *giving* you the chance, Mr. Orkle, so get on with it," Jason said impatiently.

"Yes, me lord, I will." Mr. Orkle cleared his throat in the manner of a musician tuning up his instrument and began. "Y'see, me lord, I'm in the employ o' a fine gentleman, a Mr. Tylerman by name, but in matters o' dress, 'e ain't no Pink o' the Ton, I can tell yer. 'E's too clutch-fisted by 'alf, an' 'e don't know nesh from dash—"

"*Nesh* from *dash*?" Jason asked, looking bewilderedly from Coyne to Peter. Peter, equally puzzled, shrugged, grinned and shook his head. Coyne, frowning in distaste, explained. "I believe he means that his employer is overnice in his taste—that he doesn't know the *timid* from the *stylish*."

Mr. Orkle nodded at Coyne approvingly. "That's it exac'ly. 'E 'as no sense o' style at all, which is, I can tell yer, very mortifyin' to such as meself, who 'as a very remarkable talent for style in gentlemen's apparel, which is to say a good eye for color an' a good sense for puttin' on'y the right things together. Besides which 'e pays me on'y ten pounds per annum, out o' which I finds me own tea and sugar. So this mornin' when I takes 'im 'is breakfast, I takes a peep at 'is paper—I always takes a look when I stops on the landin' for a bit o' relaxation—"

Jason and Peter were attending to Mr. Orkle's account with fascination, but Coyne observed it all with an expression of extreme distaste. At this point he could bear it no longer. "Can't you get on with it, man? I'm sure his lordship is not interested in how you spend your time."

Mr. Orkle stared coldly at the butler, turned back to face Lord Mainwaring and calmly continued. "As I was sayin', I takes a peep at the paper and sees this 'ere advertisemint for a gentleman's gentleman. Soon as I sees it, I makes up me mind to apply, and I axes Mr. Tylerman for the day out. I can tell yer that it ain't a simple thing to get Mr. Tylerman to agree. But I finally manages it, and then dresses meself up in me best—which as y' can see ain't very good, but what can y' expect on ten pounds per?—an' I takes meself all the way 'ere on shanks' mare. An' what do I get for me pains when I gets 'ere but a snub from that there whopstraw—"

"Now, *see here*!" Coyne sputtered in exasperation.

"I'll say it again—*whopstraw*! Tellin' me I ain't qualified! I axes yer, me lord, when I been a gentleman's gentleman since the eighties, 'ow  can 'e say I ain't qualified? What *I* say is that this is all a *'oax*!"

"A what?" Jason asked, looking with strangled amusement at Peter.

Peter fought back a grin and merely shrugged again.

"A 'oax," Mr. Orkle repeated. "If a man comes to yer door 'ere and says to yer butler—in 'is engagin'est manner, mind!—that 'e's been a valet for more 'n twen'y years, and the butler don't ax 'im nothin' but tells 'im to take hisself off 'cause 'e's not qualified, well, I axes yer, wouldn't *you* think it was a 'oax?"

Coyne drew himself up in proud disdain. "I am not obliged to ask you anything. I could tell *immediately* that you were not qualified, no matter *how* long you've been in service. The advertisement, my good man, is no hoax!"

"It sounds like a 'oax to me," Orkle declared stubbornly. "else how could y' tell so 'immediately' that I ain't qualified?"

"From the way you *speak*," Coyne answered promptly, taking great pleasure in playing his trump card. "My instructions are to hire someone who looks and *talks* like a *gentleman*."

Momentarily daunted, Mr. Orkle blinked. But it took no longer than a moment before he recovered. He waved his newspaper in Coyne's face. "Then where, can y' tell me, does it say so in the advertisemint, eh? Does it say *anywheres* that I'd 'ave to talk like a gentleman? No, it don't. Not anywheres in this advertisement. I axes you, me lord, is it fair to expec' me to know that? If I'd a' know'd, would I 'ave come all this way for nothin'?"

"I...suppose not," Jason admitted in spellbound amusement.

"O' course not!" Mr. Orkle said vigorously. "So, as far as I'm concerned, this is as good as a 'oax!"

"I reckon it is," Jason agreed.

"Then what 'ave yer to say for yersel's, eh? *What*, I axes yer?"

Jason, his eyes brimming with suppressed mirth, looked up at the butler. "Well, Coyne, *have* we anything to say for ourselves?"

"If you are speaking of the advertisement, my lord, all I

can say is that it is not necessary to list all the qualifications. If Mr. Orkle has been inconvenienced, I'm sure I'm very sorry, but—"

"Sorry! What good's *sorry*?" the valet cried. "That don't pay be back for me trouble and me day's pay. I oughta summons yer!"

"Summons?" Jason asked. "Do you mean *sue* us?"

"Yes, me lord. I oughta take meself to a lawyer and see if I can't summons yer. But I won't."

Jason, who had been ready to offer the valet a guinea (which would be the equivalent of more than a month's wages) in appreciation of the fellow's histrionic talents, looked at him with some surprise. "You won't?" he asked. "Why not?"

"Because," Mr. Orkle said proudly, "I am a man o' dignity. A man o' dignity don't stoop so low. An' I don't blame *you*, me lord, 'cause you 'ad nothin' to do wi' this. But as for yer man 'ere, that's another tale."

"Oh?" Jason asked. "Do you intend to... er... summons *him*?"

"No, me lord. I on'y intends to turn me back on 'im, like this, an' take me leave like the man o' dignity which I am, me message to 'im bein' expressed by me posture." And he put his nose in the air, brushed by the butler with a marked sniff and marched to the door.

Peter bit his lip and choked. Jason, laughter brimming in his eyes, nevertheless managed to keep his countenance. "*What* message is expressed by your posture, Mr. Orkle?" he asked, enthralled.

"Couldn't y' tell, me lord? That was *silent contempt*!"

With the natural sense of timing of a comedic actor, Mr. Orkle closed the door behind him just as he completed his last words. The effect was devastating on both Peter and Jason, who promptly succumbed to their long-suppressed urge to roar with laughter. Coyne, who saw nothing funny in the entire scene, headed for the door wrapped in his *own* sense of dignity, but he was arrested by the sight of Lord Mainwaring making peculiar hand signals. Jason, doubled over with laughter, was unable to speak, but he was evidently trying to convey to Coyne by hand signals that the butler was to remain.

With the air of superiority which the unamused adopt when observing people made helpless by untrammeled merriment, Coyne shook his head. "Did you want something, my lord?" he asked disdainfully.

Lord Mainwaring nodded and tried to catch his breath. But a renewed paroxysm from Peter sent him off again, and it was some time before he was able to convey his wishes to the disapproving butler. "Catch him!" Jason said breathlessly. "Catch him, quickly. I want you to hire him."

Coyne gasped. "*Orkle*, your lordship? You can't mean it! You want him as your *valet*?"

"Jason, you're a great gun!" Peter exclaimed.

But Coyne would not budge. "Miss Anne will not approve, my lord," he cautioned. "Her instructions on the qualities of the man I was to engage were quite specific."

"Don't worry about Miss Hartley, Coyne. Just hurry and catch Mr. Orkle before he gets away!"

Coyne had no choice but to do as he was bid, even though he found the task utterly repugnant. Not only had he taken Orkle in extreme dislike, but he knew that Miss Anne would take him to task for permitting his lordship to so much as *glimpse* the fellow. But, the milk being spilt, there was nothing he could do but go after Orkle as Lord Mainwaring had ordered. When he peered out-of-doors, there was no sign of the fellow on the street. Coyne had to run a considerable distance to catch up with the volatile valet. Placing his hand restrainingly on Orkle's arm, Coyne stood puffing and heaving until he could catch his breath. Then he informed the valet coldly that Lord Mainwaring had decided to make use of his services.

Orkle's delight was boundless. He hooted, gave a little dancing step, turned himself around, jumped up and down and clapped his hands in delight. His exuberance was so infectious that even Coyne felt a surprising softening toward the fellow. In untrammeled enthusiasm, Orkle offered to run all the way back to his present abode, promptly resign from his position, find a replacement and return to the Mainwarings all within the next two hours. "No need to run, Mr. Orkle," Coyne informed him magisterially. "You are now in the employ of a nobleman. A carriage will be provided to convey you."

"A *carriage*? For *me*?" The full realization of his rise in the world seemed suddenly to burst upon him. "*Blimey*!" he breathed, awed at last.

Peter and Jason had returned to the chess table, but before they resumed their game, Peter felt obliged to add his warning to the dire prediction Coyne had made before he left. "Anne won't like your man a bit, Jason. If you really intend to make that fellow your valet, you'd better prepare yourself to face her wrath."

"And how do I do that," Jason asked wryly, "your sister's tempers bein' what they are?" He looked across at Peter with a mock-suspicious scowl. "Or, you slyboots, have you brought the matter up just to put me off my game? You know that the prospect of your sister's temper has me quaking like a rabbit."

Peter laughed. "Yes, you're in a terrible fright, I can see. Really, Jason, you're the most complete hand. Stop pulling my leg and pay attention to my move. I'm about to castle."

They turned their attention to the chessboard. Since chess strategy requires single-minded, serious concentration, they soon forgot the entire matter of the valet. By the time they neared the completion of their second game, a couple of hours later, they were taken by complete surprise when a furious Anne burst in on them. "Have you lost your *mind*, my lord?" she demanded curtly.

Jason blinked up at her innocently. "Not that I know of. Why?"

"Then how, sir, do you account for the presence in this

house of that mustachioed creature who claims to be your valet?"

"Oh, is Orkle here already? Good. I'm glad you've seen him. I knew you wanted me to have someone—"

"Stop playing the innocent! You know perfectly well that I wanted you to have someone of taste, of refinement, someone appropriate to a gentleman of your rank, not a . . . a poor *parody* of a gentleman's—"

"Come now, Anne," Peter put in fairly, "the fellow's not so bad. In fact, he has a remarkable talent for style in gentlemen's apparel."

The mischievous glint sparkled in Jason's eyes. "A good eye for color, I think he said, didn't he, Peter?"

Peter, trying to suppress his laughter, gurgled. "And a good sense for putting the right coat and waistcoat together, too."

"Now, what more could one want from one's valet?" Jason asked her reasonably.

Anne glared at her brother and Jason in turn. "I can see that you refuse to take this matter seriously. I wonder, Lord Mainwaring, why you sought my advice on these matters in the first place, since you seem to take a perverse delight in scorning whatever counsel I offer. Very well, sir, have your own way, if you must. If you insist on taking as a valet a person who would be more fittingly employed in a Soho tavern, dispensing quips and grog to the regulars, *you* will pay the consequences, not I!"

"But at least I will not be more *nesh* than *dash*," Jason offered placatingly.

Anne had turned on her heel and started out, but this stopped her. "What?" she asked, completely bemused.

"True," Peter agreed, nodding his head thoughtfully at his sister, "and Jason won't be 'summonsed' either."

She glowered. "I don't know what you two are talking about!"

Jason and Peter exchanged laughing glances. "No, Peter, you're out there. Orkle said he wouldn't summons me in any case," Jason reminded Peter.

"Right," Peter said. "Too much dignity."

The two men nodded knowingly and, ignoring Anne, turned back to the chessboard.

"How delightful that you two are thick as thieves," Anne said, her voice dripping with sarcasm, and she turned back to the door.

"I hope your sister doesn't say anything to offend Mr. Orkle," Jason remarked to Peter, making sure she could overhear.

Peter followed his lead. "I know. It would be too bad."

"Yes," Jason said, ostentatiously moving a pawn up a square, "he might find it necessary to deal with her as he did with Coyne."

"Mmmm," Peter nodded, studying the board carefully. "He might certainly do so."

After a moment's struggle, during which she made to step out the door, Anne capitulated to curiosity and turned back. "How *did* he deal with Coyne?" she asked, elaborately casual.

"He said it was the only way for a man of his dignity to handle opposition," Jason explained, looking up at her.

"*What* way?" Anne asked impatiently.

"With *silent contempt*, of course," Peter said. Then, both men grinning, they bent their heads over the chessboard again, leaving Anne to stand in the doorway agape.

# *Eleven*

THE TIME OF JASON'S INTRODUCTION into
Polite Society—the night of Lady Dabney's ball—was
fast approaching. Anne, with a generosity of spirit she
didn't know she possessed, put aside her irritation with
the Viscount for flaunting her advice in so many instances
(especially in the matter of choosing a valet) and
benevolently continued to prepare him for the forthcoming event. She tried to teach him how to bow with grace
and without obsequiousness, how to address the Regent,
how to approach a lady and ask her to dance, how to lead
her to the dance floor, and how to restore her to her
chaperone. He had to learn the differences in addressing
maiden ladies and married ladies, young girls and elderly
dowagers, dukes and barons. He had to become familiar
with the relative intoxicating capacities on females of
orgeat (none), punch (variable), and champagne (danger-
ous). And he most certainly had to be able to recognize
the difference between innocent flirtations and licentious
dalliance. "It's all so complicated," he complained. "I
doubt that I shall ever get it all straight."

"If only you would pay close attention to me (instead of

regarding me with that mocking gleam that makes me wonder if you are taking any of this at all seriously), I'm sure you'd have very little difficulty," Anne answered with asperity.

"Oh, I take it *very* seriously, I assure you," he declared, a very slight smile belying his words, "but you must admit that it's difficult to know exactly when a man crosses over the boundary of mere flirting into what you call licentiousness."

"The best gage of that, sir, is your *intent*," she said flatly.

"Oh, but my intent is *always* licentious," he retorted promptly.

"There, you *see*?" she asked in annoyance. 'You won't be serious."

"I'm sorry. Seriously, then, I can understand that, while a man is standing in the ballroom with a young lady, with crowds of people all around, he may tell her how lovely she looks, and no one would think it more than innocent flirting. But what if she's asked him to take her outside for a breath of air? There, alone in the darkness of the evening, would those words *still* be mere flirting?"

Anne considered. "I don't know. Are they sitting or standing?"

"Does it matter?"

"Yes, I believe it does. If they are standing where they can be seen from the windows, for example, and not very close to each other, I would say the words would still be acceptably innocent. If, however, they were seated together on a bench, with shoulders or knees touching—"

"How? Like this?" he asked, drawing her down beside him on the sofa so that they were close enough for shoulders *and* knees to touch. "Is *this* acceptable?"

"Well..." she hesitated.

"Have you never sat beside a man like this?"

"Of course, but—"

"But if we're sitting like this, I mustn't tell you that you look lovely?"

"I ... I suppose it would be ... acceptable," she said, growing uncomfortably flushed.

"Would I be permitted to take your hand—like this—and say it? 'How lovely you look tonight, my dear,'" he said, acting out the scene.

She tried to withdraw her hand. "I don't think so," she said decisively.

"Don't tell me that takin' your *hand* is licentious! Has no one ever held it so?"

"Well, I suppose it's not *licentious*, exactly—"

"Then I have not yet passed the bounds. What if I put my other arm around you, *so*, and drew you close. Then, droppin' your hand, I lifted your chin like this ..."

She found herself pressed against him, his face close above hers. He was smiling down at her with an expression in his eyes that was not at all mocking. Why, the ... the ... *madman* was going to *kiss* her! For a fleeting moment she considered the possibility of permitting him to do it—she was conscious of a sharp desire to feel his mouth on hers—but almost immediately her fury overtook her, and she pushed him away, enraged. "You ... you detestable *sneak*!" she cried, jumping to her feet. "How *dare* you try to play your vulgar American tricks on me!"

He looked up at her in exaggerated innocence. "But, ma'am," he drawled, "how else am I to *learn*—"

"I'm sure I don't care *how* you learn! But I'll tell you this, my lord—that's the very *last* lesson you'll have from *me*!" And with a wrathful toss of her head, she strode from the room and slammed the door behind her.

Despite her resolve to have nothing further to do with his debut, Anne found herself, on the day of the ball, giving Jason instructions on what to wear. The whole family was lingering over luncheon when the subject of his evening dress came up. "I hope your fool of a valet knows how to tie a neckcloth properly," Anne said worriedly. "And be sure to tell him to press the gray loretto waistcoat. That should do well with your evening coat."

"Orkle thinks the gray waistcoat is *nesh*," Jason ventured in his irritatingly innocent tone.

Peter, about to swallow a bite of cold ham, choked. Lady Harriet raised a questioning eyebrow. "*Nesh*?" she asked, puzzled.

"I believe it's Orkle's way of saying that something is insipid," Peter explained.

"Insipid, is it?" Anne asked in frozen accents, putting down her fork and rising. "I can only hope, my lord, that your so-discriminating valet doesn't turn you out tonight looking like a Bond Street Beau!"

Lady Harriet watched with troubled eyes as her stepdaughter stalked from the room. "I don't know what ails Anne," she murmured, "but, Jason dear, don't be disturbed by what she says. I'm sure you'll be quite up to the mark tonight in every way." As they all rose to leave the table, she gave Jason's hand a comforting squeeze. Nevertheless, knowing that no one but his peculiar valet would be supervising his dressing, Harriet, like Anne, was feeling distinctly uneasy. "I must remain calm," she warned herself and went upstairs to take a nap.

There followed a few hours of silence in the household, but by late afternoon the activity in the upstairs hall was hectic. Abigails ran back and forth in the hallways between Lady Harriet's room and Anne's, carrying freshly laundered petticoats, ribbons, curling irons, perfume bottles and sundry other necessities for female evening attire. Orkle was seen running up and down the stairs at various intervals on mysterious errands in connection with Lord Mainwaring's attire. Every servant in the household, including Coyne, found an excuse to hang about the corridors, hoping to catch a glimpse of his lordship, all of them having heard that this was the night Lord Mainwaring was to make his mark. Even Peter was seen pacing the corridor, something no one in the household had ever seen him do before.

Peter, too young to be invited to *ton* parties and too

scholarly to have an interest in them, found himself for
the first time in his life piqued by this social ritual. His
affection for Jason made him concerned. He was dimly
aware that such affairs could make a difference in one's
life. He wasn't sure how, but one's friendships, one's
*affaires du coeur*, even one's self-confidence could be
affected by one's success or failure at a ball. He did not
want Jason to be changed or hurt in any way by the
experience he was about to undergo this evening. For that
reason he paced the corridor nervously, hoping that Orkle
was indeed the man he claimed to be and was capable of
sending Jason off in style. Once Jason arrived at the ball,
he had to handle himself on his own, and Peter hoped that
the people Jason would meet would be perceptive enough
to recognize the excellent qualities which Peter had found
beneath Jason's easygoing, informal American exterior.

The Mainwarings had been invited by the Dabneys to
partake of a small dinner before the ball, and the carriage
was therefore ordered for seven o'clock. When the hour
struck, the carriage arrived at the door, Coyne took up his
position at the front doorway, and Peter waited in the
drawing room for the party-goers to make an appearance.
Anne was the first to come down, nervously peeping in the
doorway for her first glimpse of her charge. "He's not here
yet," Peter told her.

Anne came into the room, buttoning her long white
gloves. She had not neglected her own appearance, and
she looked very lovely in a ball gown of rose-colored
Tiffany silk cut low over her shoulders and clinging softly
to the lines of her body. Her hair was tied back with a gold
ribbon, *à la Sappho*, with tantalizing little curls escaping
to frame her face. The only decorations she wore were a
simple gold necklace at her throat and ornate little gold
slippers that peeped out from below the hem of her dress.
Although Peter noted that his sister was in excellent
looks, he didn't comment on her appearance, his mind
and eyes being fixed on the doorway where Jason would
soon appear. Anne took no notice of the omission of

compliments. Absorbed, herself, in watching for Jason, she didn't even notice his lack of attention to her costume.

Harriet hurried in eagerly. "Is he down yet?" she asked, the answer apparent even before she'd finished the question. She, too, was looking festive in an embroidered gown of dark blue lustring and a silver turban decorated with a diamond brooch and an enormous ostrich feather. Also occupied with worry over Jason, she did not exhibit any more interest in her own appearance than Anne had shown in hers.

They did not have long to wait. Within five minutes of Harriet's entrance, Jason appeared in the doorway. He paused and cleared his throat importantly. His aunt and his two cousins turned and stared. From the top of his carelessly brushed curls to the bottoms of his black leather dancing shoes, Jason was every inch the immaculate, exquisitely-turned-out Corinthian. His black evening coat, cut short at the waist across the front and falling in long tails at the back, fit across his shoulders to perfection. His frilled shirt gleamed, his neckcloth was elegantly tied, his knee-breeches and silk stockings showed his shapely legs to advantage, and his waistcoat, of Italian silk with subtle stripes in three shades of green, added a needed touch of color which made a masterly blend of the whole ensemble.

There was a moment of appreciative silence. Before it was broken, Jason, with a wide grin, removed from his pocket an enameled snuffbox, flipped it open with his thumb and, with an air of insouciance, took a pinch of snuff. Lady Harriet squealed delightedly, rushed across the room and flung her arms about his neck. "Oh, Jason, you're *perfect*!" she cried.

Jason signaled Orkle, who was hovering about in the hallway behind him, to come in. The valet stepped into the room proudly. In his hand he held two nosegays. One, a small bouquet of surprisingly blue violets, Jason took and presented to his aunt with a small bow. "For you, my dear," he said smiling, and he leaned over to kiss her cheek.

Lady Harriet blushed with pleasure. "How very thoughtful," she murmured, putting her nose to the bouquet.

Jason took the other nosegay from the valet, a charming confection of pink and white rosebuds, and brought it to Anne. "If I may say so without being *licentious*," he said with his mischievous grin, "you look lovely tonight, Miss Hartley." He presented the bouquet with a bow. "Do I meet with *your* approval, ma'am?"

"Yes, you do," she said warmly and turned to Orkle. "I owe you an apology, Mr. Orkle," she said generously. "He is complete to a shade. A nonpareil. And the waistcoat is an excellent choice. Even the neckcloth is magnificent. What do you call that fold?"

"It's one o' me own devisin', miss, but akin to the Trône d'Amour. I calls it Knight's Reward, 'cause I invented it for Sir Timothy Knightsbridge, but 'is lordship 'ere, 'e wants to call it the Nuisance, 'cause I used up four neckerchiefs afore I tied it proper."

"Well, whatever it's called, it's beautiful. You've done a superb job with that great gawk," Anne said with a smile. "And if, as I suspect, these nosegays were your idea, I have a great deal for which to be grateful to you."

"Thank yer, me lady, for all yer kind words, but I 'as to admit that the flowers was 'is lordship's idea."

"You don't say!" Anne said, looking up at Jason saucily. "Will surprises never cease?"

As Anne walked gaily out of the room to don her cloak, she did not dream that her words were prophetic—that surprises would not cease during the entire evening ahead of them.

Coyne helped the ladies on with their cloaks, and they started for the carriage. Left alone with Jason for a moment, Peter fixed his eyes on his cousin earnestly. "I hope you have a successful evening," he said shyly, shaking Jason's hand, "but even if you make a cake of yourself, it won't matter a bit, you know. Not to people who count."

Jason looked at Peter affectionately and ruffled his

hair, but he said nothing. Then, with a grin and a wink, he tucked his chapeau-bras under his arm and went out to meet his fate.

# Twelve

THE SURPRISES IN STORE for Anne were not all to be as pleasant as the first sight of Jason in his evening clothes had been. But at least the early part of the evening turned out beautifully. Jason, athough he ignored or forgot many of her instructions, seemed to do very well indeed. In fact, before the early dinner party had ended, it was clear to Anne that Lord Mainwaring was on his way to making a spectacular success.

Ostensibly, the guest of honor at the dinner party Lord and Lady Dabney held before the start of the ball (an intimate gathering of twenty-four diners, consisting of several members of the Dabney family and a few special guests) was the dowager Duchess of Richmond, but the guest who received most of the attention was the new Viscount from America. Lord Mainwaring drew all eyes the moment he entered, and the eyes rarely left him. When he was brought by his host to meet the guest of honor, the Duchess remarked in her piercing voice that the fellow certainly was "a big 'un." She promptly asked the Viscount the question which everyone was wont to ask and which he was fast learning to dread: "Heavens, my lord, are *all* American men so tall?"

"Shucks, your grace," he replied promptly, "*this* ain't tall. I'm nothin' but a runt back home."

Anne froze, expecting a shocked silence, but Jason's quip was greeted by loud guffaws from the gentlemen, giggles from the ladies and an appreciative snort from the Duchess herself. The Duchess demanded his arm for the march to the dinner table (an honor which should have been given to her host, Lord Dabney, but which that neglected gentleman took in good part) and addressed most of her remarks to Jason all through dinner. The other guests vied with each other for his attention, asking him questions about America and hanging on his answers with flattering concentration. Lady Dabney's daughter, Amanda, clearly smitten, asked him coyly what he thought of English ladies as compared to American. "I find *all* ladies appealin', ma'am," he said, as the others fell silent, listening in fascination to his response. "Of course, American girls don't look quite so slim as you English ladies."

"Do you mean," the girl persisted, "that American girls are...er...rounder?"

"Well, they appear so, I think. Their dresses don't seem to *cling* so closely to their forms. You English girls dress to look slim and make the *men* look 'round."

Over the roar of laughter that greeted this sally, Anne distinctly heard the Duchess remark to Lady Dabney that the new Mainwaring was a wit.

By the time the dinner guests rose to go upstairs (for the ballroom, on the upper floor, was beginning to fill with newly arriving guests), Anne and Lady Harriet were light-headed with relief and gratification. Jason's success at dinner had been greater than either one of them had hoped. "Wasn't he marvelous?" Harriet whispered to Anne as they left the dining room. "He's bound to be the hit of the evening."

"Yes, I think he may be—if only he doesn't spoil it all by saying something too outrageous or tripping over his feet on the dance floor," Anne acknowledged.

"Then take him aside and *warn* him," Lady Harriet suggested and, with a smile to Lord Dabney who had come alongside her, took his arm for the climb up the stairs.

Anne caught up with Jason before he'd started upstairs and drew him to the shadows behind the stairway. "I just want to compliment you. You are doing beautifully, my lord," she whispered.

He cocked a suspicious eyebrow at her. "Butterin' me up, ma'am? I'm well aware that I said 'shucks' at least twice."

"I'm surprised to have to admit to you, sir, that no one seemed to mind that in the least. In fact, I believe they *like* your barbarous American tongue. Now, if you'll but remember to dance only the simplest of the country dances and to refrain from making any outlandish remarks when you're introduced to the Prince, I think we may brush through this evening very creditably."

His eyebrows lifted. "Do you think so, ma'am?" he asked, his tone rather cool. "I reckon—I mean I *suppose* that is high praise, comin' from you. What sort of outlandish remarks do you think I'm likely to make that I should avoid?"

The expression lurking in the light-eyed, penetrating gaze he fixed on her face caught her attention. But she couldn't read it. "I think that if you merely answer 'yes, your highness,' or 'no, your highness,' to any remark the Prince makes, you'll be certain to make no slip."

"I'll try to remember that," he said drily and turned to go. But the expression in his eyes troubled her. Was he disappointed in her in some way? Or had she offended him?

She caught his arm. "Is anything the matter, Jason?"

"No, nothin'," he answered shortly. "Nothin' at all."

She searched his face, vaguely troubled. "Are you sure?"

"Yes. I had only hoped—" But he stopped himself.

"Hoped—?" she prodded.

His piercing look discomfitted her. "I'd hoped, ma'am," he said wryly, "that by this time you'd have learned to feel some confidence in me." He turned and went quickly up the stairs, leaving her staring after him in rather breathless and shamefaced confusion.

In the ballroom upstairs, the twenty-five musicians were already playing, and several couples were circling the dance floor. Lady Dabney's balls were always lavish to the point of ostentation. Thousands of candles glittered and twinkled, their light caught by the crystal prisms of the chandeliers and scattered in shimmering pinpoints all around the room. Liveried servants poured bubbling champagne into hundreds of glasses arranged on a number of refreshment tables. And streaming into the room in large numbers were the new arrivals, dressed in rich silks and velvets, sporting jewels and gold ornaments and adding to the air of opulence.

By the time Anne had recovered herself sufficiently to make her entrance, Lord Mainwaring had already taken a place on the dance floor, very properly squiring the daughter of his hosts, Miss Amanda Dabney. Anne found a chair near her stepmother and sat down to think; she needed a moment to mull over the meaning of Jason's remark. But she could not concentrate. She found her eyes riveted on her pupil on the dance floor. The figures of the country dance which they were performing were not difficult, but even so, Anne noted with surprise that Jason was executing them with remarkable aplomb. Her pupil was indeed a credit to her tonight, she thought, and she should certainly feel proud. But she didn't feel proud—it could not have been *she* who had taught him to dance like that!

Before she could solve what was beginning to seem like a puzzle, she became aware that someone was standing before her. She looked up to find Arthur smiling down at her. "Good evening," he said happily. "I had hoped to see you here. Will you stand up with me for the next dance?

The sets will form in a moment or two."

The sight of Arthur Claybridge always made her heart flutter. Any girl's would. He was, as usual, the handsomest man in the room. His black evening coat set off his blond locks to advantage, and the grace of his carriage and the sweetness of his smile were enough to drive away the confusing depression which had settled upon her spirits since her bewildering conversation with Jason behind the stairway.

Anne gave Arthur her hand, and they walked slowly toward the dance floor. "I thought your mother objects to your standing up with me," she reminded him.

"I don't care," he said boldly. "I haven't seen you in more than a week, and I can't pass this opportunity by. Speaking of that unpleasant matter, however, reminds me that Lady Harriet may scold *you* for this. I don't wish to cause you unpleasantness. Shall I go away?"

"I doubt that Mama will even notice us," Anne declared with a touch of resentment. "Her whole attention is fixed on Lord Mainwaring this evening."

As the new sets formed, Anne noticed with surprise that Jason had joined the set with Cherry on his arm. The dance was a *boulangère*, which required figures that Jason had never sufficiently mastered. With a sinking heart, Anne whispered a warning to Cherry to help him as much as possible. As the music began she offered a little prayer that Jason might not disgrace himself.

During the dance, she could not observe Jason well. Not only was she forced to pay attention to her own performance, but she had to converse with Arthur as well. He was attempting to use their meagre time together to discuss their plans. Anne tried to follow what he was saying, but the movements of the dance and her own attempts to see how Jason was performing prevented her from comprehending. "Please, Arthur," she pleaded at last, "let's talk about this later, when we can find someplace out-of-the-way in which to sit down and converse properly."

At the dance's end, Cherry, breathless and in high color, confided to Anne that Jason had managed the steps quite unexceptionally and had, at the same time, kept up a lively—indeed a flattering—conversation with her which she had very much enjoyed. "Really, Cherry?" Anne mused. "I can't understand it. I *know* that I was not so gifted a teacher as to have caused results like *this*!"

Arthur, noting that his mother was watching him from the sidelines, and not wishing her to fall into a state of apoplexy, relinquished Anne to a portly dandy named Percy Livermore for the next dance, promising to return to her side as soon as possible. But the dance had scarcely begun when it stopped abruptly. The musicians broke into "Rule, Britannia," and the Prince Regent entered the room. He was followed by his entourage, a large group which included such notables as his brother Frederick, the Duke of York, and Lord and Lady Hertford.

Lord and Lady Dabney hurried to greet him. While they made their effusive obeisances, the entire assemblage formed two lines across the length of the room, leaving a wide aisle down the center. The Prince proceeded slowly down the aisle, acknowledging a friend here, kissing a lady's hand there, stopping to exchange pleasantries with his cronies or pausing to permit his host to introduce him to those whose acquaintance he had not made.

The Prince could, when he wished, behave with cordial familiarity, and this was one of those times. This sort of assemblage (where the surroundings were opulently tasteful and the guests glitteringly elegant) was the very thing he enjoyed. He beamed heartily as he walked down the line. As he approached the place where Lord Mainwaring was standing, Anne noticed with chagrin that Jason was accompanied by the obnoxious Alexandra de Guis. Lexis was looking breathtaking in a gown of silver gauze over green silk that clung so closely to her figure that Anne knew her petticoat had been damped.

The Prince was quite tall himself, and he took particular note of the stranger in the room who stood taller than he. "And who is that young giant?" he asked his host.

When the introduction had been made, and Jason had stepped forward and executed a faultless bow, the Prince smiled at him warmly. "So *you* are the American Viscount I've heard so much about. They tell me you're a bruising rider. I should like to ride with you one day."

"I should be honored, your highness," Jason answered comfortably.

"Tell me, Mainwaring, are all you Americans so tall?" the Prince asked inevitably.

"Yes, your highness, we are," Jason answered with a twinkle that caused Anne (who knew that look meant mischief) to hold her breath in dread. "We *have* to be, you know."

"*Have* to be?" the Prince asked, puzzled.

"Yes, indeed, your highness. If you British continue to molest us on the high seas, we shall have to trounce you again, so we encourage any and every physical asset in our men—even exaggerated growth such as mine."

There was a moment of shocked silence while the Prince stared blankly at Lord Mainwaring. Then he burst into hearty laughter. "I say, Mainwaring, that's *good*!" he boomed jovially. "That's very good indeed."

The rest of the assemblage was now free to join in the merriment, and while they gave way to their laughter, Anne breathed a sigh of heartfelt relief. But her ordeal was not over, for the Prince was not through with Jason. He became serious and fixed a sharp eye on the Viscount. "Were you trying to suggest, sir, that America intends to engage us in another war?" he asked interestedly.

"Well, your highness, as to that, I can't say. I don't believe America wants war. President Madison is trying hard to avoid it, being gifted with the two senses (beyond the usual five we all have in common) which Americans have in abundance but which, if you will forgive me for being blunt, I haven't noticed as being very evident in the British character."

"Is that so?" demanded the amused Prince, recognizing the humorous glint in Lord Mainwaring's eye. "And which two senses are those?"

"*Horse* and *common*," Jason responded brazenly.

The Regent roared, and all the onlookers joined in. Those people not close enough to hear pressed forward and asked the more fortunate ones to repeat the story, and for several minutes laughter continued to sound around the room. "I *like* this fellow," the Regent announced to his retinue, putting his arm around Jason's shoulder. "Do you play cards, old fellow? Let's go off to the card room and test that common sense of yours."

As the Prince and his circle made for the card rooms, with Jason in tow, Lady Harriet and Anne exchanged glances that spoke eloquently to each other their intense relief and sense of triumph. Jason's success was assured.

Some time later, Arthur found an opportunity to escort Anne to a small sitting room off the ballroom where they might have a moment of seclusion. There he sat down beside her on a sofa and faced her eagerly. "At last we can converse," he said urgently. "I've thought of nothing all week but your news that Lord Mainwaring has agreed to support us. Anne, I cannot like it. It goes against my nature."

"I've thought about it, too, my dear, and I think you are being over-nice," Anne said placatingly. "To accept his support seems to me the wisest thing we can do."

"It is the *weakest* thing we can do," he replied earnestly. "Can't you see that my being so greatly beholden to another man for my wife's—and even my own—support would be abhorrent to me?"

Anne looked at him with dawning comprehension, then lowered her eyes to the hands folded in her lap. "Oh, Arthur," she murmured, shamed, "you are so *good*! I begin to think that you are much *too* good for me."

Arthur took her hand in his and lifted it to his lips. "You are being gooseish, you know. But I'm pleased that you are beginning to understand how I feel."

"But, Arthur, if we refuse Lord Mainwaring's offer, what *are* we to do?"

"I've told you. Only say yes, and I shall write to Shropshire and arrange to take the vicarage." Noting the look of dismay that came into her eyes, he leaned toward her urgently. "Please don't look so downcast, love. You will be happy there, I promise! What would we give up by leaving London which can possibly compare with what we shall gain by having each other? This life is all so shallow and meaningless, after all. What are balls and parties and the whole social whirl but activity for superficial minds? In Shropshire, we shall have simplicity, and peace, and good works..."

"Oh, Arthur, I don't know..."

"We haven't time for further vacillation, my dear."

"Please, Arthur, don't say any more. I must think—!"

At that moment, Lord Mainwaring appeared in the open doorway. "Ah, there you are, ma'am," he said cheerfully. "I've been searchin' for you. I hope you'll pardon this interruption, Claybridge, but I've not had one dance with my dance-instructor. I believe they're goin' to play a waltz. Will you stand up with me for this one, ma'am?"

"A *waltz*?" Arthur asked, shocked. "You must be mistaken."

"No, he may be right, Arthur. Amanda told me that her mother might be persuaded to dare. After all, this is not Almack's. Waltzing is not so terrible, really it isn't. Many people are beginning to learn it, and it's become the rage in Paris."

"I think it's a shocking display," Arthur declared in disapproval.

"Not at all," Anne argued. "I've tried it myself, several times, and have found it an enormously pleasant experience. But, Lord Mainwaring, you cannot perform the waltz without a great deal of skill and practice."

"Why don't you chance it?" Jason urged. "It's danced even in America, you know."

Anne laughed. "Don't let your success this evening go to your head, my lord. Until you've had more experience in the ballroom, you should avoid a dance of such difficulty. I don't believe you're quite ready for it."

"I see," Jason said quietly, his smile fading. The strange, disappointed look that had troubled her earlier came back into his eyes. "Well, then, please forgive me for interruptin' your conversation." With a short bow, he was gone.

"How strange," Anne said, puzzled. "He almost seemed . . ."

"Hurt," Arthur ventured. "I think his feelings were hurt."

"But . . . he could hardly have expected me to prance around the floor with him in a dance he doesn't know!"

"And such a vulgar dance, too. At least so it seems to me. However, you might follow him and promise the fellow the next country dance. After all his goodness to you and your family, it would not be kind in you to give him pain."

"Oh, Arthur, you are truly too good for me," Anne sighed. She gave him a quick kiss on the cheek and ran after Jason.

The waltz had begun, and the guests had crowded around the floor to watch the few couples who were courageous enough to perform the daring new dance in public. Anne's eyes searched the crowd, but Jason was not to be seen. Then she turned to watch the dancers. There he was—he was *waltzing*! She moved to the edge of the floor to have a closer look. There in the center of the floor, with the beautiful Lexie in his arms, Jason was twirling around with an expertise and grace remarkable in so tall a man. The two of them looked magnificent together, and even those onlookers who disapproved of the intimacy of the dance could not help but admire the picture they made.

Anne's blood turned cold as the realization burst upon her that she'd been tricked. *Jason knew how to waltz*! He had known all along—and all the other dances as well. He had handled himself with easy confidence all evening. Why, he had probably never required her instruction for *anything*! It had all been a *trick*—a trick to make a fool of her! The blackguard had let her believe he was a bumpkin from the wilderness, when all the while he'd been as comfortable and at ease among the *ton* as if he'd been born to it! He'd been laughing to himself all along. And not only at *her* but at Harriet and Peter as well! Her throat began to burn and her knees to tremble. He was a deceitful, dishonest, fraudulent *wretch*, and she wanted nothing more than to slap his arrogant face!

"For a fellow who doesn't know how to waltz," Arthur's amused voice came from behind her, "he is certainly doing well."

"I don't need you to point it out to me," Anne snapped at him. Arthur, startled at her vituperative tone, gave her a stricken look. Anne immediately regretted her words. "Oh, dear, I didn't mean... I'm sorry, Arthur."

"Is anything amiss, my dear?" he asked her gently.

Anne was very close to tears, but she couldn't permit herself to make a scene. What she wanted more than anything else was the privacy of her bedroom. "Will you t-take me home, Arthur?" she asked, struggling to keep her voice steady.

"Of course, if you wish. But do you think it wise to leave now? Lady Dabney will think it strange if you take your leave before supper is served. I believe people are starting to go down to supper now. We need stay only a little while longer."

At that moment the waltz came to an end. Anne watched as Lexie laughed breathlessly up into Jason's face. The Viscount tucked her arm in his and, still laughing, they headed for the stairs which led down to the lower rooms where the supper tables had been set. Although they passed within inches of Anne's position, neither of them noticed her, so absorbed were they in their intimate raillery. Anne's fingers curled into tight little fists. What a perfect pair, she thought with furious venom—the Detestable and the Deceitful! Let him have her—Jason and Lexie deserved each other.

She bit her lip and turned to Arthur. "I don't feel much like eating now," she said in a carefully controlled voice. "Why don't you go down without me? I see Cherry sitting over there with her mother. Why don't you offer to escort them?"

"But I don't wish to leave you. I have no great desire for supper either," he assured her.

"I think you'd be *wise* to leave me for a while. If your mother takes notice of the time we've spent together this evening, she'll be bound to serve you a severe tongue-lashing when you return home tonight."

Arthur looked at her with raised eyebrows. "Is something wrong, Anne?"

"No, of course not. I merely think we must be particularly careful at this time not to bring difficulty upon ourselves."

"Very well, then, I'll do as you say. But will you permit me to escort you home later?"

"I don't think so. Don't look so distressed, Arthur. I was hasty in asking it of you. If I must wait until after supper, I may as well leave with Mama." She gave his hand a reassuring squeeze and walked quickly away.

When she neared the door, she looked round to make certain that Arthur was safely occupied with Cherry and that no one else had taken notice of her, and she slipped out of the ballroom and down the stairs. She ordered her cloak from the footman stationed at the front door and quickly ran out into the street.

The night air was quite cool, and the sounds of the city were hushed and remote. Even the music and the din of revelry coming from the Dabney house behind her sounded muted and far away. She raised the hood of her cloak and began to run, trying to flee from the feeling of humiliation and confusion which threatened to overcome her. But as she ran, the tears began to flow, and by the time she arrived at her own doorstep her eyes were stinging and red, and there was an ache in her chest which could not be explained by her physical exertion alone.

# *Thirteen*

ANNE, keeping her face well hidden by her hood, attempted to slip by Coyne without a word when he admitted her into the house. But the butler was not easily avoided. "I'll take your cloak, Miss Anne," he said firmly, following her to the stairs.

"Never m-mind, Coyne," she said, in a valiant attempt to steady her voice. "I'll take care of it m-myself. Just go to b-bed."

The butler stared at her suspiciously. "Is anything wrong, Miss Anne? Where are the others? You haven't come home *alone*, have you?"

She shook her head and tried to wave him away, but the gesture made her hood fall back and gave him a glimpse of her reddened eyes. "*Miss Anne*! What's happened? What's amiss here?" he asked in alarm.

One glance at his troubled face was all that was needed to undo the weak hold she had managed to clamp on her emotions, and she burst into fresh tears. In great agitation, the butler took her arm and led her, unresisting, into the drawing room where he helped her into an easy chair near the fire and went quickly to the table to pour her a glass of brandy. "Is there something I can do for you, Miss Anne?" he asked worriedly as he hovered over her and handed her the drink.

The warmth of the fire was comforting, and she wiped the tears from her cheeks. "No, no, C-Coyne, thank you," she said, determined to regain control of herself. "It is nothing. T-truly, I'm just being missish. I don't want any brandy."

Coyne bit his lip, feeling helplessly inadequate. "Isn't there *anything* I can—?"

He was interrupted by the sound of the front door which opened and shut with a crash, followed by the clatter of hurried footsteps in the hall, and Jason, his face tense with worry, strode into the room. At the sight of Anne, he stopped in his tracks. "Oh, *here* you are!" he exclaimed angrily. "See here, girl, don't you know better than to run off without escort? What a fright you've given me! Whatever possessed—?" Suddenly, taking note of Coyne's agitated expression, the glass of brandy in the butler's hand and Anne's swift movement to turn her face away from him, he paled. "Good God! Something *has* happened!"

He crossed the room in two strides and knelt before her chair, his face agonized. Taking both her hands in his, he asked in a choked voice, "Were you accosted on the street? If anyone's harmed you, I'll—! Anne, please, *tell me*!"

Anne turned and stared at him in considerable surprise. "Nothing of the sort has occurred, my lord, I assure you. There is no reason at all for you to be so... agitated."

He peered closely at her face. "Are you *sure*, my dear? You seem so... upset..."

She turned her face away and tried to free her hands from his grasp. "I'm *quite* sure. You and Coyne... you're both making a to-do about absolutely nothing."

He stared at her, disbelieving, for a long moment. Then he released her hands and stood up. "Very well, we'll take

your word for it. Thank you, Coyne, for your assistance.
I'll take that brandy, if you don't mind, and then you may
go to bed."

Coyne handed Jason the brandy. "Yes, my lord, thank
you. But Lady Harriet has not yet returned—"

"Don't worry about Lady Harriet. I'll go to fetch her
shortly. I'm sure she won't require anything else tonight."

"Very well, my lord," Coyne said and bowed himself
out.

Jason, his eyes on Anne's averted head, drained the
brandy glass in a gulp. Then, with a deep breath, he said,
"When I saw Claybridge taking supper without you, and I
couldn't find you anywhere, I was nearly beside myself
with anxiety. If the footman hadn't told me—"

"I don't see why my absence should have been any
concern of yours," Anne said coldly.

"You attended the ball under my escort. That makes
me responsible for your safety."

"But as you can see, I am quite safe. You need trouble
yourself no longer."

Jason turned to the fire and, leaning his arm on the
mantelpiece, he stared into the flames. "I can see you've
been crying, my dear," he said softly. "If the cause is
something that occurred on your way home, I wish you
would tell me. However, if the cause is personal—having
to do with young Claybridge, for instance—then, of
course, I have no right to interfere..."

Anne's head came up abruptly. "This has nothing
whatever to do with Arthur!" she said furiously. "In all
the time I've known him, he's *never* caused me to shed a
single tear! This is all because of *you*!"

He turned. "*Me*?"

"Yes, my lord. I've been crying because I realized
tonight that I've been completely taken in. I now know
that you are a lying, deceitful *imposter*."

"I don't know what you're talking about," he said, his
brow wrinkled in bafflement. "Do you mean that you
think I'm not the real Mainwaring?"

"As to that, I have no idea," she answered nastily, "but I wouldn't be at all surprised to learn that your identity, too, is a lie."

"I'm not aware of *any* occasion when I lied to you, ma'am. As to my identity, they say it's a wise child who knows his own father, but as far as I know, Henry Hughes *was* my father and the late Lord Mainwaring my uncle."

"Since I assume that Mr. Brindle investigated you thoroughly, I shall not question your word on *that* score," she grudgingly acknowledged.

"Then I don't see—"

"Oh, don't you? Are you going to pretend *now* that you have always been open and aboveboard with me? Don't look at me with that sham innocence! Will you deny that you led me to believe that you'd never taken tea in a refined drawing room? Or that you'd never asked a lady to dance? All that backwoods ignorance! Why, you almost had me believing we were lucky you could *read*!"

"Oh, *that*!" Jason said, his brow clearing with relief. "Is *that* all that's botherin' you?"

"Is that *all*?" she echoed. Jumping up from her chair, she faced him with trembling rage. "Do you mean to imply that this is *unimportant*? A paltry little *misunderstanding*?"

"Yes, ma'am, that's *exactly* what I mean to imply. It was no more than a little joke."

"A joke? A *joke*? For more than a month you tricked me, lied to me, evaded and deceived me at every turn! You let me instruct you, coach you, attempt to teach you to bow, to speak, to dress, to dance . . . when all the time you *knew* you were more than adequately capable of performing your role without any help from me!"

"Oh, come now, Anne," he said placatingly, putting a hand on her arm in an attempt to restrain her fury. "Where's your sense of humor? I only meant to tease you a bit—"

"*Tease*?" she cried, thrusting his hand away. "Is *that* what you call it? You have used me shamefully, abused

my trust and made a fool of me, and you call it teasing!"
She turned her back on him and put her head in her
trembling hands. "And what makes it all so *ugly* is that
you've done the same to Mama and Peter, too!"

This last thrust was more than Jason's good nature
could stand. "Now look *here!*" he exploded, pulling her
around to face him. "I've heard enough of this nonsense.
You listen to *me* for a moment! In the first place, Lady
Harriet, whatever she may have thought of me before
tonight, certainly never considered me as *primitive* as you
did, and therefore she is perfectly delighted—not upset, as
you are—by learning that I am adequately civilized. And
as for Peter, he never doubted it from the first, so your
remarks about him are completely unfounded. But the
most important point, my girl," he said, emphasizing his
words by grasping her shoulders as if he were about to
give her a good shaking, "is that, if I've *really* used you
shamefully, you have only yourself to blame! Yes, my
dear, you brought all this on *yourself*, by your mindless
assumption that Americans are all untutored clods
without taste or familiarity with the civilized world. What
do you think America *is*—an aboriginal jungle? Did it
never occur to you, ma'am, that we have books and
schools and drawing rooms and teacups in the United
States?"

She stared up at him, trembling and confused. For a
moment their eyes locked, his glaring and hers uncertain.
Then she wavered and lowered her head. 'Let me go, sir,"
she muttered. "If this is the way you were taught to treat a
lady in the United States, it is not as civilized a place as
you seem to think. You are hurting me."

He dropped his hands with a reluctant laugh. "Touché,
ma'am. But I was *not* taught, in America, to handle ladies
roughly. You seem to bring out the savage in me."

"I suppose," she remarked petulantly as she returned to
her chair, "that since you blame me for misjudging you,
you expect *me* to apologize to *you* for this imbroglio."

"Not at all. I merely hope to reestablish a sensible

perspective of our relationship."

"We *have* no relationship, my lord. We *never* have had one. What little bond we may have built up in the last few weeks was based on dishonesty and false assumptions, and it no longer exists."

"Then let's build a new one. And you can begin by calling me Jason instead of the 'my lord' you insist on using."

"It was at *your* insistence, my lord, that I so address you."

"You knew perfectly well that I was joking."

"I have no liking for your jokes. And I have no wish to establish a relationship with a man who finds it amusing to deceive—"

Before the last word left her tongue, she found herself being abruptly hauled to her feet. With only one hand, he caught both her hands behind her and pinioned her against him with his arm. "I did *not* deceive you!" he muttered angrily. "You deceived yourself." With his free hand he cupped her chin and forced her to face him. "Look at me!" he commanded. "Take a good look! It's time you began to know me. I'm neither the American primitive you thought I was nor the English dandy you tried to make me. I'm merely a man—an *individual* with a character uniquely my own. I won't be forced into a mold of your devising—not the *cloddish* one, or the *lordly* one, or the *deceitful* one. So look at me, ma'am. It may be worth your while to open your stubborn mind and learn to recognize the man I really am."

She tried to respond, but couldn't find the words. Her heart was pounding with something akin to terror, but she didn't feel afraid. He, too, was in the grip of some strong emotion, for she could feel his heart pounding as loudly as hers. But the lightly colored eyes looking down at her revealed nothing to help her identify this bewildering sensation.

For several seconds neither of them moved. Then Anne became embarrassingly aware of the intimacy of their position. No sooner had the feeling struck her than she recognized a responsive flicker in his eyes—a spark of amusement flared into life in their blue depths. He had read her mind! She reacted with a blush. She made a movement to break free of his grasp, but his arm tightened around her and the gleam in his eyes brightened.

She remembered another time that he'd held her like this. He'd been about to kiss her, then, but she'd been furious with him and had pushed him away. Now, more angry than ever, she felt the same unexpected and sharp desire for his kiss, and the same irritation with herself. Again, she tried to push him away, but this time she was completely helpless. A smile dawned slowly on his face. "Jason," she warned breathlessly, "don't you *dare*!"

There was no question in her mind that he'd been about to kiss her. But the question of whether or not he would have heeded her warning was never answered, for the door opened and they quickly jumped apart. It was Peter who stood in the doorway, his eager smile quickly fading into a look of astonished and acute embarrassment. "Oh...sorry," he mumbled awkwardly. "I didn't know...that is, I didn't mean to—"

"Come in, Peter," Jason said with casual aplomb.

"No, it's all right. I don't want to interrupt...that is, I mean I only wanted to find out how things went. I'll talk to you tomorrow."

"No need to wait till tomorrow. Your sister and I have finished our talk, have we not, ma'am?"

"Quite finished," she answered icily.

"You see?" he said cheerfully to Peter. "Besides, I was about to go out. I must pick up Aunt Harriet—she's still at the Dabneys'."

With that, he went quickly from the room, closing the door behind him. "That *blackguard*!" Anne hissed, throwing herself into the chair. "That odious, insufferable *toad*!"

Peter regarded her in some perplexity. "Who, *Jason*? I

had the distinct impression, when I burst in here so inopportunely, that you rather *liked* him."

"If that was your impression," she told her brother roundly, "you have completely misunderstood the situation. The fellow is a dastardly *imposter*, and I have never disliked anyone more."

"Jason? An imposter? I don't believe it. What's he done?"

"What hasn't he done! The wretch *tricked* me!"

"If you mean that he made an improper advance to you, my dear, I don't in the least blame you for being angry. I would not have thought it of him, although he's often told me that he finds you a deucedly pretty girl."

"Don't be a gudgeon. He made no improper advances. The episode you burst in on was a mere nothing. What I learned about him this evening was much, much worse."

"Good lord, what *was* it?"

"I found out that everything he's done since he arrived has been an enormous *pretense*. Everything! The backwoods manner, the drawling speech, the outlandish clothing, the blunt manners, the clumsy dancing...everything!"

"Oh, is *that* all? You can't mean that you've got yourself in this state of agitation over Jason's *raillery*."

"Raillery? How can you call it raillery? It was nothing but lying and deceit!"

"Really, Anne, you seem to be making much out of nothing much. Anyone having the least knowledge of Jason can tell that his greenheaded-foreigner performance is play-acting."

Anne stared at her brother in some dismay. "Do you mean to say that you knew *all along* that he was perfectly capable of meeting the *ton* and talking to the Prince and dancing with ladies?"

"I may not have realized that he could dance, but I knew he was no fool. From the first I could see that he was well-educated and knew his way about. Very clever fellow, Jason. Holds an advanced degree from a Virginia college, I believe. William and Mary, I think he said. I take it he did himself proud dancing with the ladies tonight?"

"He was the most spectacular success. He danced superbly! You should have seen him. He moved around the ballroom as if he'd been *to the manner born*! You wouldn't have believed it—everyone *adored* him! Even the Prince was enchanted with him."

"Well, good for old Jason!" Peter looked at his sister in mild concern. "One would think you'd be overjoyed, instead of sitting there looking like a thundercloud."

"Why should I be overjoyed? He lied and deceived and tricked me at every turn. I spent *weeks* trying to instruct a man I believed to be an artless innocent to face the lions of society, and all the while the fellow was a lion himself!"

"Yes, my dear, I understand that. What I *don't* understand is why you're so angry about it. As far as I can see, he didn't actually lie to you—he merely permitted you to believe what you wished to believe. I don't see that as such a terrible crime. Can it be that there's something *else* which angers you? Is it because he wasted so much of your time?"

"No...no, it's not that. It's because...because..." She hesitated, trying to sort out the confusion of her feelings. "It's because...he made such a *fool* of m-me," she said tremulously.

Peter shook his head. "No, I don't think that's true," he said thoughtfully. "Neither Mama nor I found him to be an artless innocent. I don't feel *I've* been made a fool of, and neither, I'd wager, does Mama. Perhaps you should have been a more careful observer."

"Are you trying to tell me," she demanded in chagrin, "that *I'm* at fault in all this?"

"I don't think *anyone's* at fault. I admit that I don't have any great understanding of these man-woman affairs, but—"

"*Man-woman affairs*! Really, Peter, I assure you that there is no such thing between Jason and me," she said with some asperity.

He shrugged. "Are you sure? Well, as I said, I don't know much about such things, except what I read in books. I only wanted to suggest that you're far too upset over nothing. The evening went well, and Jason is a success. It seems to me that you should try to forget the rest of it. Come on, let's go up to bed."

"I don't see how I can forget being made a fool of," Anne muttered glumly.

Peter went to the door. "Whenever someone says, 'He made a fool of me,' I tend not to believe it."

"Oh? Why not?"

"Because no one can easily make another a fool." He opened the door and added gently, "When one feels foolish, it's usually because one has made a fool of one's self. I'm not saying that is necessarily the case with you, though. You must decide that for yourself. Good night, my dear."

# Fourteen

ANNE LAY AWAKE most of the night, brooding over her brother's last words. *Had* she made a fool of herself? Was *she herself* to blame for misreading Jason's character? She painfully remembered a number of times when she *should* have recognized—by Jason's inate politeness, his sensible attitudes, his quips, his self-confidence, his relationship with her brother Peter and his easy manner with her stepmother—that he was a cultivated, urbane gentleman. But she brushed these thoughts aside. The fact was that he had consistently and deliberately hoodwinked her. His clumsy performances during the dancing lessons, his tendency to slip into the drawling speech of a country boy, his pretended ignorance of the manners of the drawing room and modes of dress and behavior of the *ton*—all these he had enacted with the uncanny ability of a born deceiver. Why, then, was she to be blamed for not recognizing the fraud?

Of course, she had to admit to herself that she'd jumped to false assumptions about him from the first. But she could scarcely be blamed for those mistaken first impressions—why, *everyone* believed that Americans were roughnecks and oafs! Jason should have taken it upon himself to *correct* the misconceptions, not encourage them by wantonly and dishonestly playing up to them. For that dishonesty, he could not be forgiven. She would not forgive him to her dying day!

That was her conclusion, and that was just what she told Cherry the following afternoon as she sat pouring out her heart to her friend in Cherry's pink-and-gold bedroom. "I shan't forgive him, ever! Not as long as I live!" she declared vehemently.

"I don't blame you a bit," Cherry said staunchly, sitting beside Anne on the bed and patting her shoulder. "It was dreadful of him to have misled you so."

"Oh, Cherry, you're the only one who understands. Even Mama turned a deaf ear to me this morning, telling me that I should have known better than to take a pet over his 'teasing.' Teasing, *ha*!"

"Do you think Anne, that his lordship will still expect you to find him a bride?"

"I don't care *what* he expects! I'm through with him. As far as I'm concerned, he can marry La Belle Lexie, if she's what he wants."

Cherry recoiled. "You can't mean it! Not *Lexie*! I know the gentlemen all dangle after her like moonlings, but none of them seem to *marry* her, do they? What would their mamas say? Even Lord Mainwaring wouldn't want a wife everyone knows is fast."

"I don't care a jot if the future Lady Mainwaring is fast or not. The matter no longer interests me."

"Yes, but Anne," Cherry pointed out worriedly, "if you don't keep to your part of your bargain with Lord Mainwaring, he may not keep his part either. And then there will be no settlement."

"I don't *want* a settlement, and neither does Arthur. I intend to tell Arthur, when he comes here later this afternoon, that I shall go to Shropshire with him, just as he wishes."

For a moment, Cherry gaped at Anne in shocked

silence. "Anne!" she breathed, rising and facing her friend awe-stricken. "You don't mean... you've *decided* at last?"

Anne shook her head in acquiescence.

Cherry's face seemed to freeze in an expression of shock. "Oh, Anne," she whispered in a trance-like monotone, "I can't believe it!"

"Why not? What's the matter with you, Cherry? I always told you I would marry Arthur."

"Yes, I know, but..." She turned away and wandered abstractedly to the window where she stood staring out at the spring-dressed trees. "You didn't think that you'd enjoy being a vicar's wife in a little country village..."

"I still don't think so. But *you've* been telling me and telling me how lovely it will be."

"Yes, I'm sure it will be..." Cherry said.

"So I've decided to believe you. There, now, aren't you going to come here and wish me happy?"

"Of c-course I w-wish..." Cherry began, but as she turned from the window, she burst into tears.

"Heavens, Cherry, what *is* it?" Anne cried, jumping up in alarm and running across to embrace her friend.

"I d-don't *know*! I s-suddenly f-feel so l-lost! Oh, Anne, whatever shall I do when you've g-gone?" And she put her head on Anne's shoulder and sobbed.

"Cherry, don't! Here, come and sit down. You know that nothing will ever really separate us. Why, you must promise to ask me to come down to London every spring, to stay with you for at least a month! And you must come to me twice a year for weeks and weeks! This exile to Shropshire would be completely insupportable if I could not count on your company some of the time."

Cherry sniffed and wiped her eyes. "I know I'm a g-goose. Of course we shall visit. B-But you and Arthur are my dearest f-friends. I shall be so l-lonely!"

"What rubbish! Before you know it, you shall be married, too, and we shall both be busy with *babies*."

"I shall *never* be married," Cherry said funereally. "I've

only had one offer in all my life."

"Yes, I remember it. That gentleman from some country place or other, with the stooped shoulders and the elongated arms. What *was* his name?"

"Howard. Howard Mildmay." Cherry gave a little, reluctant giggle. "Can you imagine what sort of babies I would have had if I'd married him?"

"Monkeys!" Anne laughed. "Darling little monkeys! You should have accepted him."

Cherry's smile faded. "You're joking, but perhaps I should have. There have been no other offers at all, and it's been more than three months since Howard made his."

"Three whole months without an offer?" Anne teased. "That is positively shameful. Any girl who does not receive at least one offer every six weeks is not worth her salt."

"You may laugh, but it's very lowering to think that I haven't *one* prospect."

The friends fell silent, each suddenly engrossed in her own thoughts. Anne tried for the thousandth time to envision the country vicarage, with herself as mistress, dressed in solemn colors befitting the dignity of her station and guarding her tongue to keep from shocking the elderly parishioners with her arrogant London ways. Cherry was sunk in an overwhelming, sickening guilt. She glanced surreptitiously at her friend, wondering if Anne had any inkling of the treachery Cherry nourished in her heart. She had begun to realize, in the last few days, that she did *not* want Anne and Arthur to marry. Arthur had come to her so often of late, to unburden his heart to her and seek her comfort. It had been enormously satisfying to be able to console him. She'd held his hand and stroked his shoulder and offered him maxims of the virtues of patience and restraint. Every moment with him had been sheer joy. Once Anne married him, all that would be over. Cherry ached with shame that she could harbor such selfish desires.

Determined to expunge this wickedness from her soul, she jumped to her feet. She would set to work immediately to find herself a passably acceptable suitor and marry him. She would busy herself with her duties, have half-a-dozen babies and never think of Arthur again. Crossing the room with a decisive step, she opened a drawer in her dressing-table, and took out a large pair of shears which she held out to Anne while she covered her eyes with a dramatic gesture. "Here," she said in a voice of doom, "go ahead and do it!"

"Do what?" Anne asked, bewildered.

"The time has come. It's now or never. *Cut my hair*!"

Two hours later, two severed braids lay curled on Cherry's dressingtable, the floor was littered with tendrils of hair, and Anne stood over Cherry (who was seated before her mirror staring at her face in horrified fascination) with a curling iron in her hand. Cherry's heart-shaped face, which as far back as she could remember had been framed in a neat band of braid, was now topped with a myriad of short, dark curls. Her face looked smaller, younger and a little less full in the cheeks. Her eyes looked enormous.

"Well, do you like it?" Anne asked.

"I . . . I don't know," Cherry said, frightened. "I wonder what Mama will say."

"*I* think you look wonderful. Completely up to the mark. The braids made you look like a governess—more nesh than dash."

"What?"

"Never mind. That's something Lord Mainwaring's man likes to say. But no one could say you are not dashing *now*!"

"Am I?" Cherry asked shyly.

"As dashing as Caro Lamb," Anne declared.

"Good heavens, don't let Mama hear you say *that*!" Cherry said, scandalized. But the comparison between timid little Charity Laverstoke and the notorious Lady

Caroline Lamb (she had been known to dress up like a pageboy, aided by her slight figure and short-cropped curls, in order to escape detection while on her way to or from an assignation) gave Cherry such a lift that she decided to show her new coiffure to her mother immediately.

Lady Laverstoke, an indefatigable card player, was discovered at the doorway, adjusting her bonnet before a wall mirror in preparation for her departure for one of her frequent engagements for a card-game with her similarly addicted cronies. "Look, Mama," Cherry clarioned, "I've cut my hair!"

Lady Laverstoke's hands, adjusting the angle of her bonnet, were stayed. "Charity Laverstoke," she demanded in quelling accents, "how *dared* you do such a thing without my permission?"

Cherry's face fell, and Anne, who had followed behind her, felt her fingers clench into fists. Couldn't Cherry's own mother show a little enthusiasm? No wonder Cherry had so little self-confidence. "Don't you like it, Mama?" Cherry asked plaintively.

"Whether I like it or not does not signify," Cherry's mother declared, turning her attention back to her bonnet. "I am very displeased that you should have taken such a step without my permission. But I shall say nothing more, since I am fully aware that your friend—yes, *you*, Miss Anne Hartley—encouraged this act. It seems to me, miss, that you have quite overstepped the bounds of friendship by encouraging Charity to take this rash step."

Anne sputtered furiously, but before she could defend herself, Lady Laverstoke had opened the door.

"But, Mama, aren't you going to tell me if you like it?" Cherry asked again.

"The change makes very little difference in your appearance, as far as I can see," her mother responded without looking round, and she shut the door behind her.

A woebegone Cherry turned away from the door and walked back to the sitting room, followed by an enraged

Anne. Anne spent the better part of the next hour trying
to convince Cherry that her mother was really pleased
with her appearance but didn't want to admit it because
she hadn't been consulted. Anne thought she had
succeeded in convincing her friend that she did indeed
look lovely, when the butler entered the sitting room to
announce Arthur's arrival. Cherry gasped, screamed, put
her hands to her head in a vain attempt to hide her hair
and tried to flee.

Anne grasped her arm and forced her into a chair. "Sit
down, Cherry, and don't behave so foolishly," she
ordered.

Cherry would have jumped up again as soon as Anne
turned away, but Arthur entered at that moment. Cherry
drew back into the protective shade of the wings of the
chair and tried to make herself inconspicuous. Arthur, his
mind on his own problems, gave her an abstracted nod in
greeting and turned a worried face to Anne. "I hope you
have some word for me, my dear," he said without
preamble. "If I don't send some response to Shropshire
soon, I may lose this opportunity."

Anne, without going into the details of her quarrel with
Lord Mainwaring, gave Arthur the news he'd been
waiting for—that she was at last in agreement with him
that a Gretna Green marriage and a life in the vicarage in
Shropshire were the most satisfactory solutions to their
problems. Aware that Cherry was in the room, Arthur
restrained his impulse to seize Anne in his arms. He
contented himself with smiling at her warmly and lifting
her hand to his lips.

Cherry, not wishing to be in the way, tried to rise from
the chair and slip from the room, but Anne would not
permit it. "Stay where you are, Cherry, because you must
help us make plans. We shall need your help if we're to
leave for Gretna without detection."

The next half-hour was filled with discussion of the
ways and means for the elopement: the clothing and
personal effects to be packed, the type of equipage which

would be necessary for the journey, the number of weeks needed for preparations, the measures to be taken to insure secrecy, and the content of the notes to be left behind. When all these matters had been thoroughly gone over, Cherry again made an attempt to take her leave. This time Anne did not stop her, and Cherry made for the door.

So engrossed had she been in the discussion that she'd quite forgotten about her shorn hair. As Arthur turned to thank her for her aid and advice, he caught his first glimpse of her altered appearance. "Good God!" he exclaimed in horror. "What have you *done* to yourself?"

Cherry stared at him, her eyes filling with tears and her lips trembling. Then her hands flew to her hair, she gave a little moan and, with tears splashing down her cheeks, she ran from the room.

"Confound it, Arthur," Anne said in disgust, "you've really done it! Couldn't you have said something a bit flattering? I shall never be able to convince her *now* that she looks well."

And without waiting for a response from the astounded and shaken Lord Claybridge, she ran after Cherry to offer what comfort she could.

By the time she arrived home, Anne was in no mood to talk to anyone. She had not been able to console Cherry, and although she had finally left the girl to cry out her frustration alone, she felt responsible for having made her best friend miserable. In addition, she was about to embark on a carefully planned program of deceit, a necessity which was the dark side of an elopement. Anne had no liking for it, and she knew that she would find the next six weeks (the time she and Arthur had allowed for preparations) repugnant. Handing her bonnet to Coyne, she headed for the stairs without a word.

But she was not to escape to her room so easily. First Peter emerged from the library to inform her excitedly that Jason had taken him to Cribb's Parlour, where Peter had been matched with a sparring partner of his own weight and had shown some small prowess with his fists. He added that, from the moment they'd appeared, Jason had been surrounded by several of the patrons and had been fussed over all afternoon.

Anne received this news coldly, merely remarking that Jason's doings did not interest her and that she could find little to delight her in learning that her brother showed a talent for fisticuffs. Boxing was, in her view, a disgusting and vulgar sport, and if her brother cared to indulge in such displays, he was not to expect her to applaud.

Having thus delivered a set-down to her brother, she went up the stairs and came face-to-face with her stepmother. "Oh, Anne, dearest," Lady Harriet cried excitedly, "I've been waiting all afternoon to tell you—I've the most delightful news. Jason has received a veritable mountain of invitations, even one from the Regent himself to dine at Carlton House, and *we* are included as well!"

"Delightful," Anne muttered drily, hoping to escape without further conversation.

"Isn't it?" Harriet chirped happily. "I'm so completely in alt over his success, I had to retire to my room *four times* today to calm my nerves and to regulate my breathing."

"I wouldn't fly into alt over this, Mama, if I were you," Anne cautioned, "or you'll have his lordship so puffed up with his own consequence that there will be no living with him."

"Nonsense, there's no danger of that. He seems to be handling all this attention with remarkable aplomb. It may be that his unfamiliarity with London society prevents him from fully realizing the extent and importance of his success, but this afternoon he sat with me for a while, and he seemed quite unmoved by all that's happened." Lady Harriet paused, her smile fading. "There is only one thing I cannot like."

"Oh? And what is that?"

"Did you know that he's taken a fancy to Alexandra de Guis?"

"Yes, I'd noticed that."

"Do you think he is serious? I believe I've heard that Miss de Guis' reputation is not quite what it ought to be."

Anne shrugged. "Lexie de Guis is a calculating, man-eating, odious *cat*! As far as I'm concerned, she and your American nephew should deal perfectly together." She turned on her heel and strode down the hall to her bedroom, leaving Harriet staring after her with a troubled frown.

Anne slammed her door irritably, ruefully aware that, in a mere twenty-four hours, she'd managed to deflate her mother, offend her brother, scold her betrothed, bring chaos on her best friend, and quarrel bitterly with the head of the household. Another day like this and there might be no one in the world willing to speak to her!

## Fifteen

LADY HARRIET WATCHED with a troubled expression as her stepdaughter stalked off down the hall. What was the matter with the girl? After Jason's triumph of the night before, one would think that Anne would be a bit pleased. Instead, she was ill-tempered and sulky and not at all like herself. The girl's explanation—that Jason had made a fool of her—was really quite absurd. A tempest in a teapot, nothing more. Harriet hoped that Anne did not intend to bear a grudge against Jason for such a trifle.

Harriet had not forgotten her earlier intention to encourage a match between her nephew and her stepdaughter. Although she no longer felt the need to force Anne into an advantageous match (having every confidence that Jason would do all that he ought for the family in regard to their finances) she nevertheless firmly believed that the two were well-suited. Anne was not the sort of girl to be happy with a man like Lord Claybridge. She was too spirited to be expected to endure life with a fellow who was so oppressively proper as Arthur Claybridge appeared to be. It was too bad that Claybridge was so breathtakingly handsome—his looks tended to blind a girl to the colorlessness of his personality.

Harriet had, for a while, nurtured the hope that Jason, on his part, felt an attraction to her stepdaughter. She'd noted an expression in Jason's shockingly light eyes when they'd rested on Anne's face when he thought no one was watching. Those eyes had held a glow which Harriet was sure signified a dawning affection. But last night at the Dabney ball, he'd taken no notice of Anne. Instead, he'd stood up for three dances with the beautiful Alexandra de Guis. Harriet shook her head in disappointment. She certainly hoped that Jason would not fix his affections *there*. Miss de Guis was not considered to be at all the thing.

Harriet shrugged and started down the hall to the sitting room where she'd left her embroidery. There was no use in brooding over the matter, she told herself. There was very little she could do about it.

She had no sooner settled herself with her needlework when Peter came in. "There's something I'd like to ask you, Mama," he said in a rather troubled voice.

"Of course, dear. Come and sit down. Is something the matter?"

"I'm not sure. It has to do with a subject on which I'm woefully ignorant, and my books don't help at all."

"You have me agog with curiosity," Harriet said, tucking her needle safely into the fabric and thrusting the embroidery aside. "What subject can it be for which books are insufficient?"

"Love," Peter said succinctly.

Harriet stared at him. "Good Lord! Have *you* met a *girl*? I cannot imagine when you could have done so without my being aware of it."

"Met a girl? *Me*? Don't be gooseish, Mama. I'm speaking of . . . someone else."

"But who?"

"Never mind who. Just listen. Suppose you came into a room and saw a young lady being held by a man . . . and saying 'Don't you dare!' And then, when they saw you, they jumped apart, and the fellow went away. Then, the lady said he was detestable, but not because he'd been...er...making *overtures*, but for an entirely different reason."

Lady Harriet studied her son closely. "I'm afraid I'm not following this very well. What is it you're asking me?"

"What I *suppose* I'm asking is if the lady was making excuses for the gentleman so that *you* would not make a scene."

"I still don't understand. All these hypothetical people...it makes the situation so confusing. Did you come upon a couple embracing? And if so, why should it concern you?"

"You see, if the man was behaving in an ungentlemanly way, shouldn't I...the observer...*do* something about it?"

"Do what? Call him out?" Harriet asked in some amusement. "I don't see why it is your affair."

"Well..." Peter paced about the room in some awkwardness, trying to find a way to explain his predicament. "...suppose the girl in question—and we're only *supposing*, mind—was the observer's sister."

"Peter! Did you come upon someone mauling *Anne* about?" Harriet asked, getting to the root of it.

"I wouldn't call it 'mauling' exactly..."

"Was she upset about it?" Harriet asked interestedly.

"She was upset, but she claimed it was not about that. She said the embrace was nothing."

"I see." Harriet paused, her mind busy with speculations. "You know, Peter dear, that Arthur Claybridge and Anne have been...close...for some time. Even if he *were* to make an advance, I don't believe it should be considered improper. She would not be in any danger from him, you know."

"But...the man was not Lord Claybridge..."

"*Not*—? You don't mean it!" She stared at her son with dawning comprehension. "It *couldn't* have been...you couldn't mean *Jason*!"

"I will not say," Peter declared, coloring in chagrin.

Lady Harriet peered at her son closely. "Can you tell me when this incident took place?"

Peter hesitated for a moment and then shrugged in self-disgust. "I've made such a mull of this already, I suppose I may as well tell you, although I don't see the relevance. The incident occurred last night."

"Last night? But they were at the ball."

"Anne came home early, remember?"

"Yes, but Jason remained. He took me home after Anne had already gone to bed."

Peter lowered his head, feeling very much like a traitor to a man whom he held in great affection. "Jason came home to ascertain that Anne had arrived safely. Then he went back to the Dabneys' for you."

"Did he really?" his mother asked. To his astonishment, her eyes brightened and a smile dawned on her face. "What *interesting* news! I was beginning to lose hope." She jumped up, ran over to Peter and kissed his cheek. "Thank you, dear. You've brightened my day considerably."

Peter was completely confused. "Mama, what are you talking about? You cannot *like* learning that Ja—that a certain gentleman has made improper advances toward your daughter!"

"I know this will be hard for you to understand, my dearest boy, but not *all* advances should be considered improper. It depends entirely on who the gentleman *is*. If the gentleman were, let us say, someone like Lord Claybridge, I would find the circumstances unremarkable and untroublesome. If he were a notorious rake like, for example, Sir Miles Minton, I would be considerably upset. And if it were Jason, I would be quite delighted."

Peter frowned at his mother in utter stupefaction. "If you don't mind my saying so, Mama, I find that explanation both repugnant and illogical. However, if Anne were likely to agree with your analysis, then I suppose I should not have to trouble myself about the matter any longer. *Would* Anne be likely to agree with you?"

"That, dearest, is a very good question. I wish I knew the answer. You have no idea how very interested I am in learning the answer to that question."

"But, then, what is *my* responsibility in this matter? As Anne's brother, isn't it my duty to protect her?"

Harriet patted his cheek affectionately. "When a lady is in distress and cries out for help, *any* gentleman should certainly go to her assistance. But otherwise, I think the wisest course is to ignore the situation."

Peter sighed in considerable relief. "Good. I'm glad I need do nothing about this. I didn't relish having to speak to Ja—to this person like a Dutch uncle. I would have felt a damned fool. Thank you for your help, Mama." He started for the door. "I didn't understand very much of what you were saying, and I admit that these matters of love are beyond my comprehension, but I *did* surmise, from your remarks, that you are hoping that Jason and Anne will make a match of it."

"Yes, I am," his mother admitted frankly. "It was very clever of you to have deduced that."

"Not so very clever. You see, I'm of the same mind myself," he said with a grin and left the room.

Later that evening, in spite of a heavy downpour, Arthur Claybridge returned to Half-Moon Street. Hatless, nervous, and soaked through, he appeared on the doorstep of the Laverstoke house and requested the butler to send for Miss Charity. He was left cooling his heels in the drawing room for almost half an hour. Finally, the door opened and Cherry entered timidly. Her eyes were red-rimmed, and she had covered her shorn locks with a lace cap like those worn by widows and elderly ladies. "Did you wish to see me, Ar—?" She gasped at his appearance, her question forgotten.

"Heavens, you're *soaked*!" she cried in consternation.

"It's nothing. I walked here, you see. It's been raining," Arthur explained abstractedly.

Cherry was immediately transformed into a bustling *hausfrau*. "Come here to the fire *at once*," she ordered, "and let me have your coat. I'll hang it here near the fire and see if it will dry off."

"No, thank you, Cherry. I'm fine, truly. I don't want to sit in your drawing room in my shirtsleeves," Arthur demurred.

"Oh, pooh, who cares for that? I insist that you take it off. I don't want it on my conscience that I permitted you to take cold."

Arthur obediently did as he was bid. Cherry hung the coat over the back of a chair and pushed it close to the fire. Then, inviting Arthur to take a seat equally close to the fireplace, she urged on him a large brandy which she'd poured for him herself. "Now we may be comfortable," she said and took a chair opposite him. She looked across at him questioningly and waited for him to tell her why he'd come.

Arthur gulped a mouthful of brandy, coughed, shot a glance at her and spoke quietly. "I had to come, Cherry, to tell you how sorry I am..."

"Sorry?" she asked, puzzled.

"For making you cry this afternoon. I don't know what to say...to explain..."

Cherry blushed. "There's no reason at all for you to explain," she told him hastily. "It was all my fault. I never should have given way to the impulse to..." She raised her hand to her head nervously and dropped it again. "...to cut it. I don't know why I did it."

"But you don't understand! I want to explain that I didn't mean that you didn't...*don't* look perfectly fine—"

"I l-look *hideous*!"

"That's not true! You *couldn't* look hideous, *ever*, no

matter what you did to your hair! That's what I've come to tell you."

"You are very kind, Arthur, b-but it's not necessary to tell me t-tales..." Cherry said, her head lowered.

"Please believe me," Arthur begged. "You see, it's only that I've always thought your braids were so beautiful—"

Cherry fixed a wide-eyed gaze on Arthur's face. "Oh, Arthur, *did* you?"

He nodded glumly. "Yes, so much so that I couldn't *help* crying out when I saw what you'd done. Forgive me. I never should have presumed to express my feelings on so personal a matter."

Cherry lowered her head again. "That's all right, Arthur. I never sh-should have cut them off. If I had known..." Her voice trailed off in a pathetic little sniff.

Arthur got up and crossed to her chair. Kneeling down before her, he took her hands in his. "I hope you will forgive me for offending you. I assure you I never meant to disparage your appearance. I didn't even take a proper look, you know, for you ran away so abruptly."

Cherry kept her head lowered, although she made no attempt to free her hands. "I don't want *anyone* to have a proper look. I shall wear c-caps for the rest of my l-life!"

Arthur couldn't help smiling. "Little ninny, of *course* you won't. I'm sure you look charming." He reached up and pulled the cap from her head. Cherry lifted her head in fright and pulled her hands from his grasp, raising them to try to cover her hair again. He grasped her wrists and held them tightly against his chest while he stared at her face. She was more enchanting than he'd ever seen her, the dusky curls tousled about a face that looked more wide-eyed, full-lipped and vulnerable than he could bear. "Why, you're...*beautiful*," he whispered.

Cherry's eyes widened even more as she stared in growing wonder at his face. His entire expression attested to the sincerity of his words. His eyes were glowing, and his lips were very slightly smiling. Her heart lurched, and she yearned to brush the damp lock from his forehead and stroke his cheek. Unconsciously, she leaned toward him. Suddenly their faces were so close that their lips met in a kiss that neither one of them was aware of initiating. For a long while, neither one could think. They floated on a cloud of blissful emotions: surprise, elation, sweetness, forgiveness and promise. It was so good, so inevitable, so *right* that his hands should be clutching hers to his chest, that their lips should meet in soft longing, that they should be sharing this unexpected joy.

It was Arthur whose mind awoke first. With a start, he released her and jumped to his feet. "Oh, my God! What am I *doing*?"

Cherry covered her mouth with her hands. "Oh, *Arthur*!" she said in a horrified whisper.

He turned away and stared into the fire. "I'm so sorry... so terribly sorry! I don't know what... possessed me...!"

Her sympathetic instincts were instantly aroused. "Don't upset yourself, Arthur. It was an *accident*. I... scarcely regard it..."

He turned to look at her, his eyes unconvinced. "Thank you. You are very good," he murmured, reaching for his coat. "I am truly sorry. I seem to be doing all the wrong things today. I've never *done* such a thing before. Cherry, I don't know what to say except to assure you that it will not happen again."

"Of course. There's no need to say any more," Cherry said in a small voice. "We shan't speak of it again."

She accompanied him to the door. "You've been very kind, Cherry," he said quietly. "I don't deserve... I only hope that you will forget this whole evening ever happened."

After he left the room, Cherry ran to the window and watched as he hurried away along the wet street, his collar turned up and his head down. She knew that she would never speak of what had happened—not to anyone. But she would never forget it, either.

# Sixteen

THE WEEKS THAT FOLLOWED were exciting ones in the Mainwaring household for all but Anne. Lord Mainwaring was invited twice to ride with the Prince. Peter was happily neglecting his studies to make frequent trips in Jason's company to Cribb's Parlour and Jackson's Saloon to watch the boxing matches and to practice the skill himself. Harriet had the pleasure of becoming the envy of her friends for her relationship with the nobleman who was rapidly becoming the darling of the *ton*.

Everything Jason said was picked up and repeated in all the clubs and salons of London, some young men even going so far as to use "shucks" in their own conversations. The story of Jason's race with Miles Minton was again repeated, and he was challenged to repeat the event by every rider who had a hope of success. He was offered membership in all the best clubs, and his appearances at White's, although infrequent, were greeted with eager attention. Matchmaking mamas began to call on Harriet and press her to entice her "interesting" nephew to attend their dinners and balls. Harriet began to wonder if Anne could be right after all; perhaps all this attention would turn Jason's head.

But Jason remained curiously unmoved. He seemed to avoid making close associations with other men, although he was cordial to all whom he met at sporting events or social occasions. He refused most of his invitations, modestly deferring to his Aunt Harriet's advice about those few which she deemed important for him to attend. He didn't spend money rashly, he made no changes in the household, and he did not attempt to rule the roost. If he *were* going to have his head turned, as far as anyone could see, the process had not started yet.

Harriet could find only one real difficulty in their lives since Jason's debut—his relationship with Anne. Although he was as pleasant to her as he'd always been, greeting her at the dinner table, trying to joke with her when they sat together in the drawing room, or offering to escort her to her social engagements, she responded coldly, refusing his invitations, answering his greeting with monosyllables and reacting to his quips with cold disgust. She showed no signs of softening; her anger at what she called his unforgivable deceit continued unabated.

Anne, however, did manage (without revealing her interest to anyone else) to take notice of the females in whom Jason developed an interest. She knew whom Jason escorted to the theater or danced with at the various assemblies. Except for his undisguised interest in Lexie de Guis, there was not one girl of the dozens who had been paraded before his nose who seemed to attract special attention from him. Although he had accompanied Amanda Dabney to Covent Garden, had stood up for two dances in one evening at Almack's with Cynthia Deverill and had shown polite attentions to several others, there was not one who could flatter herself that he was as interested in her as in the detestable Lexie.

If the young ladies of London seemed to hold no special interest for Jason, politics did. He spent the better part of each morning carefully perusing both the *Morning Post* and the *Times*. To Lady Harriet's horror, she discovered that Jason had become a subscriber to a notorious weekly called *The Examiner*, a journal edited by the essayist and poet Leigh Hunt and his brother John, and markedly liberal and reformist in its opinions. When she requested Peter to ask Jason to cancel his subscription, Peter laughingly refused, telling her she was being childishly timid. Finally she broached the subject to Jason himself. "You don't want people to take a notion that you're *revolutionary*," she warned him.

Jason couldn't help laughing. "But, my dear, how can an American be anything else?"

"Really, Jason, I think it's time you stopped calling yourself an American. You are now an English peer, and it's time you remembered that fact."

Jason, his smile fading, opened his mouth to respond, but evidently thought better of it and shut it again. "Never mind, Aunt Harriet," he said at last in his easygoing way. "Reading *The Examiner* has never caused anyone to be drummed out of the House of Lords, as far as I can ascertain."

With that Lady Harriet had to be content. Jason had explained to Peter that it was only in *The Examiner* that he could learn anything about the real situation between the United States and its problems with England. The other English newspapers devoted very little attention to the upstart little nation across the sea.

It was in *The Examiner* that Jason learned about the *Little Belt* affair; neither the *Post* nor the *Times* had bothered to report it. Jason chortled as he read that the forty-four-gun *President*, a newly commissioned American ship, had attacked and defeated the British *Little Belt*. Ever since 1807, when the British *Leopard* had set upon and defeated the smaller American ship *Chesapeake*, American pride had been smarting. This situation was exactly the reverse, and Jason understood how delighted the news must have made the Americans.

That very evening, Jason dropped in at White's. There in the foyer, handing his hat to a footman, was an acquaintance of Jason's, Lord Castlereagh, the British Secretary of War. "I notice that the press is silent on the *Little Belt* affair," Jason couldn't resist remarking to Lord Castlereagh after they'd exchanged greetings.

Lord Castlereagh raised an eyebrow. "Do you imply, Mainwaring, that we are *ashamed* of the affair? The *Little Belt* was hopelessly outweighed and outgunned by the *President*, you know."

"Not any less than the *Chesapeake* was outweighed and outgunned by your *Leopard*, if you remember," Jason pointed out. "I suspect that the British papers were full of *that* affair."

Castlereagh laughed. "You have me there, old fellow. Your point!" He put an arm across Jason's shoulders as the pair walked to the card rooms. "But, if I can tell you in strictest confidence, I'm just as happy to see nothing of the affair in the newspapers. No good can come of arousing the public. We don't want war with America."

"On *that* point," Jason assured him, "I'm in whole-hearted agreement. America doesn't want war either."

Castlereagh sighed. "I hope you're right. But I hear that the American Congress is full of hotheads, like that fellow Clay. Do you know anything of the new firebrand the south has elected? His name is Calhoun, I believe."

"No more than you, I'm afraid. I've been away from the States for almost six months," Jason answered. But he was impressed with Lord Castlereagh's knowledge of the happenings in America. He could only hope that the Americans were equally well-informed about the British.

The night of the Prince's dinner party was, in many respects, as exciting to the people in the Mainwaring household as the night of Jason's debut. After all, it was not every day that one was honored with an invitation to dine with the man who was, in all but name, the King of England. The magnificent, colonnaded façade of the Prince's London residence, Carlton House, was familiar to everyone in London, but of the three members of the Mainwaring party attending the Prince's dinner, only Lady Harriet had ever seen Carlton House from the inside. It was, therefore, an evening they all knew would be memorable.

When they arrived, Jason and Anne looked about the rooms with fascination. The rooms were dazzlingly decorated. The Prince received his guests in a room whose walls were hung with blue silk covered with gold fleur-de-lis. After being received, the guests could wander through the rooms at will. Each room they saw was lavish with beautiful paintings: there were van Dykes and Vernets, Le Mains and Greuzes to be seen and admired wherever one turned. The apartments were lavishly furnished with objects d'art: girandoles, clocks, looking-glasses, bronzes, Sevres china and Gobelin tapestries. The cabinets, chests and tables had been made by the finest craftsmen in Europe. There were marble busts by Coysevox, bronzes by Keller and candelabra by Thomire. As Anne moved through the magnificent rooms on Jason's arm, she couldn't help wondering if he found the rooms too ornate for his simple American taste. But his face gave away nothing of his feelings, and she did not have an opportunity to question him in private before dinner was announced.

The guests were seated, and Anne found herself at some distance from the head of the table, while Jason had been placed quite near the Prince. With the forbidding Lord Hertford beside her, and the imperious Lady Holland opposite, she relapsed into an unaccustomed shyness and rarely lifted her eyes from her plate.

Her shyness, however, did not prevent her from taking note of the sumptuousness of the dinner. The footman behind her chair offered her so many dishes that, when the number passed sixty, she lost count. After four different soups were offered, there followed a large number of fishes, among which were a fish stew, trout Provencale and a piece of delicious English turbot with lobster sauce. These were followed by broiled ham, braised goose, pheasant, partridge and several other fowl, as well as beef smothered in glazed onions and succulent little lamb cutlets. The number of side dishes was stupefying: truffles Italienne, cabbage flowers sprinkled with Parmesan cheese, tomatoes with sauce Hollandaise, stuffed mushrooms, puree of kidney beans, a salad of fish filets with oysters, little puff-pies filled with mince-meat and a memorable chicken sausage with Bechamel sauce.

As if these were not enough, the footman offered all sorts of rolls, breads and pastries from among which Anne selected a biscuit flavored with orange rind which she found remarkably light and tasty, and a cheese roll which looked delectable but which she found she was too full to eat. Reluctantly, she had to refuse all the cakes and desserts which were passed before her eyes—a *Charlotte Americaine* (which the Prince announced was named in Lord Mainwaring's honor), a nougat cake, a French banana cream, an apricot souffle and a little basket of sweetmeats.

Anne was able to observe, too, that Jason was continuing to enhance his reputation by his quips and witticisms, for the laughter from his end of the table was frequent and prolonged. She wished she had been seated closer to him and could hear what he'd said. But Harriet was not very far removed from the head of the table and would undoubtedly repeat his *bon-mots* when they returned home. Anne could not guess that by the time they returned, Jason's social success would be shockingly reversed.

It was Lady Hertford, acting as the Prince's hostess, who rose and invited the ladies to adjourn to the music room. As soon as the gentlemen were alone with their port, the conversation turned to politics. Jason had heard rumors that the Prince favored the Whigs, who expected to be returned to power the following year when the Prince would have the authority to change the government. But as Jason listened to the talk around him, he was struck by the strong Tory sentiment expressed by the guests, and the Prince's lack of Whiggish feeling. Jason refrained from expressing his own opinions, however, until the subject of America's stiff-necked opposition to England during this difficult time was mentioned.

All eyes turned to Jason. "If you're askin' me if American sentiment is with Napoleon, I'd say probably not. If you're askin' me if America will ever get into this war on the side of the French, I'd say it depends."

"On what?" asked Lord Castlereagh promptly.

"On how far you British go to drive us into the arms of the French," Jason answered.

"Are you saying that America's actions depend on *us*?" Lord Hertford asked naively.

"Of *course* our actions will have an effect on the American policy," Lord Castlereagh interjected impatiently. As Secretary of War, he was the one gentleman in the room fully cognizant of the tensions existing in the current international scene. "But you'll have to admit, Mainwaring, that President Madison is inclined to favor the French, no matter how little tangible evidence he has that Napoleon is a real friend of America."

"You are thinking of the Cadore letter, I suppose," Jason said. "I agree that the President has shown a certain leaning toward the French, but I believe he no longer places any trust in the Cadore letter or in Napoleon's pledges. What he truly wishes—as most Americans do—is to preserve American neutrality. But, may I add, *not* at the expense of the freedom of our ships to trade, both with you and with other European nations."

"Lord Wellesley tells me," Lord Castlereagh put in, "that the Foreign Office is considering revoking the Orders in Council. By that action, American ships will be free to trade with us, unhampered."

"I'm delighted to hear it," Jason said, "but if British ships continue their impressment of American sailors, the revocation of the Orders in Council will not be enough."

"Impressment?" the Prince asked in annoyance. "I very much dislike that word. Our Navy knows nothing of impressment. If you speak of our right to reclaim British deserters serving on American ships, it is one right the British Navy will *never* surrender."

"But your highness cannot deny," Jason persisted, "that many *American* sailors are caught in that net."

"Then tell your merchant marine not to employ British deserters on their ships!" the Prince declared angrily.

Lord Castlereagh, recognizing the choleric color rising in the Prince's face, tried to attract Jason's attention by coughing warningly. But Jason had warmed to his subject and would not be deterred. "Most Americans would reply to that, your highness," he went on, "by sayin' that *you* should tell your Navy to pay your sailors a bit more and use the cat-o'-nine-tails a bit less, and you'll have fewer deserters." A glance at the Prince's face told him that the Prince had little liking for that position. "Oh, well, I see that this point of view will win no likin' in this company. We'd best drop the subject, since we'll not reach agreement. This kind of talk is as useless as a snake makin' love to a buggy whip—nothin' can come of it."

There was a burst of laughter from the listeners, but it died out quickly as one after the other of the men around the table caught sight of the Prince's face. His color was high, his mouth stretched in an angry grimace and his eyes flashing. The Prince was not amused. It was apparent that Jason had gone too far.

The Prince Regent, infuriated, rose and stood silently at his place for a moment. Then, deliberately turning away from Jason, he said to the others, his accent icy, "Well, gentlemen, shall we join the ladies?"

# Seventeen

IT WAS IMMEDIATELY APPARENT to Harriet and
Anne that something had gone wrong. The atmosphere in
the music room, when the gentlemen rejoined the ladies,
was suddenly tense. Jason insisted that they take their
leave. Despite Harriet's whispered admonition that a
leave-taking so soon after dinner was too abrupt, he
herded them to the Prince to say their good-byes. When
they made their adieus and murmured their appreciative
thanks for the evening's entertainment, the Regent's
coldness was unmistakable in the stiffness of his
acknowledgment. And when they passed out of the room,
the other gentlemen, speaking in low voices to their wives,
seemed to avoid meeting their eyes. It was all bewildering
and dreadful.

In the carriage, Jason was irritatingly unconcerned. He
merely explained that he'd done what Anne had always
warned him against—talked too much. Then he leaned
back against the squabs and tried to change the subject.
But the ladies persisted in their questioning until they
eventually drew from him a somewhat clearer account of
what had transpired. When the full import of what he'd

done burst upon them, Harriet moaned and clutched her breast. "Oh, heavens, we are undone!" she uttered.

"Do you mean to say," Anne asked, horrified, "that you made disparaging comments about the British *Navy*? *Good God*! Have you never heard of our defeat of the Armada? Have you never heard of *Trafalgar*?"

"I believe word of those encounters *has* reached America," Jason responded satirically, "but you should have warned me, ma'am, that the British Navy is so *sacred*. It seems that I've *blasphemed*.

"There, do you *see*?" Anne exploded, turning to her stepmother. "I *told* you that he makes a joke of everything!"

"We must remain calm," Harriet murmured without conviction.

"The man's *impossible*," Anne said disgustedly.

"I think, Jason," Harriet said worriedly, "that Anne is in the right this time. This is no laughing matter, you know. He is the *Regent*. I very much fear that we shall live to regret this night."

Harriet's fears were more than justified. The door knocker of the Mainwaring house became distressingly unused. The number of callers dropped markedly; the flow of invitations almost ceased entirely (and those that *did* come were not the kind that Harriet wished Jason to accept); the gentlemen who had fawned on Jason at White's were now quite cool; even the eager mamas, who had once pushed their daughters into Jason's path, were suddenly hesitant. Overnight, Jason's life altered.

The entire household became depressed. Orkle remarked in confidence to Coyne that he very much feared his lordship's evening clothes "was goin' to moulder wi' lack o' use." It had been exciting even to the servants to find Mainwaring House the center of a social whirl. Now the inactivity and gloom were doubly discouraging because of the comparison with the previous exhilaration. Everyone, from Lady Harriet to the lowliest scullery maid, was affected. Only Jason seemed unperturbed. He rode in the park every day, as usual, played chess and took his weekly trips to Jackson's Saloon with Peter, and maintained his accustomed air of untroubled amiability.

In addition to the members of the household, there were two others who remained loyal to the ostracized Viscount. One was Cherry, who followed Anne's lead in almost everything and who therefore spoke up loyally in Jason's defense whenever anyone mentioned his name in her presence. Cherry had been having a difficult time since she'd cut her hair. It was not that her new appearance was in any way detrimental to her social success—on the contrary, her daring new coiffure was much admired and had won her the attentions of two new swains. One was a pudgy-cheeked youth who spoke with a stammer and followed her around like a devoted puppy whenever she sojourned on foot through the park. The other was more impressive—none other than Captain Edward Wray, the cavalry officer who'd been Alexandra de Guis' escort that day in the park. Captain Wray, tired of the high-handed indifference he'd received from Lexie, had turned his eyes to Cherry.

With a persistence that should have been as flattering as it was unexpected, Captain Wray, who was on protracted leave from his regiment while he recovered from a wound he'd received in Spain, spent a good part of his free time in Cherry's company. Tired of the spirited but superficial flirtation he'd endured with Lexie, he found Cherry pretty, sweet and comforting. The sympathetic attention with which she listened to his accounts of his military adventures was alone enough to make him her devoted admirer.

But Cherry's attentiveness to Captain Wray's monologs came more from habit than from her heart. Inside, her feelings were focused elsewhere. For her part, the relationship with Edward Wray had only one thing to recommend it—it helped to keep her mind from dwelling on the events of a certain rainy night, the memory of which filled her with longing and guilt but which she nevertheless could not resist reliving over and over again in her dreams.

The other person who remained loyal to Jason was Lexie herself. It was Cherry who discovered Lord Mainwaring's continued relationship with Lexie and reported it to Anne. "Captain Wray had taken me up in his curricle, and we were tooling about the park when I saw them," she related. "They were both on horseback, and they were laughing and talking together in a manner which . . ." Cherry hesitated, trying to find the right words to describe the comfortable intimacy of their demeanor.

". . . which is only developed when two people are much in each other's company, is that what you're trying to say?" Anne asked shrewdly.

"Yes, that's it, exactly. I must tell you, Anne, that they were very much absorbed in each other and seemed completely unaware of the number of gossips who were watching and whispering behind their fans."

Anne listened to Cherry's report with increasing vexation. Jason seemed to be determined to behave in a manner deliberately designed to discompose her spirits. Wasn't he aware that he'd done enough harm to himself and the family by offending the Regent without adding to society's disapprobation by attaching himself to a female whose reputation was no better than it should be? Every time she reviewed Cherry's words, she found herself fuming. She was in a terrible mood, and it was all Jason's fault.

Lying awake at night, she asked herself why Jason's problems should affect *her* so deeply. Even Harriet, who had learned to hold Jason in the highest regard, seemed less affected by his ostracism than she. Harriet had simply cautioned herself to remain calm, had done her breathing exercises and had managed to maintain her serenity. But Anne was somehow deeply disturbed, and Jason's indifference to his situation and his involvement with

Lexie made that disturbance even more acute. She began
to speak shortly to the family and the servants, her temper
flared easily and even her sleep was restless and troubled
by disturbing dreams.

The future for the Mainwarings and the Hartleys
seemed to her to be very glum indeed. If Jason remained
ostracized, the effect would be felt by Lady Harriet and
Peter as well. They, too, would be subject to social
disapproval and neglect. And it was only logical to
assume that, if Jason continued to be ignored by the
matchmaking mamas of eligible young ladies, the
likelihood of his making an offer to Lexie would become
more certain. Poor Mama and Peter would be forced to
live in the Mainwaring house under Lexie's dominion—a
fate which was beginning to seem an imminent and
horrible possibility.

The fact that Anne would be far away from the scene
by the time this repugnant possibility should become an
actuality was of no comfort at all. Although she tried to
tell herself that all this was not really her affair, and that
she would soon be living in Shropshire, completely out of
touch with and uninformed about the goings-on at home,
the thought only seemed to exacerbate her tensions.
Could she possibly permit herself to run away, callously
leaving behind all familial feelings? Could she embark on
a new life, knowing that the family she'd left behind was
enmeshed in a coil of problems? Had she no responsibility
for their happiness and well-being?

The date of her elopement loomed very near. In just
over a week, she would be starting for Gretna Green. If
only she could do something to reestablish Jason in
society before she left. But the dark hours of the night
offered no inspiration, and she eventually fell asleep
without having found a practical solution to the problem.

She awoke the next morning heavy-eyed and depressed. Pulling aside the curtains, she discovered that the
weather exactly matched her mood. The sky was gray and
lowering, and a distant rumble promised the coming of a

storm. As if to spite herself, she dressed in a drab, puce-colored muslin round-gown (which she absolutely detested) and made her way to the breakfast room. There she found Jason seated at the table cheerfully sipping a cup of coffee and reading his newspapers. She sat down without speaking a word and reached for the teapot.

"Good morning, my dear," Jason greeted her with a smile.

She looked at his newspapers in annoyance. "Haven't you had *enough* troublesome news from America? Or are you searching for *new* material with which to offend your friends?" she asked maliciously.

Jason laughed. "Oh, I'm quite capable of inventin' offensive comments without referrin' to my newspapers at all. For example, I might remark that you are not in your best looks this morning."

She glared at him. "*Offensive* is quite right. It wanted only *that*, my lord, to make my morning complete. If you will be good enough to pass me the jam, I shall refrain from speaking to you further."

"But I have no wish for you to refrain from speaking," he said, grinning and handing her the jam pot. "I enjoy listenin' to you, even when you're churlish."

She did not deign to respond but stirred her tea in silence. With a shrug, he returned to his newspaper. But after a silence of several minutes, during which the only sounds were the rattle of his newspaper and the clink of her spoon against the cup, she could endure it no longer. "I wonder, my lord," she ventured, "how you can be so cheerful and unconcerned when your position in society has been so seriously injured."

"But I've told you before," he explained, putting aside his paper readily, "that I don't care a fig for my position in society."

She leaned her chin on her hand and surveyed him wonderingly. "Yes, so you have, but I can't quite believe you. You are not a fool—you *must* realize that the rest of your *life* will be adversely affected."

"My life does *not* depend on the good will of the *ton*, my dear," he declared firmly.

"But, Jason, it *must*," she said, leaning forward and speaking with an intensity and sincerity she had not shown since their estrangement. "In your position as a peer of the realm, you must live your life among us. Didn't you enjoy the attentions of society before, when they made so much of you?"

"Yes, I suppose I did. But I knew it was only a temporary phenomenon. I didn't take it seriously. Just as I don't take its loss very seriously either."

"Temporary phenomenon? *Why* did you assume their good will was only temporary?" Anne asked.

"It was not their good will I assumed to be temporary, but my stay among them. You see, I never intended—and don't intend now—to remain here in London."

"I don't understand. Do you mean you intend to spend your days buried away on our estate in Derbyshire, as Uncle Osborn did?"

He gave her a strange look. "No, my dear. I shan't be going to Derbyshire. I shall be going *home*," he said with a small, rather patient smile.

"*Home*?" She stared at him incredulously. "You can't mean . . . *America*!"

He gave a wry laugh. "I'm constantly amazed, my dear, at your persistent tendency to regard the place of my birth as some sort of untamed, indigent backwater from which one would wish only to escape."

There was something in his tone that made her peer at him closely. "I didn't mean to offend you, Jason," she said quickly. "I *honor* you for feeling an attachment to the place of your birth. And I shall have to admit," she added, lowering her eyes to her cup, "that you've quite convinced me that your country is adequately civilized . . ."

"Thank you for that," he said with a half-smile. "*But*—?"

She flicked a quick glance at him and nodded. "Yes, there is a *but*."

"I was sure there would be." He made a mocking gesture, as if bracing himself for an attack. "Go ahead."

"Don't joke, Jason. I'm quite serious. I only want to say that . . . to be a *peer of England*, and especially in this time of our history . . . why, that is the most *fortunate* position to hold in all the *world*! You cannot expect me to take seriously the notion that you would give it all up and return to America!"

"I can't seem to make you take *anything* I say seriously." He reached across the table and took one of her hands in his. "I wish . . ." He paused and fixed his eyes on her hand, its fingers lying relaxed and unresisting in his large palm.

"*What* do you wish?" she prodded encouragingly.

His hand closed over hers. ". . . that one day I might be able to show you my home," he said softly.

The sincerity of his tone caught her unaware. Her throat tightened unaccountably. "I would like to, very much," she answered. "Tell me about it."

"I'm not much good at describin' things with words," he said, lifting his eyes to her face. "It's somethin' you have to see for yourself. America is so vast, you know, that when you travel from north to south it's like travelin' from one world to another. New England is mountainous and craggy, with violent changes in weather and a kind of harsh, strong face. But where I come from, in Virginia, it's all soft and green, with rollin' hills and blue-shadowed mountains and wispy mornin' fog. The changes of the seasons kind of sneak up on you. One mornin' you look around and all the colors of spring have burst out—the white dogwood's in bloom all through the woods, and the azaleas have gone crazy. Or it turns autumn, and suddenly the trees look like they're goin' up in flames. One time, I remember, I'd been trekkin' through the Shenandoahs, and I'd slept in the forest. Durin' the night, there'd been a touch of frost. When I woke, there were the pines with drops of ice hangin' from every needle—it looked like the forest had grown a beard!"

"It sounds . . . very beautiful . . ."

"It *is* very beautiful."

She sighed. "But England is beautiful, too, you know," she suggested gently.

"I don't deny that, my dear."

"Don't you see, Jason, what's troubling you? You've come all this way, from a land that you obviously love, to find yourself pushed and coaxed and prodded and coerced into taking on the role of an English nobleman. And just when you'd finally convinced us—yes, I'm willing at last to admit it—that you could be perfectly acceptable just the way you are, you are suddenly and heartlessly ostracized! No wonder you want to chuck it all away. But you're only *homesick*! It's perfectly understandable under the circumstances, but I assure you it will pass."

"Anne, when will you ever *listen* to me?" he asked rather plaintively. "This ostracism has nothing whatever to do with how I feel."

"That's what you think *now*. But just you wait." Withdrawing her hand from his clasp, she rose and went to stand behind his chair, putting a comforting hand on his shoulder. "I'll find a way to end this situation in which you find yourself. And when I do, you'll feel quite differently."

He let out a long, discouraged breath. "Don't trouble yourself, girl," he said shortly. "Nothin' you do in *that* direction is likely to cause me to change my mind."

"We'll see about that," she answered airily and went to the door. But before leaving, she paused and looked back at him curiously. "Did you mean to suggest by your last remark that there is some *other* direction I could take which would cause you to change your mind?"

"Well, I doubt if *anything* you did could really change my mind about leavin', but there *is* somethin' that might make me *postpone* my departure for a bit."

"And what would that be?" she inquired archly.

He turned in his chair and regarded her speculatively. "Can't you guess, ma'am?"

"I'm sure I don't know what you're talking about," she responded decisively and was immediately disconcerted by feeling a rush of blood to her cheeks. What *was* there in the expression of his eyes that caused her color to rise?

His light-colored eyes seemed to penetrate her thoughts, and his lips curled in a mocking smile. "If you really don't know, it won't do for me to tell you, girl. At least, not yet," he said. And he turned, picked up his newspaper and resumed his reading.

She stood in the doorway watching him for a moment, but he didn't look up. Finally, with an exasperated sniff, she left him alone.

# *Eighteen*

ANNE SAT on the window seat of her bedroom and watched the rain, but her thoughts were on the surprising conversation with Jason. He couldn't have been serious when he said he intended to return to America. She could not believe that. No, she *wouldn't* believe it! The thought of his leaving, she suddenly realized, was intolerable. She had become accustomed to his presence in the house; it made her feel protected and secure.

She tried to imagine the America he had described. He had spoken so lovingly of it, she almost longed to see it for herself. She closed her eyes and tried to imagine a voyage through the United States, with Jason as guide and companion. The prospect set off little bubbles of excitement in her blood. But of course it was an *impossible* prospect—she would be in Shropshire before long. All at once, a question occurred to her which made her very uncomfortable: why was the prospect of seeing the green hills of *Virginia* so much more exciting to her than that of seeing the green hills of *Shropshire*? Before she permitted herself to search for an answer, she banished the question from her mind.

But one thing become increasingly clear to her as her musings continued. Jason was not to be permitted to leave—for Harriet's and Peter's sakes, if not for her own. They needed him. She must see Jason reestablished. Once he found contentment in his new life, his homesickness would fade—of that she was certain.

Her first step in her attempt to reestablish Jason in society was to give herself ample time to accomplish her goal. To that end, she went immediately to her writing desk and penned a note to Arthur, telling him that the family crisis necessitated a brief postponement of their elopement. That done, she found her spirits amazingly lightened—so much so that her puce-colored dress seemed suddenly inappropriate, and she promptly changed into a shirred muslin creation the color of jonquils.

Arthur, who had not seen his betrothed for weeks, had been having a difficult time. He couldn't tear from his memory the image of a heart-shaped face topped with dusky curls. In all his twenty-five years, Arthur Claybridge had been a model of manly rectitude, the pride of an evangelical mother and the despair of a dissolute father. Arthur considered himself an honorable man. An honorable man, however, did *not* spend his days and nights dreaming of *one* young lady while betrothed to *another*.

Arthur took stern measures to cleanse from his soul what he feared was a tendency to profligacy. He took long walks. He gave up meat. He immersed himself daily in a tub filled with cold water. He studied scripture for long hours at a time. Before he fell asleep at night, he tried to picture himself in a cottage in Shropshire, gazing contentedly across the table at a countrified Anne with a baby in her arms and a child at her knee. Somehow the vision seemed too unreal to give him comfort.

When Arthur received Anne's note, his first reaction was one of relief. But as soon as he recognized the feeling for the unworthy thing it was, he banished it from his mind. In its place came a wave of resentment. How dared she *use* him in this way? Why should everyone else in her life come before *him*? His rancor was not a feeling he found to be worthy of a man about to take holy orders, but he could not banish it. Thrusting the note in the pocket of his coat, he rushed out of the house into the rain.

Anne was sitting in the library, engrossed in concocting schemes to reunite Jason with the Prince, when she was interrupted by Coyne, who informed her that she had a caller.

"What? In this downpour? Who is it, Coyne?" she asked.

"It's a Miss Alexandra de Guis, Miss Anne. Shall I send her in?"

"*Lexie*? What on earth—? She can't want to see *me*. You must have misunderstood. It's probably his lordship she's come to see. Just tell her he's gone out."

"She particularly told me it was *you* she wanted to see, Miss Anne," Coyne insisted.

"Really? I wonder what—? Well, send her in, then, Coyne."

In a moment Lexie entered the room. Anne rose to greet her, and the two touched cheeks. "What a surprise, Miss de Guis," Anne murmured with affected politeness. "Here, let Coyne have your pelisse—it's quite damp."

Lexie removed her stylish cape and handed it to the butler. "What a charming room," she said, looking about her with what Anne thought was a proprietary interest.

"Thank you," Anne said coldly. "Coyne, bring in a tea tray, will you? Miss de Guis would not doubt like a cup after having ridden out through such a downpour."

"No, thank you, Miss Hartley. I can only stay a moment. I'm keeping my coachman waiting at the door. Please don't bother with tea."

The butler left, and Anne motioned Lexie to a chair.

Lexie settled back gracefully and watched while Anne
took a chair facing her, her almond-shaped eyes searching
Anne's face and her lips curled in a slightly sardonic smile.
"You don't like me very much, do you, Miss Hartley?" she
asked abruptly. "Don't bother to deny it—most women
don't like me. I attribute their dislike to simple jealousy,
but in your case, I admit to being puzzled. You are quite
lovely enough not to have to be jealous of anyone. And
you've already won your heart's desire, have you not?
Lord Claybridge is quite besotted over you, they say."

Anne, very uncomfortable under Lexie's direct gaze,
tried to avoid an answer. "I suppose you've come to call
on Lord Mainwaring," she said irrelevantly, trying to
change the subject. "I'm sorry, but he's gone out."

"I know that. It's his afternoon for the boxing saloon.
Amazing, isn't it, how many otherwise sensible gentlemen
are addicted to that barbarous sport? But never mind
that. I came purposely to see *you*, my dear, and I
particularly did *not* want Jason to know."

Lexie's words indicated a degree of intimacy with
Jason which irritated Anne in the extreme. "Is that so?"
she inquired cooly.

"Yes. You see, it's because of him that I've come to see
you."

"Because of Lord Mainwaring?"

Lexie raised an eyebrow. "Lord Mainwaring? Dear
me, how formal you are. Come now, Miss Hartley, may
we not speak comfortably with each other? I've come
merely as a friend of the family. I believe you all have need
of a friend at this time."

"I wasn't aware, Miss de Guis, that we are short of
friends."

"My, my. We *are* at sword's point, aren't we?" Lexie
murmured, half to herself. "May I ask, Miss Hartley,
what it is about me that sets up your bristles? I have never
done you a disservice that I'm aware of, have I?"

"No, of course not," Anne answered hastily, Lexie's
bluntness making her decidedly uncomfortable.

"Then what *is* it that stands between us? Is it my reputation? I assure you that any gossip you may have heard regarding my being 'fast' is nothing by nonsense. Why, the worst thing that may honestly be claimed against my character is that I damp my dresses. But I venture to guess that there have been times when *you* have done so."

Anne had to smile. "More than once, I must admit. Although I caught the most dreadful chill the last time I tried it, and so I've given up the practice."

"There! You *see*? So why does *my* doing it set all the tongues wagging? It is because Mama was so imprudent as to run off with a French emigré? And how long must I be blamed for my mother's headstrong behavior?"

Anne tried to remember when and for what cause she had first believed that Lexie was "fast." Could she have been misjudging Miss de Guis all these years? She looked with dawning compassion across the room at the lovely creature sitting opposite her. "No one blames your mother in the least, as far as I know," she assured the girl. "Why should they? The Compte de Guis is a most respected gentleman. You must not imagine that your parents are the subjects of malicious gossip. I assure you they are not."

"Then why am *I* the subject of malicious gossip?" Lexie asked in sincere perplexity.

Anne looked down at her hands in shame. "Perhaps you were right in your first suggestion—that we are all jealous cats when we see so beautiful a creature as you in our midst."

"No, it's utter nonsense! Charlotte Firbanke is more beautiful by far, and no one says a *word* about her!"

"But Charlotte is such a *good* little mouse . . ." Anne began.

Lexie drew herself up indignantly. "And what makes you think that I am *not*?"

Anne couldn't help giggling. "Really, Lexie, you're not comparing your behavior with Charlotte Firbanke's, are you? Why, Charlotte never opens her mouth unless her mama prompts her."

Lexie's lips quivered and a reluctant laugh popped out. "I suppose my behavior cannot be described as quite so discreet as all *that*," she admitted with a guilty smile.

"Well, you must own, Lexie, that you are frank to a fault," Anne said, feeling a sudden warmth for the young woman opposite.

"That's true," Lexie nodded ruefully. "My wretched tongue. Mama always cautions me about it. But I can't seem to control myself. If a thought leaps into my mind, I blurt it out at once. But it hasn't been such a bad thing today—I'm glad I've been so frank with you, Anne. (I may call you Anne, may I not? You called me Lexie a moment ago.) At least it's broken the ice between us."

Anne looked at the girl before her with new eyes. She had never realized that the beautiful Miss de Guis could be so vulnerable. Remembering all the unkind thoughts she'd harbored against the girl made her quite ashamed. "I'm glad, too, Lexie. Frankness is a quality I very much admire."

"That's what Jason says, too. And that brings us back to the reason I've come. Jason's situation with the Regent is the outside of enough, and I've come to enlist your help in putting an end to it."

Lexie's proprietary tone when she spoke of Jason was enough to cool Anne's feeling of warmth toward her. Nevertheless, her interest was piqued. "Have you some plan in mind which would end the situation?" she asked curiously.

"Yes, I have. If we could bring Prinny and Jason together at a party small enough to cause them to come face-to-face with each other, I feel sure that Jason could charm the Prince out of the sullens. However, my father and mother are not important enough to entice the Prince to attend one of their soirées."

"I don't see how *I* can help you there. The Prince is hardly likely to accept one of *our* invitations either."

"No, I've solved *that* problem myself. My maternal grandmother, Lady Lychett, sits high with Lady Hertford, and they've already, between them, arranged a dinner party for the Prince in two weeks' time. The problem is that Jason refuses to attend. He says he has no desire to ingratiate himself with the Prince. I need your help in persuading him to go."

Anne shook her head. "If *you* were unable to persuade him, I don't see how *I* can do it," she admitted honestly.

"Do you suppose Lady Harriet might succeed? Perhaps, between the two of you, you might contrive."

"All I can promise, Lexie, is that we'll try. But Jason is a rather stubborn fellow, I'm afraid."

Lexie sighed and rose to leave. "Yes, I've noticed that. He keeps insisting that he intends to return to America. I've begun to believe that he really means it." She started for the door. "Not that I blame him—he makes his homeland sound very inviting."

Her words smote Anne like a blow. "Oh, has Jason told you... much about America...?" she asked in a small voice.

"Good heavens, yes," Lexie answered lightly. "He talks about it all the time. Well, good-bye, my dear. I'm so glad we had this chance to become better acquainted."

Anne accompanied Lexie to the door and said her good-byes with proper politeness, but her mind was in a whirl. She walked back to the library in a daze. Jason's conversation about America that morning had seemed to Anne to be meant for her alone. It had been a moment of shared intimacy. It had made her feel so close to him. Now that feeling was completely destroyed. He had evidently shared *many* such moments with Lexie. Perhaps the relationship between them had developed much further than Anne had suspected. Perhaps—and the thought filled Anne with agony—they were in love!

Anne stood at the library window and watched the rain with unseeing eyes. Lexie and Jason. She remembered them whirling around the floor at the Dabney ball, a spectacularly striking pair. Perhaps they would make a well-matched couple. Lexie was not the detestable girl that Anne had thought. Why, then, was the prospect of a marriage between them so painful to her?

But Anne knew the answer to that question. She had known it for weeks. This thing inside her had been growing since the first day she'd seen Jason looming in the doorway of the upstairs sitting room. She loved him. If she did not want Lexie to have him, it was only because she wanted him for herself! What a fool she'd been. She'd bullied him and criticized him and underestimated him and offended him until he couldn't help but hold her in dislike. And all the while, Lexie had frankly and openly admired him. Who could blame the man for choosing Lexie to wed?

Besides, she had no right to think about Jason in this way. She was promised to Arthur. Arthur was so good, so true and loyal—she couldn't hurt him. There was nothing for her but to wish Jason well, go off with Arthur to Shropshire and begin the demanding task of accepting her fate with good grace. She had no other choice.

Arthur, meanwhile, looking like a sodden and abstracted ghost, appeared on the doorstep of the Laverstoke house on Half-Moon Street just as Cpatain Edward Wray was emerging. The Captain's face wore a self-satisfied smile, and Arthur could immediately discern that the Captain had immensely enjoyed his call on Cherry. He glared at Captain Wray with smoldering animosity as he brushed by him on the steps and reached for the door-knocker. The Captain did not understand why he'd been glared at and cut by the disheveled Lord Claybridge, but the matter was of no concern to him. He jumped into his waiting carriage and drove off.

When Arthur was admitted by the butler, Cherry was just about to climb the stairs to her room. However, after taking one look at Arthur's tempestuous expression, she flew to his side, quickly drew him into the drawing room and closed the door in the butler's disapproving face. "Arthur, you really must cease this running about in the rain," she scolded. "You will surely contract an inflammation of the lungs if you are not more careful."

"Never mind that," he burst out angrily. "What was Wray doing here?" Then, taking note of Cherry's startled expression, he immediately became contrite. "No, don't answer. I've no right...! I don't know what I'm saying." He dropped into a chair and stared at Cherry miserably. "Here, read this." And he thrust Anne's note into her hand.

Cherry scanned it quickly. "Oh, Arthur," she murmured in her most consolatory tone, "how disappointing! A *postponement*, when the date of your departure was so *near*!"

"It is not the postponement which troubles me, I assure you. It is the tone of that note. Is *that* the letter of a lady who is in love and eager to be married?"

Cherry looked at him in perplexity. "I don't know what you mean."

"Is there a single 'dearest' in the entire epistle? Is there a 'my love' to be found anywhere? Is there a 'sincere regret' expressed either within or between the lines? *Is* there, Cherry?"

"Well, I..."

"Don't be afraid to speak honestly to me, my dear. Too much has passed between us to hold back now. Is this the sort of letter *you* would write if you had to postpone our wedding?"

Cherry's eyes filled with tears, and she turned away. "I don't think it's fair to ask me that, Arthur," she said quietly. "Perhaps this letter *is* a bit... hasty. But Anne has a great deal on her mind these days, you know."

"Don't try to defend her to me. She may have a great deal on her mind, but I venture to guess that *I* do not figure prominently in her thoughts!"

Cherry turned back to him, dismayed. "Are you trying to suggest that Anne doesn't *love* you?"

"Yes, that's *just* what I'm suggesting. And I want your advice on what to do about it."

Cherry dropped down on the sofa aghast. "You *can't* believe what you're saying! She has been completely devoted to you for *years*! I am her very best friend, and she's *never* given me any indication of a decline in her love for you. You cannot let yourself forget your feelings for her merely because of a hasty note."

"Let us not speak of my feelings for her," Arthur said bitterly, turning his face away from the earnest eyes staring at him. "You, at least, should have guessed that my feelings have undergone a change."

"Arthur, you mustn't—!"

He wheeled about, crossed the room and confronted her. "Don't you think I *know* I mustn't? I've wrestled with myself for days and days. I am quite prepared to sacrifice myself...I am quite prepared to give you up...! Don't look at me so, Cherry. I *love* you! Let me say it just this once!" He sat down beside her on the sofa and grasped her hands. "I love you! But I know that a gentleman can never go back on his word. I am ready to honor my obligations to Anne. But I begin to suspect that her wishes to go through with our plans are no stronger than *mine*."

Cherry's full lips trembled pathetically. "That's not *true*. She most truly loves you. I know it. You are...I hate to say this, Arthur, but I must!...you are letting your own wishes interfere with your judgment, I fear."

He lowered his head. "Is that what you think? That I'm clutching at straws?"

"I...I'm very much afraid so, my dear," she said tenderly.

He sighed deeply. "What am I to do, my love? I'm at my wit's end over this affair."

"There's nothing you *can* do but wait until Anne is ready and proceed with your plans. She will be ready soon, I'm sure."

"Yes, you're right, of course." They gazed at each other sadly. "I can see no hope. No hope at all."

"Don't say that, Arthur. You will be happy. I know you will."

"Are *you* going to be happy married to Captain Wray?"

Cherry smiled wanly. "I'm not going to marry Captain Wray."

"Oh, Cherry," Arthur sighed, much moved, "is it because...of me?"

She nodded her head.

"Will you tell me, just once, that you love me? Just once...before I go?"

She lifted his hand, still holding hers, to her face and rubbed her cheek against it. "I love you, Arthur," she whispered tearfully, "and always will."

They sat for a moment in silence. Then Arthur rose abruptly and ran to the door. "Arthur," she cried, "wait, just a moment. I must not...you must not...ever..."

"I know," he muttered in a choked voice. "I must not ever come here again." And he ran out into the unfeeling rain.

# *Nineteen*

THE COMBINED EFFORTS of Lady Harriet and
Anne to coax Jason into attending Lady Lychett's dinner
for the Prince were unavailing. Jason adamantly refused
to attend. In desperation, Harriet suggested to Anne that
perhaps another plan might succeed. "What have you in
mind, Mama?" Anne asked interestedly.

"I wonder if perhaps a *gift* might do the trick. If Jason
bought a magnificent mantel-clock, for example, of
bronze or that ormolu that the Prince likes so much, and
sent it to the Prince with a little note—"

Anne frowned. "It sounds like a *bribe*. I don't think
Jason would approve of such a plan."

"Perhaps we can convince Jason that giving a gift to
the Prince is a gesture which is *expected* of a peer."

"But for what reason? The Prince's birthday was more
than a month ago..."

"I'll think of a reason," Harriet promised.

"Even if we *could* convince Jason to do it, do you think
the Prince would be influenced by such an obvious
device?"

Harriet shrugged. "I believe he might be. He does *love*
beautiful things, you know."

"I suppose there's no harm in *trying* to persuade Jason to do it. Go ahead, Mama, and see what you can do."

Not ten minutes after this conversation had taken place, Anne was surprised by a light tap at the sitting-room door. It was Mr. Orkle who answered her call to come in. The valet entered the room with unusual hesitation and stood regarding Anne dubiously before he spoke. "Is something on your mind, Mr. Orkle?" Anne asked encouragingly.

"Yes, miss, beggin' yer pardon. Y'see, I been puttin' me brain to work on a ticklish problem. It's this 'ere disagreemint 'tween 'is lordship an' 'is 'ighness, the Prince. It's a rotten shame wot 'appened, ain't it, miss?"

"Yes, Mr. Orkle, a very rotten shame," Anne agreed, studying the fellow in some surprise. "Do you have some ideas on the subject?"

"Jus' one, miss. Y'see, I've invented this 'ere new fold—for a neckcloth, y'know. An' if I may say so as shouldn't, it's the grandest fold since Mr. Brummel devised the famous Trône d'Amour."

"How very interesting. But I don't quite see what—?"

"Well, I been thinkin' . . . what if 'is lordship'd go about town sportin' the new fold. Everyone'd be bound to ax 'im about it . . . wot's it called an' all. An' 'e'd say it's called the *Regent*! Now, I axes yer, wouldn't *that* be pleasin' to the Prince?"

"I don't see how it could *fail* to please him," Anne said with a smile.

"Right!" Orkle nodded in self-satisfaction. "The thing is, though, that Lord Mainwarin' don't seem inclined to go along wi' the idea."

"No? Why not?"

"Says it'd be cuttin' too much of a dash for 'im. Lord Mainwarin' don't like 'is clothes to attrack any partickler notice, y'see. 'E says 'e likes to be unobtroosive."

Anne couldn't help laughing. "As if a man his size could ever be unobtrusive!"

"That's me thought exackly! Wot 'arm, I axes yer,

could come from the fold of a neckcloth? That's why I
'oped that *you* ..."

"...that I could persuade him?"

"Yes, miss, that's the ticket."

Anne sighed. "My influence with his lordship is not at
all great, Mr. Orkle. I'm very much afraid I've not been
successful of convincing him of *anything*. However, I
shall certainly try."

Mr. Orkle thanked her effusively and withdrew,
leaving her smiling broadly at his naive but ingenious
plan. While the smile still lingered on her lips, Peter came
looking for her. "I've been thinking," he said without
preamble, "about this silly ostracism that Jason's had to
endure—"

"Not you, too?" Anne interrupted with a laugh.

"Oh? Has it been worrying you also?" Peter asked
innocently.

"It seems to have been worrying *everyone*. Don't tell
me you've thought of a solution."

"Perhaps I have," Peter said, taking the chair facing his
sister and leaning toward her with purposeful earnestness.
"The Prince is quite interested in the Royal Academy of
Arts, you know. He made a speech there last month and
even gave them a rather splendid bronze lamp as a gift.
My thought was that Jason should do something similar."

"I don't think I follow—"

"What if Jason presented something to the Academy in
honor of the Regent? Word of the presentation would be
bound to get back to the Prince, wouldn't it? And he'd be
bound to be pleased."

"I don't know," Anne mused. "What sort of thing
could Jason present to the Academy?"

"One of the family portraits, perhaps...or a piece of
sculpture from the manor house at Derbyshire. You know
the sort of thing the Academy collects."

"Mmmm. It certainly *sounds* like a good plan," Anne
said thoughtfully. "At least it appears to be less servile or
obsequious than some of the others I've heard, for the gift

would be made to the Academy and not to the Prince. On that basis, you may have a *hope* of convincing Jason. Why don't you ask him at dinner tonight?"

"I can ask him this afternoon, for he's taking me to a cricket match," Peter suggested, "unless you think it would be more advantageous to wait until dinnertime when we can make the proposal together."

"Ask him at the cricket match, by all means," Anne said decidedly. "I don't think my presence at dinner would be of any strategic value at all."

If Anne imagined that her interview with Peter was the last one in which a suggestion to bring about the desired reconciliation between the Regent and Jason would be made, she was to be proved mistaken. For shortly after Peter and Jason had left the house for the afternoon, Anne had another visitor. It was Cherry, and no sooner had Anne seated her in the sitting room and perched on the sofa beside her when Cherry broached the very same subject. "I've been thinking about Jason's problem," she began eagerly, "and I believe I've a suggestion to bring about a solution."

"Oh, Cherry, not you, *too*!" Anne exclaimed with a gurgle of laughter. "I've been receiving suggestions for the past two days!"

"Have you really? How fortunate! Have any of them been promising?"

Anne shrugged. "How can they be, when Jason is so adamantly set against making an effort in his own behalf? But, pray, don't keep me in suspense. What is *your* contribution?"

"It is not very substantial, I'm afraid, but it is the only thing I could think of . . ."

"Really, Cherry, you're always so lacking in confidence. Tell me your plan, and without these unnecessary reservations."

"Well, then, you know how fond Mama is of cards—whist and hearts and games of chance. She holds a card party at least twice during the season. I've heard that the Prince is fond of cards, too, so I've persuaded her to send him an invitation to her next. Of course, I don't know if he'll accept, but Mrs. Fitzherbert is fond of play, and Mama expects *her* to be present, and you know that the Prince often accompanies her. So we have every hope..."

"I don't know if the scheme will work, Cherry. Jason doesn't indulge in card games very often. Perhaps he may be persuaded, if you don't tell him that the Prince is expected. Why don't you ask him? If you turn your large, melting eyes on him, he may not be able to refuse you."

Cherry blushed. "Oh, Anne, you're a dreadful tease. You know very well that Lord Mainwaring takes no special notice of me."

"Well, if it's any comfort to you, he takes no special notice of me, either."

"When shall I ask him?" Cherry inquired, determined to complete her mission. "Is he expected home shortly?"

"I couldn't say. He neither asks my permission to take his leave nor informs me of his intentions in the matter of his return. Jason, my dear, is nothing if not independent. I think these Americans drink independence with their mothers' milk. I believe, however, that he's gone to a cricket match and is not expected back until dinnertime."

"In that case, will *you* ask him for me? I've brought along an invitation."

Anne nodded, but without enthusiasm. "I'll deliver it, Cherry, but you shouldn't count on his attending. Jason is not easily persuaded."

Cherry's face fell. "Oh, dear, then you don't think he'll come?" she asked tragically.

"I must say, Cherry," Anne remarked in some surprise, "that, although your sympathetic nature is well known to all the world, I had not thought you would be *quite* so troubled about Jason's problems."

"I'm *not* troubled about Jason's problems. It's *you* I'm troubled about," Cherry said flatly.

"*Me*? I don't understand. What have *I* to do with this?"

Cherry faced her friend with an expression of profound disapproval. "Really, Anne, I sometimes fail to understand you. Did you not postpone your *elopement* because of this?"

"Yes, but—"

"Didn't it occur to you to wonder if Arthur is upset by your—I hope our friendship is strong enough to withstand blunt speaking—your *neglect*? For how else is he to view your request for postponement except as neglect of him? How can you love him and have no sympathy for his pain?"

Anne's eyes flew to Cherry's face in mortification. "Oh, Cherry, I'm a *beast*! I don't *deserve* Arthur. And I don't deserve a friend like you." She jumped up and began to pace the room, her feelings of guilt and remorse overwhelming her. "But I shall make it all up to him! I shall be ready to leave with him the moment this business with Jason is resolved." She sat down beside her friend and grasped Cherry's hands. "And, Cherry, I shall do my best . . . my *very* best . . . to make him a good wife. I shall be as devoted and patient and loyal as I can possibly be, I promise you."

Cherry, struggling with her own guilt, took no notice of the tone of self-sacrifice in Anne's words. Moved to tears, she held out her arms, and the friends embraced. "You will be happy," Cherry said in a quivering whisper. "I know you will. But you must leave for Gretna *soon*!"

"I'll leave with him *very* soon," Anne assured her. The girls broke apart and wiped their eyes. "Surely, with so many suggestions for bringing about a reconciliation with the Prince, *one* of them is bound to work."

But Anne and Cherry were about to learn that the more carefully humans plan to take control of their fates, the more likely it is that Fate herself will step in to take matters into her own capricious hands.

The cricket match was held at the Artillery Ground, Finsbury, and Jason was surprised at the number of people who turned out for the game. Londoners of all classes arrived on foot, on horseback, or in every conceivable type of equipage on wheels. Jason, who had driven a light phaeton, had to spend a good deal of time finding a place to leave the vehicle. By the time they'd found a proper place and instructed the tiger on caring for the horses, the match was under way. Peter thought he'd heard the sound of a band playing "Rule, Britannia," indicating that a member of the Royal Family was present, but he gave the matter no thought in his eagerness to get to the playing ground to witness the game.

Peter found the match quite exciting; he'd shouted himself hoarse by the end of it. But Jason, who had never witnessed a cricket match before and was not familiar with the finer points of the game, found the match rather a bore. He saw nothing very fascinating in a wild melée of twenty-two men running back and forth across a field in a meaningless confusion. He kept his feelings to himself, however, for he had no wish to dampen Peter's enjoyment.

But it was with considerable relief that he greeted the finish of what had seemed an endless game. "Does it always take *four hours*?" he asked Peter.

"Sometimes much longer," Peter said proudly. "I've heard of a game that lasted two whole days!"

They tried to make their way back across the field toward the phaeton, but the excited, milling crowd all about them impeded their progress. Suddenly, Peter gasped. "Good Lord! It's the *Prince*!"

Jason followed Peter's eye to the right, where the crowd was particularly thick and excited. In the midst of the throng, shaking hands with one of the players, was the Regent, evidently enjoying the carnival atmosphere. "Quickly, Peter, let's turn off this way," Jason muttered. "I've no wish for the embarrassment of coming face-to-face with him."

They turned and moved as quickly as the crowd would

permit to their left. But they'd not gone four paces when a stentorian voice stopped them in their tracks. "I say, Mainwaring, is that you?" the Prince called.

Jason had no choice but to turn around. Taking Peter's arm, he approached the royal presence as the crowd drew back to make a passageway for them. "How do you do, your highness?" Jason said politely when he was near enough to be heard. Then, bowing, he added, "May I present my cousin, Peter Hartley?"

The Prince smiled at Peter with warm condescension and shook his hand. Then he turned back to Jason. "I haven't seen you for quite a while, old fellow. Where have you been keeping?"

"Close to home, I fear," Jason murmured.

"I shouldn't do that, if I were you," the Prince said, wagging a finger at him. "Not at the height of the season, you know. Not at all the thing. But you are the *very* man I wanted to see."

"*I*, your highness?" Jason asked in astonishment.

"Yes. I've been told that you're an excellent judge of horseflesh. Is that right?"

"I don't know about that, your highness," Jason demurred.

"Don't be so modest, man. I remember distinctly being told that you won a race against Minton with a horse you'd just bought. Not an easy man to best in a race, Miles Minton. So come along with me...yes, right now...I want to show you the horse I have with me. He's a prime bit of blood I've just acquired. I'd like to know what you think of him."

Jason had just time enough to cast Peter an astonished glance before the Regent placed an arm about his shoulders and walked off with him through the crowd. The members of the Prince's retinue and those members of the *ton* in the crowd who were privy to the events at the Prince's dinner party gaped in surprise. As the crowd surged along in the wake of the Prince, there were several who smiled at each other in knowing amusement at the caprices of royalty.

Peter followed along, grinning widely. What a tale he had to tell when he got home! He could easily imagine Anne's and his mother's faces when they heard that the Prince had embraced Jason like a long-lost brother. "He didn't even *remember* that there had been a rift!" Peter would tell them with a chortle. It was all so ridiculous. It was all so baffling. But the conclusion was inescapable—one astounding fact was clear: Jason's ostracism was over!

# Twenty

THE DOWAGER DUCHESS of Richmond, paying a
morning call on Harriet, expressed her delight at Lord
Mainwaring's success in achieving so envied a place in the
very heart of society. The Prince had taken him under his
wing with renewed enthusiasm. The Duchess had already
noticed that Mainwaring's quips were being repeated
everywhere, Mainwaring's way with a neckcloth was
being copied by all the dandies, and Mainwaring's
prowess on horseback was being universally praised.
"Reminds me of the time that Franklin fellow took
London by storm, back in the nineties. Remember,
Harriet?"

Many elderly Londoners were beginning to remark, as
did the Duchess, that not since the days of Benjamin
Franklin had an American made such a mark. The
Corinthians, the Dandies, the politicians and the ladies all
found something in him to admire. His wit, his
horsemanship, his style, his Americanisms, his mischievous smile and easy address were again noticed and
remarked upon. And in the Mainwaring household, the
doldrums had miraculously disappeared, completely

dispelled by the dazzling glow created by his lordship's renewed and heightened popularity.

The Duchess' morning call was merely the latest coup in a series of triumphs which Lady Harriet had scored in the fortnight since Jason had found himself reunited with the Prince. First there had been a visit from the Countess Lieven. Then she'd received a much-prized invitation from Lady Hertford. There had even been a proposal of marriage from the ludicrous but socially prominent, thrice-married Earl of Stanborough. But the most significant of all these indications of Lady Harriet's newly elevated importance was the considerably increased deference shown to her by her dressmaker.

Thus, when the Duchess took her leave, Harriet entered the dining room for luncheon with a dance in her step and a smiling countenance, completely unprepared for the news which Peter was about to relay to her. The two of them were alone at the table, for Jason was rarely home these days and Anne had left to take luncheon with Cherry. "Did Jason tell you, Mama," Peter asked, "that he plans to return to America soon?"

Harriet, who was about to reach for a biscuit, froze. "Return to *America*? You must be *mad*!"

"No, I'm afraid it's quite true. He told me himself, last evening, when we were playing chess."

Harriet felt her pulse begin to race. Steadying herself by regulating her breathing, she tried to brush the matter aside. "What nonsense! He was only teasing. You know how Jason enjoys a little joke."

"He wasn't teasing, Mama," Peter said earnestly. "He truly means to go."

"But... but by *why*? The fellow has become society's *darling*! He's living a completely enviable life! Are you telling me he doesn't *like* it here?"

"I don't think he sets much store by his role as 'society's darling,' although I do believe he's greatly enjoying himself."

"Then I don't see why—"

"America is his *home*, you know. Perhaps he misses it," Peter suggested gently.

"Rubbish!" Harriet declared. "*This* is his home. We are his *family*! How can he *think* of deserting us?"

"I believe he is very fond of us, my dear, but his attachment to his birthplace is very strong. I've often remarked on it. It's my belief that he never meant to remain here. He only came for a visit—to see where his father was born and to meet his father's people..."

"But what of his titles? His estates? His responsibilities?"

"I believe," Peter said quietly, breaking a slice of bread into little pieces with nervous fingers, "that he intends to bequeath them to *me*."

Lady Harriet gasped. "*Peter*! You don't *mean* it!"

Peter smiled wryly. "He said he is certain I shall make an excellent Viscount."

"And so you shall," said his mother, torn between pride and joy in her son's new expectations and dismay at the imminent loss of the man who had become a source of security and an object of her affections. "But I don't really understand. Why should he choose to live a life of deprivation and difficulty in America when he could have one here of ease and elegance?"

Peter smiled. "He's not cut out for a life of ease and elegance. And from what I've learned of his station in the United States, he is far from deprived. Not only is he the head of his father's shipping lines in Norfolk—a bustling and successful venture, I understand—but he seems to have extensive land holdings, both in Virginia and on the frontier—I think he called it Kentucky. I think our Jason is much more prosperous than we'd ever imagined."

"Is he really?" asked Harriet, wide-eyed. "My goodness, it sounds very impressive. Although I don't know why I should be so amazed. He *is* a Mainwaring, after all."

Peter laughed. "Once you thought he was nothing but a boorish rebel."

"Yes, I did, but that was before I'd met him. However, I

must admit that, even afterwards, I thought him an impoverished waif. I think it must have been that atrocious coat of his..."

They both smiled, remembering their first impression of the man who had made such an impact on their lives. But their smiles soon faded as they each tried to imagine how they would do without him. "I, for one, will be very sorry to see him go," Peter sighed.

"Oh, and so will I!" Harriet seconded mournfully. "How shall we *manage* without him?"

"Jason says we shall do very well...and I suppose he's right. He is so easy a man to learn to rely on. But he insists that we are perfectly capable of relying on ourselves. He says that when I've finished my schooling, we should plan to visit him in Virginia for an extended stay."

Harriet grew misty-eyed. "Oh, I should *like* that, shouldn't you?"

"More than I can say. That prospect is the only thing which enables me to face his departure with equanimity," Peter admitted.

Harriet worriedly bit her lip. "I wonder...Peter, what do you think Anne will say?"

"I have no idea. But, Mama, that reminds me...Jason asked particularly that we keep this to ourselves and not tell Anne. He wants to tell her himself."

"Very well, if that is what he wishes. She likes to pretend that she in uninterested in Jason's welfare, but I believe that his departure will pain her, too."

"As to that, Mama, I have no opinion. I've never understood Anne's reactions to Jason. He has never given her adequate cause—it seems to me—to explain why she holds him in such dislike."

Harriet groaned. "She does hold him in dislike, doesn't she? Oh, dear...I had so hoped that the two of them would..." Her voice trailed off in a melancholy sigh.

"So did I, Mama," Peter said glumly, pushing away his untouched plate of food. "So did I."

*       *       *

Although Anne did *not* hold Jason in dislike, that fact was not at all in evidence as she faced him that evening in the library when he'd stopped in to bid her good night. For the eighth evening in a row, Jason was on his way out. He had not had dinner with the family since his reinstatement in the Prince's good graces. The Regent had taken Jason under his wing, and Jason's nights had become as busy as the most roisterous pleasure-seeker in London. During the past week, the Prince or some other "friend" had insisted on his companionship for a bachelor dinner, two or three card parties, an evening of gambling at Watier's, and one wild rout-party at an unidentified abode. On each of these occasions he had rolled in during the wee hours of the morning, making his first appearance of the day well past noon. He had begun to look weary-eyed and pale, and Anne viewed his dissipation with complete disgust. "Are you going out *again*?" she asked in thinly veiled abhorrence.

Jason nodded. "A musical evening at the Hollands, and then, I believe, I'm expected at White's for cards."

"I suppose this will be another occasion when you totter home in the early morning," she said in icy disapproval.

"Do I detect a note of disapprobation, ma'am? Do you not approve of my association with Prinny?"

"Oh, is he 'Prinny' to you now? How enviable to be part of the inner circle—the brightest star in the Regent's firmament!" she said, her voice dripping sarcasm.

Jason looked at her in injured innocence. "I don't see why you're takin' on so. Isn't this what you wanted for me? Isn't this what you trained me for?"

"If you think that I intended to prepare you for this sort of activity, my lord, you're completely out in your reckoning! I neither desire nor deserve any credit for your amazingly rapid and spectacular descent into dissipation and debauchery."

He took her chin in his hand and tilted her face up. "Call me dissipated and debauched if you will, but it was

for *you* that I took this path. No, don't try to turn away,
my girl—you may as well face it. I'm no more dissipated
than any other 'gentleman.' That's what you wanted me to
be, isn't it—a London gentleman? I'm only bein'
*obligin'*!"

She shook herself free. "Don't bother to oblige *me*, sir.
Your behavior is no concern of mine, I assure you. 'Ain't
no skin off my nose.'"

Jason laughed. "Can it be that while you've made a
gentleman of me, I've made a backwoodsman of you?"

"No, not at all, for I'm no more a backwoodsman than
*you* are a gentleman."

"Are you implyin'," Jason asked, exaggeratedly
offended, "that I'm *not* a gentleman? Look at me, girl!
From the tip of my perfectly polished shoes to the top of
my coiffed head, I'm what you made me! Look at the
starched points of my shirt-collar! Look at the fold of my
neckcloth! Look at the gold fob hangin' on just the right
length of chain from my waistcoat pocket! What *more* do
you want?"

"Do you think these trappings make you a *gentleman*?" she asked in frozen hauteur. "Do you sincerely
believe that the clothes you wear, or the style of your hair,
or even the dissipated, corrupt company you keep has
anything to do with being a gentleman?"

Glaring up at him, she noted with some surprise that he
was regarding her with a half-smile and a strangely
approving gleam in his penetrating eyes. "As a matter of
fact, my dear," he said softly, "I don't think so at all. I *did*
think, however, that those were your very standards for
judgin' gentlemanliness." He leaned down and planted a
gentle, affectionate and completely unexpected kiss on
her forehead. "It's a real pleasure to me to realize that
you've learned somethin'." Placing his chapeau-bras
under his arm, he executed a faultless little bow and
sauntered from the room.

As Anne watched him go, a number of painful feelings
swept over her—anger and frustration, impatience and

irritation, and, most distressing of all, an overwhelming sense of disappointment and loss. This was not the way she'd planned to take leave of him. Jason couldn't know it, of course, but this was the last time she would see him. Tonight was the night she was leaving for Gretna Green. As Cherry had pointed out to her many times since Jason's reinstatement, there was no longer any reason for Anne to keep poor Arthur dangling.

She had a strong desire to run after Jason, to stop him and tell him—but what? What was there she could say to him? With flagging spirits and a throat which burned with unshed tears, she turned and climbed the stairs to her bedroom. She would use the half-hour before dinner to finish her packing and to prepare herself for the ordeal of sitting down to dinner with Mama and Peter and pretending that nothing extraordinary was happening.

But her hands were trembling and her will was too weak to make much headway on her packing, and she found herself sitting on the edge of her bed staring at the petticoat in her hands as if she didn't know what to do with it. What was she *doing*? She had not the least desire to run away to Shropshire! How could she leave her dear stepmother and brother and the London house which had been her home for as long as she could remember? How could she leave Jason, whose challenging ways and cheerful spirit had brightened her days, filled her thoughts and awakened her to the possibilities of zest and joy that days could hold when spent with him and that were so completely absent when he was not with her?

But this kind of thinking was mere self-indulgence. She had to make herself stop. She had to bury her feelings for Jason. She had no right to them. Even if he had shown an interest in her beyond the brotherly, she could not encourage him. She couldn't betray Arthur, who loved her so loyally. She was *promised*, and a person with character does not ignore promises. No matter what it cost, she would go to the Scottish border with Arthur, endure the hasty, runaway wedding and settle with him in his vicarage. And by making him happy, perhaps she would find a measure of contentment for herself. At the very least, her conscience would be clear.

With Jason to care for them, Mama and Peter would do quite well without her. They would miss her, she knew, but in time they would forgive her. They might even pay her a visit once in a while. She, however, would not be able to permit herself to visit this house, ever again. It would be too painful, and she might never be able to force herself to return to her Shropshire home.

Jason, she supposed, would marry Lexie. They'd have a wonderful life together. Lexie had taste and style—she'd redecorate the Mainwaring house and make of it the center of a social whirl. With Jason's political leanings and Lexie's social talents, they would become the most sought after couple of the *ton*. Lexie would make an excellent political hostess. Anne admitted to herself that Lexie would undoubtedly be a far superior Lady Mainwaring to the one *she* would have become if she'd been given the chance.

As for Jason himself, she didn't think he would continue to pursue his present, dissipated course. Once he married, he would no doubt settle down. A man was entitled, she supposed, to sow some wild oats for a time. He was too sensible, too level-headed and energetic, to be content to waste himself on gambling and carousing. He would soon tire of these shallow, frivolous pastimes and turn to serious preoccupations. If Lexie had any sense, she would encourage him to enter Parliament. That was the place for a man like Jason.

But these things could not be Anne's concern. Jason's future was now out of her hands. She had to admit that, while she *had* had an influence on his fate, she had not done very well. It was too late now for her to make amends. She must put Jason and his interests out of her mind. With a shake, she roused herself from her reverie, folded the petticoat carefully and placed it in an already overcrowded bandbox, trying unsuccessfully to brush away the tears that kept falling upon it as she worked.

# Twenty-One

ANNE STOOD JUST INSIDE her bedroom door with her ear pressed against it, trying to hear the sounds in the corridor. She couldn't leave the room until she was sure everyone was asleep. She had heard Harriet's door close some time ago, and Peter's step could just now be discerned as he passed her door on his way to his bedroom from the library. It would not be long now before he, too, would be asleep. Anne tied her light cloak at the neck, raised the hood carefully and turned to check her portmanteau. In less than fifteen minutes—on the stroke of midnight—Arthur's carriage would be waiting at the corner of the street. The time of her elopement was at hand.

She listened at the door again. All was silence. Even Coyne and Orkle, who had been given strict orders from Jason never to wait up for him beyond midnight—must have gone to bed. Jason was, of course, not at home and it was unlikely that he would return from his nightly carousing early enough to interfere with her plans. By the time he *did* return, she and Arthur would be well along on the Old North Road.

Anne checked over in her mind the various tasks which were to be attended to before her departure. She had packed all the clothing and toilet articles necessary for the trip. She had closed the portmanteau and tied the bandbox. She had left for her abigail a list of other things to be sent to her in Shropshire. And she had written a note to Cherry and sent it out earlier in the evening. *By the time you read this,* she had written, *I shall be on my way to Gretna. It is only to you, my dearest friend, that I can admit my unhappiness on this occasion. Life in a cottage in Shropshire will be nothing more than an Exile for me. I would not for the world hurt Arthur by admitting to him my overwhelming doubts about my ability to Exist in such surroundings, but to you I do not hesitate to confess that my expectations for my future Happiness are small indeed. My only comfort will be the hope of seeing you again in the near future. Please, dearest Cherry, promise to come to me in Shropshire before the month is out! If you do not, I shall undoubtedly die of Loneliness and Despair. Until we see each other again, I remain your Loving and Devoted Anne.*

There was only one task left, but it was the most difficult of all. She had to write to her stepmother. What could she say that would not cause dearest Harriet a great deal of unhappiness? Biting her underlip in distress, she sat down at the writing desk and picked up her pen. *Dearest Mama,* she wrote, *I hope you will find it in your heart to forgive me for what I am about to do. Arthur and I are leaving for Gretna Green. Because of his mother's Opposition, we have agreed that this is the only way. Please wish us Happy, and believe that I love you too much to have done this unless I was Certain that you and Peter will go on quite well without me. I know that you will be Happy and Secure, for Lord Mainwaring is devoted to you both and is certain to take excellent care of you. In time, when you've forgiven me, I hope you will come and visit us at the Vicarage in Shropshire where we will be living. In the meantime, you and Peter have my*

*Undying Love. Your Devoted Anne.*

Wiping away a tear, she sealed the note and placed it on her pillow. Then, with a last fond look about the room, she picked up her portmanteau and the overstuffed bandbox and stealthily crept from the room.

She had great difficulty in carrying the heavy boxes down the stairs, but she was almost at the bottom when the front door opened. Jason stood on the threshold, his hat set at a precarious angle on his tousled head, his neckcloth loosened, his cheeks flushed and his eyes overbright with drink. And under one arm he carried what Anne eventually identified as the parts of a complete suit of armor. "Ah! 'S *you*!" he exclaimed thickly. "Evenin', ma'am. Look at th' present th' Prince has given me!"

He stumbled into the entryway, shut the door with a thump and proceeded to assemble the armor noisily. As Anne stood frozen on the stairs, Jason clumsily connected the parts and hung the entire apparatus on a stand especially made for that purpose. "There!" he crowed. "Won'erful, ain't he? Always dreamed of havin' a suit of armor." He put an arm around the metal figure. "Goin' t' take 'im back t' America with me."

"You're *foxed*!" Anne exclaimed in disgust.

He put his index finger to his lips in a gesture of exaggerated caution. "Shssssssh!" he whispered hoarsely. "You'll wake everyone. An' don't look so fierce, ma'am. I'm... only a bit... disguised..."

"*Disguised*? You're completely cast away! I've never even *seen* anyone so drunk!"

Jason executed an elaborate and unsteady bow. "Happy t' con... tribute to y'r education, ma'am."

"I think," she said in cold reproof, "that you'd better take yourself to bed at once!"

"Tha's jus' what I intend t' do, ma'am. If you'll be... good enough... t' step out o' the way..." He came toward the stairs unsteadily.

Anne stepped hastily aside, and for the first time Jason

noticed the baggage on the stairway. His eyes narrowed, as if he were trying to get them to focus, and he stared at the portmanteau with unblinking concentration. Then he turned to look at Anne, who found herself flushing hotly. "Goin' somewhere, m' dear?" he asked with frightening intensity.

"I can't discuss it with you now," she retorted nervously. "You're in no condition to understand. Go to bed. It will all be explained in the morning."

He came to the bottom of the stairs and looked up at her, the movement causing his high-crowned beaver to fall off his head and roll away across the floor, completely unheeded. "No need t' explain. I'm not so drunk that I can't ... tell wha's happenin.' Y'r runnin' off wi' Clay-bridge."

"Please, Jason," she entreated, the smoldering look in his eyes making her distinctly uneasy, "go up to bed."

He shook his head. "Won't let you!" he declared mulishly.

"You won't let me? Don't be foolish—you don't know what you're saying."

"Yes, I do. Y' don't really *want* t' go, so I won't let you."

Anne frowned down at him, nonplussed. She was well aware that the hour of midnight had already struck. Arthur must be waiting. She could not stand here and argue with a drunken *sot*. Squaring her shoulders with determination, she picked up her bags and went down the few remaining steps. Avoiding his eyes, she attempted to brush past him. "No!" he snapped. He grasped her by the shoulders so fiercely that she dropped her bags. "I tell you y' can't go! Won't ... permit it!"

Before she quite realized what was happenin', he pulled her to him in a crushing embrace. She was lifted quite off the ground, and his lips were pressed furiously against hers. It should have been quite revolting—he was hurting her, and he reeked of liquor. She should have fought him off like a tiger. But for a moment, while her pulse raced and her head swam, and a tremor of something she'd never felt before swept over her from head to toe, she lay against him unresisting. Then her good breeding and her sense of decorum reasserted themselves, and she began to pummel his chest with angry fists. For all the effect her struggle had on him, she might as well have been beating upon a wall.

But eventually, without releasing her from the clasp of his arms, he set her on her feet and lifted his head. "L'il fool," he muttered, "don't y' see y' can't run away?"

"You are out of your mind," she said breathlessly. "Let me go."

He tried to clear his head by giving it a vigorous shake. "Damn, I'm too befuddled for this sort o' thing. But I can't... Are you going to pretend, after all this... that you still *want* to marry Claybridge? Can I have misunderstood...? This thing between us just now... was it *nothing*?"

"Jason, you're drunk. You didn't know what you were doing. I don't even think you know who I am. Perhaps you think I'm someone else... someone like... like Lexie—"

Jason threw back his head and gave a shout of laughter. Then he pulled her to him again. "You're *idiotic*!" He lifted her up so that their faces were so close they almost touched. "Listen to me, you ninny! I know who you are! I'd know you if I were a... a thousand times drunker than I am now. I'd know you if... if I were blin'folded... an' had to pick you from among a thousand girls!" He looked at her with a crooked, slightly hazy but tender smile. "I... know the sound of your footstep... the curve of your cheek... the feel of your hair... that gurgle in your laugh... an' I even know how that... strangely muddled mind of yours works. So don't start thinkin' you can make me b'lieve you *want* to run off wi' that Claybridge fellow. Fine fellow, I grant you... but not for you..."

Anne stared at him dumbfounded. Her throat was choked with tears. Could he really have *meant* all that?

Was he trying to tell her . . . Could he possibly *love* her? She couldn't bring herself to believe it. It was the liquor he had drunk. He'd never spoken to her like this when he was sober. She must go, before he weakened her resolve. She struggled in his arms. "Jason, please . . . put me down," she begged.

He merely shook his head and pressed his lips to hers again. But this time the kiss was gently urgent. It asked for, but did not demand, a response. She closed her eyes. She felt as if every bone in her body had begun to melt. And like her bones, her will, too, became limp. If only she could remain like this forever. Oh, Jason, she thought in helpless confusion, I do love you so! But she couldn't let herself surrender to this feeling. It was all unreal—a fantasy built on her longing and Jason's drunkeness. She pushed against him and wrenched her head free. "Oh, God, Jason," she cried, "*let me go!*"

At that moment, Arthur, who had been waiting outside for an agonizing half-hour, stealthily opened the door to see what was keeping his betrothed. He was just in time to hear her pitiful cry. The sight of his affianced bride struggling in the arms of her enormous, would-be seducer made him wild with fury. Ignoring the fact that Lord Mainwaring was more than a head taller and a good deal heavier than he, he gave an animal cry of rage, lowered his head and stormed toward his target like a maddened bull.

On hearing Arthur's shout, the bemused Jason released Anne and turned to see who had intruded. Before he could grasp what was happening, Arthur hurtled, head first, into Jason's middle. Jason, the breath knocked out of him, tottered backward, falling heavily against the suit of armor. With a terrible noise, the armor, Jason and Arthur went crashing against the wall. The armor broke apart, its pieces clattering loudly upon the stone floor, the helmet hitting Jason's forehead before bouncing off across the hallway.

Arthur, unhurt, managed to maintain his balance by holding on to the wall. But Jason fell to the floor, where he lay sprawled on his back, unconscious, a great bloody gash just above his right eye already dripping its red fluid down his cheek and onto the floor.

Anne screamed in horror. Arthur, still clinging to the wall, turned slowly and stared, aghast, at the havoc he had wreaked. "Arthur, what have you *done*?" Anne asked in a fearful whisper, her eyes on Jason's pale face. "Do you think he . . . he's . . . ?"

"Dead? No, of course not," Arthur said quickly. "He *couldn't* be . . . !"

Anne walked slowly to Jason, knelt at his side and leaned over him. "He's breathing!" she murmured in intense relief.

"Thank God," Arthur breathed fervently.

Anne sat down on the floor and gingerly lifted Jason's head to her lap. "We must do something to revive him . . ." she said helplessly.

"Yes, but I'm afraid I don't know quite—"

"I'll fetch some brandy," said a voice from behind the stairs. They turned quickly to see Coyne, followed by a number of the household staff, peering at them from the shadows. They were all in their nightclothes, and a number carried candles. And suddenly, from the top of the stairs, came other voices. "What's going on down there?" Peter inquired sleepily.

Lady Harriet, her nightcap askew and a light robe thrown hastily over her nightdress, came down the stairway holding her candle aloft. At the sight of the metal apparatus strewn all over the hallway, the discarded baggage, Arthur's white face, Anne in a traveling cloak, and Jason lying on the ground, his head in Anne's lap and his blood trickling down his face, her candle began to tremble. "Oh, my God!" she mumbled. "Oh, my *God*!"

"It's all right, Mama, really," Anne said, unconvincingly. "Never mind the brandy, Coyne. I think his lordship has already had enough of that sort of thing."

Mr. Orkle pushed through the press of servants and marched firmly to his employer's side. "Wot we needs is a

basin o' warm water, a sponge an' some bandages, I says,"
he remarked calmly.

"Yes, right away, Mr. Orkle," said Coyne, shaking
himself into activity. "Hop to it, George," he said to one of
the footmen. "The rest of you, off to bed now. This is none
of your business. And don't let me hear any gossiping,
mind!"

Lady Harriet and Peter came down the stairs. "Good
heavens, Claybridge," Peter demanded, "did you and
Jason have a mill? And what's all this stuff strewn about?
Armor?"

Before Arthur could answer, Jason stirred and opened
his eyes. Anne's face swam mistily into his view. "Y' can't
go," he muttered.

"No, no, of course not," she said and smiled down at
him comfortingly.

"I m-must remain c-calm . . ." Lady Harriet whispered
tremulously, bending over the fallen warrior.

"I say, Jason, is this your armor? What did you try to
do? *Joust*?" Peter asked, amused.

Jason painfully turned his head and squinted in the
direction of Peter's voice. "M' armor! Is 't ruined?"

Peter began to gather up the pieces. "Dented a bit, I
imagine, but we'll be able to fix it," he announced
cheerfully.

"I don't know how you can worry about armor with
Jason lying there *wounded*," Harriet said querulously.

"Not . . . wounded," Jason assured her thickly. "Jus' a
bit . . . disguised . . ."

"But you're *bleeding*!" Harriet informed him.

"Oh?" Jason queried foggily. "Tha's nice." With a sigh
of contentment he turned his head back to Anne,
snuggled comfortably in her lap and went promptly to
sleep.

So deep was his sleep that even Orkle's ministrations to
his forehead did not rouse him. Once the wound was
cleaned and bandaged, Peter and Orkle shook him and
dragged him to his feet. "Come on, old man," Peter said,

struggling mightily to rouse Jason enough to gain his assistance, "let's get you off to bed."

Jason, now on his feet, leaned heavily on Peter's and Orkle's shoulders and looked around dizzily. "Anne?"

She had risen and gone to put a consoling arm about her stepmother's shaking shoulders. "Yes, my lord?" she asked.

He blinked at her whoozily. "You're not...goin' away...?"

She lowered her eyes. "Not...tonight, my lord. Good night."

Coyne took a branch of candles and started up the stairs with Jason and his assistants following. They had not gone halfway up when there was a knock at the door. Coyne looked around in amazement. "Now, who—?"

"Go on up with his lordship, Coyne," Anne ordered. "I'll see to the door."

"At this hour?" Lady Harriet cried fearfully. "You will *not* go to the door! Who knows what sort of person may be standing there! Go ahead, Coyne. I'll take the candles."

Coyne hurried down, handed the candles to Lady Harriet and hurried to the door, but no one else moved. He opened it a crack.

"I beg your pardon, Coyne," said a female voice timidly, "for waking you at this shockingly late hour...but I saw...that is, I must see Miss Hartley at once!"

"*Cherry*?" Anne cried in astonishment. "Is that *you*?"

Coyne opened the door and Cherry hurried in. She stopped abruptly as her eyes took in the confusion in the hallway. "Oh!" she gasped in confusion. "I thought...I mean...the whole *family*...? Has something gone wrong?"

Anne burst into a peal of laughter. "Yes, I think you could safely say that," she agreed. "I can't *imagine* what brings you here at this hour, Cherry, but—"

"I have to talk to you, Anne. It's *most urgent*," Cherry said.

"It must be, if you've come out alone in the middle of the night. Arthur, please take Cherry into the sitting room. I'll join you both as soon as I've helped Mama to bed."

"If you think you can shunt me off like this, young lady," Harriet said with asperity, "you've much mistaken the matter."

"Come now, Mama, you're not being reasonable," Anne said gently, taking her stepmother's arm and urging her toward the stairs. "You've been quite shaken by all this, you know. If you lie down and regain your calm, you'll be much more the thing by morning. Then, when your breathing is regular and your mind composed, I'll tell you all about what has happened here tonight."

"Very well, if you *promise* . . ." Harriet agreed reluctantly, and she turned and permitted Anne to lead her up the stairs.

While Jason and Harriet were being assisted into bed, Arthur, pale and shaken, faced Cherry in the sitting room with less curiosity than relief. "I'm so glad to see you," he said to her pathetically. "This has been the most *disastrous* night. I don't think I can bring myself to go through it again."

"But that's why I'm here, my dear," Cherry said eagerly. "Perhaps you won't *have* to."

"Why not?" Arthur asked, his curiosity piqued at last.

"I received a note from Anne tonight. Arthur, you were right about her, and I was wrong. I now am convinced that she does *not* love you as she ought." Cherry lifted her head with newfound courage. "I've decided that I won't *permit* her to run off with you and make you miserable!"

"Cherry!" Arthur said, awed, and he gathered her into his arms.

By the time Anne reappeared, Arthur and Cherry were seated side by side on the sofa, fully prepared to explain to Anne the state of their feelings. "You must be wondering, my dear," Cherry began, "why I've come at this late hour."

"Yes, it *is* a bit strange," Anne said, "but it's not important now. There's something I must—"

"It *is* important, Anne. Please let me explain. I'd been to see the play at Covent Garden tonight with Captain Wr—" She gave Arthur a quick, surreptitious glance. "Well, that part's not important, but I arrived home quite late and found your note. Really, Anne, I must implore you not to go through with the elopement feeling as you do. I hope you don't mind my saying this in front of Arthur, but—"

"But, Cherry, that's exactly what *I* wanted to say. Arthur, I've been thinking about this very thing. I can't go with you to Shropshire. I would be terribly unhappy in your sort of life, and no matter how hard I'd try, it would not fool a man as sensitive as you. In the end, you would be unhappy, too. The three of us have always been such good friends that I know you won't mind my saying these things so openly ... but Arthur, I'm not the girl for you. You are so truly *good*! You need a girl like ... like *Cherry*!"

"But, *Anne*," Arthur interrupted in astonishment, "that's just what we—"

Cherry hastily placed a restraining hand on Arthur's arm. "Anne, my dear," she said with a nervous giggle, "this is not the time for matchmaking."

"Yes, you're right. Let's leave it at that. Arthur, you *will* see Cherry home, won't you?"

"Of course," he said, giving Cherry an appreciative smile. He'd understood at once what Cherry had done. In her deep, instinctive understanding of other people's feelings, she had realized that the kindest way out of the situation was to permit Anne to make the match between them. His heart filled with pride in her. She was the perfect mate for a man in holy orders.

Cherry rose, gave Anne a quick embrace, and left the room. Anne looked at Arthur diffidently. "I hope you find it possible to forgive me someday, Arthur dear. But I know this is for the best."

Arthur nodded wordlessly and lifted her hand to his lips. Then he walked quickly from the room. Cherry stood at the door, waiting. But he would not take her home. He gave her a questioning look. She nodded imperceptibly and, hand-in-hand, they went out the door. Who would have believed, Arthur thought wonderingly, that this nightmare of an evening would end with his taking his beloved Cherry to Gretna Green?

## Twenty-Two

EVERYONE SLEPT a little late in the Mainwaring household the following morning, but by ten most of the inhabitants were up and about. Peter had already had his breakfast and was at his studies in the library as if nothing untoward had occurred. Lady Harriet had sent for her abigail and was trying, with the girl's assistance, to apply a soothing cucumber lotion to her ravaged complexion. Anne was sitting despondently over her coffee in the breakfast room, wondering what she was to do with her now-directionless life. And Jason was awake but unable to lift his throbbing, aching head from the pillow.

Coyne came into the breakfast room (his usual, stolid manner unaffected by the activities of the previous night) to inform Miss Anne that Miss Alexandra de Guis had come to call. Anne told him to send her in. Lexie's brisk entrance, in her resplendent velvet riding costume, was so exuberantly cheerful that it seemed a reproach to Anne's depressed spirits. "Where is your abominable cousin?" Lexie demanded without preamble. "He had fixed to ride with me this morning."

"I'm afraid Jason has met with an accident," Anne told her.

"An *accident*?" Lexie turned quite pale. "What happened? Has he been badly hurt?"

"No, no," Anne hastened to assure her. "He... er... fell against a suit of armor and received a cut on his head. His man tells me that he's quite all right this morning and is suffering more from the effects of having imbibed too deeply last night than from his injury."

"Oh, thank goodness!" Lexie sighed in relief and sat down at the table. "May I have some tea? I need something restorative to recover from the shock."

Anne poured the tea. "I'm sorry you had to miss your ride. If I had known, I would have sent a message to you."

"Don't trouble your mind about *that*. But, Anne, would it be very shocking—and detrimental to my reputation—if I went up to see Jason? I'd like to see for myself the extent of his injury, instead of having to imagine things. My imagination can paint very gruesome pictures sometimes."

"Yes, I know just what you mean." Anne rose and went to the door. "Let me ask Mr. Orkle if Jason is in any condition to have company."

If Anne secretly hoped that Jason would instruct Orkle to send Lexie away, she was doomed to disappointment. Orkle brought word that "'Is lordship'd be delighted," and Lexie ran eagerly up the stairs. It was more than an hour later when she came down again. Anne discovered her standing in front of the hall mirror, near the door, adjusting her very fetching riding hat.

"Are you leaving, Lexie?" she asked.

"Yes, I may as well," Lexie said with a frown. She turned from the mirror, and her eye fell on the suit of armor which had been reassembled and stood on silent guard in a corner of the hallway. "So *that's* the armor Jason's been babbling of. He's as delighted as a child with it. The fellow swears he's taking it back to America with him."

"Yes, I heard him say so—but I don't take it seriously," Anne said.

Lexie studied Anne carefully. "Didn't he tell you he plans to leave within the month?"

Anne was startled. "No . . . he didn't. I . . . do you think he *means* it?"

"Oh, he means it, all right. And I, for one, am utterly chagrined."

"Are you, Lexie?" Anne asked wonderingly. "I thought . . ."

There was an awkward pause. Lexie raised a quizzical eyebrow. "Don't be afraid to speak your mind to me, my dear. *What* did you think? That I wouldn't *mind* Jason's leaving?"

"No, not that. I hadn't thought of his leaving at all. I was sure that, now that he is ensconced in the Prince's circle, he was fixed here. But if he is *serious* . . ."

"I'm sure he is."

"Then . . . I thought . . . that you might go *with* him."

Lexie smiled bitterly. "I? I'd have been delighted to go, my dear. But you see, I wasn't asked."

"Oh," Anne said, suddenly feeling breathless.

"Did you think he would ask me?" Lexie inquired in wry amusement. "You quite amaze me, Anne. Have you lived with the man in the same house for all these weeks and learned so little about him?"

Anne stared at her. "What do you mean?" she asked in confusion. But before Lexie could frame a reply, there was a knock at the door. Anne turned, irritated at having to interrupt this fascinating conversation, and went to open the door. Captain Wray stood on the threshold. "Good morning, Miss Hartley. Forgive this intrusion so early in the day, but I've just come from the Laverstokes. I had promised to take Miss Charity riding this morning, but I found the entire household at sixes and sevens! It seems that Cherry has run off to Gretna Green!"

"Good heavens!" Anne gasped.

"Don't keep the Captain standing on the doorstep,

Anne," Lexie said smoothly. "Ask the gentleman in."

"Yes, of course," Anne murmured, trying to collect her wits. "Do come in, Captain Wray."

The Captain stepped inside and made a brief bow to Lexie. "Good day, Miss de Guis," he said with stiff politeness.

"How do you do, Captain Wray," Lexie said in wicked amusement, extending her hand to be kissed. "It has been a *very* long time, has it not?" she asked, fluttering her eyelashes at him coyly.

But Anne took no notice of the byplay. "Did you say that Cherry had *run off*? When? And how did the Laverstokes learn of it?"

Captain Wray tore his eyes from the magnificent Lexie and turned back to Anne. "Last night, it seems. Her mother received a message from Cherry this morning. I thought you might be able to tell me something more about it."

Anne smiled slowly. "The little sly-boots! It didn't take her very long to act on my suggestion. Thank you for bringing this news to me, Captain. I couldn't be more delighted!"

"But why?" the Captain asked in confusion. "Do you know who it is she's run off *with*? It couldn't be that stuttering fool who kept following her about, could it?"

"I believe, Captain, that our Cherry has gone off to marry Arthur Claybridge."

The Captain gaped. "What? *Your* Arthur Claybridge?"

Lexie gave a merry laugh. "I felicitate you, Anne. You seem to have solved *one* of your problems very neatly."

"I have no idea what you mean," Anne said with dignity, but coloring nevertheless. "The fact that Cherry and Arthur found that they suit each other beautifully has nothing whatever to do with *me*."

"I don't understand any of this," Captain Wray exclaimed.

"Don't let it trouble you, my dear," Lexie said, favoring him with a brilliant smile and taking his arm.

"Walk with me to the stables, and I shall explain it all to you."

"I'd be delighted," Captain Wray said eagerly.

"Good day, Anne," Lexie said suavely. "I hope you'll let me know when you solve your *other* problem." With a quick wink for Anne, she turned her attention to her new prey, and, giving him a honeyed smile, she swept him out the door.

Anne had no time to mull over Lexie's words, for Mr. Orkle came down the stairs to tell her that Jason was asking for her. With a racing pulse and a chest constricted with acute and almost unbearable tension, she tapped on the door of his room. "Come in," he croaked.

She opened the door timidly and peeped in. The room was shadowed, for the drapes had not been opened, but she could see Jason sitting up in bed, propped up by a number of pillows. He was unshaven, unkempt and pale. A large bandage was tied at an angle over his right temple and around his head, and his right eye was black and swollen. His left eye was bloodshot, and his expression pained. In short, he looked terrible. "Well, don't stand there starin' at me like a frightened kitten," he growled. "Come in."

She stepped in and shut the door behind her. The sound made him wince. "Are you all right?" she asked in concern.

"I'm as far from 'all right' as it is possible to be, ma'am," he responded sourly. "My head seems to contain all manner of aches and pains, and any little noise makes things worse."

"Yes, I know. Mr. Orkle explained to me that it is the result of over-indulgence in drink and will soon pass off."

"Mr. Orkle talks a great deal too much, but he's quite right. In America, this affliction is called a 'hangover.' But I will admit to you, ma'am, that as hangovers go, this one is a jim-dandy. However, let's not talk about it. Sit down, please. I sent for you because I believe we have some business to discuss which was left over from last night."

She took the chair beside his bed. "I was not aware of any leftover business," she said demurely.

'Oh, *weren't* you now!" he said sarcastically. "Listen here, girl, I've *done* with humorin' you. I've followed all your rules. I've been so restrained and polite I've hardly recognized myself. And all I got for my pains was the sight of you creepin' off to wed that drearisome Claybridge fellow."

"Arthur is *not* drearisome!" Anne said, outraged. "He's the finest, kindest, best-natured man in the world."

"Oh, he is, is he? Then why didn't you run off with him after all?"

"Because..." she confessed, lowering her eyes to her hands, "...he preferred to run off with Cherry instead."

Jason cocked his good eye at her. "He *did*? Well, well!" His lips twitched in a very slight smile. "The fellow has more sense that I gave him credit for."

Anne got to her feet haughtily. "If that's a slur at me, Jason Hughes—!" she sputtered.

"Oh, sit down," he commanded, "and don't raise your voice like that, girl." He raised a shaky hand to his forehead. "Remember my head!"

She sat down again. "I'm *glad* your head aches," she declared maliciously. "You *deserve* it. And I would be obliged, your lordship, if you'd get to the point. What is this business you wish to discuss with me?"

He gave her a one-sided grin. "I know how your mind works, you know. You think I called you here to apologize for my behavior last night."

"I don't think anything of the kind! You are not enough of a gentleman for that."

"For once you're right. I have no intention of apologizing."

"An apology is not at all necessary, my lord," Anne said with icy dignity. "I realize that you were not yourself."

"Oh, no, girl, you're quite wrong there. That excuse

won't wash. I was never *more* myself than I was last night, and you know it."

"I don't know any such thing. You would *never* have behaved so . . . so disreputably if you'd been sober."

"Maybe not, but only because of cowardice. Drink made me brave," he admitted.

"In England we call it 'pot-valiant.' It is not a quality to give one pride."

"I'm not *takin'* any pride in it. Only explaining to you that my behavior was simple honesty. *In vino veritas.*"

"What nonsense," she insisted stubbornly. "I don't believe you even *remember* anything that passed between us last night!"

"Don't bet on it, girl. Would you like me to repeat our conversation to you *verbatim*? I can even do it with *gestures*!"

She colored to the roots of her hair. "That won't be necessary, thank you," she said coldly, rising from her chair. "If you'll excuse me now, I think I've had enough of this conversation."

"No," he said, reaching out and grasping her wrist. "Please stay. We haven't yet discussed our business."

"What is it you want to discuss?" she asked unyieldingly.

"Sit down, here on the bed where I can see you better."

Reluctantly, her wrist still held in his iron grip, she sat down on the bed facing him. "Now, then, what is it?"

"I only want to know when you think you'll be ready to leave."

"Leave? Leave for where?"

"For America, of course."

"Jason, what sort of joke is this?"

"You know it's no joke. I imagine you'll want us to be married *here*, with the family and half of London present. I don't mind waiting for that. How much time do you think you'll need for all that before we set sail?"

Furiously, she tried to pry her wrist from his grasp.

"*Will* you let me go?" she raged. "I can see now that you can be quite as obnoxious when you're sober as when you're drunk!"

He lifted his free hand to his forehead dramatically. "My head!" he moaned, leaning back against the pillows and closing his eyes. "You're frettin' my head."

"And you're fretting *mine*! Let go!"

He opened his good eye. "Does this mean you *won't* marry me?" he asked innocently.

She stopped her struggle to free her wrist and stared. He was watching her from his one good eye with a rather boyish apprehension, as if his confidence had suddenly collapsed. His poor, bruised face looked so young and vulnerable that her anger disappeared. "Oh, Jason, *really*!" she said with a reluctant laugh. "Is *this* the way you propose marriage to a girl?"

His face immediately brightened. "I thought I'd proposed last night," he said promptly.

"You were *drunk* last night!" she exclaimed in disgust.

He grinned. "Not so drunk as you think." He lifted his hand and brushed her cheek with the back of it. "My lovely little fool! Don't you know that I've loved you from the first?"

"Oh, *Jason*!" she sighed tremulously and cast herself against his chest.

He enveloped her in his arms with a small sigh of contentment. "You haven't told me, my love," he said against her hair, "that you—how is it they phrase the question in your English novels?—that you return my very flattering sentiments."

Hiding her face in his chest, she said shyly, "I do very much return your very flattering sentiments."

"Enough to come with me to America?" he persisted.

She looked up at him, her smile fading. "Must we go, Jason? Are you sure you cannot like it here?"

"I like it here very much. But I'm an American, my dear. Through and through. There's a war coming, I'm afraid, and my place is at home."

She pulled herself away from him and sat up thoughtfully. "But ... what about Mama? And Peter?"

"They will be fine. Lady Harriet will be perfectly content to remain just as she is. And Peter will make a distinguished Viscount Mainwaring when he comes of age."

"You seem to have thought of everything. Do you think I will make a distinguished Mrs. Hughes in a—what sort of abode shall we live in in America? The only habitation I've ever heard you mention is a blanket under the sky."

"I think I may be able to find us a roof to settle under. And you shall make a very distinguished Mrs. Hughes. Believe it or not, before long you'll be more American than I."

"Shall I, Jason? Are you sure I shall be suitable? Am I capable of adjusting to ... to ... ?"

"... to such uncivilized customs as we have in the wilderness?" he teased. "Don't worry your head on that score, love, for you'll have me at your side to protect you from the wild animals and savage men who come your way. Besides, I've always felt that you're a courageous little chit. Doesn't your spirited nature tell you that you'll enjoy the challenge?"

She smiled at him shyly. "Yes, it does. I think ... I shall enjoy it enormously ..."

He seemed to catch his breath. "Are you *really* sayin' that—?"

"I'm saying that I shall be most happy to go to America with you."

They smiled at each other for a long while. "Do you think," he asked at last, "that to celebrate this occasion, love, you could bring yourself to lean over and kiss me?" His good eye twinkled mischievously. "Very gingerly, of course. *Very* gingerly. Remember my head."

Lady Harriet emerged from her bedroom and searched through the house for her stepdaughter. She was consumed with curiosity about the activities of the night before and could wait no longer for the answers. But Anne was nowhere to be found. Coyne was sure that she had not gone out, but the girl was certainly not in her bedroom, the drawing room or anywhere else Harriet could think of. Finally, Mr. Orkle, being asked if he'd noticed her anywhere, remarked that she'd last been seen going in to visit with his lordship. Lady Harriet promptly made for Jason's room.

When her light tap on his door was not answered, she sensibly assumed that Jason was asleep and turned away. However, in motherly concern for the condition of his wound, she turned back to take a peep at him. She opened the door and looked in. The room was dimly lit, but there on the bed she could see quite plainly that her stepdaughter and her nephew were locked in a very close, not-at-all-gingerly embrace.

With great presence of mind, she stifled the glad cry which rose in her throat and backed hastily out of the room. She closed the door with silent care. "Oh, my!" she breathed delightedly. "Oh, *my*!" She had an overwhelming desire to do a jig, right there in the corridor. "I must remain c—" she began to say automatically, but then stopped herself. "*Bother* with staying calm!" she crowed in gleeful abandon. And in complete disregard of its deleterious effect on her breathing, she went skipping down the hall to break the news to Peter.

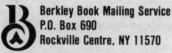